Girl on a Boat

by

Amanda Wheelhouse

Girl on a Boat

by
Amanda Wheelhouse

July 2017
First Edition

Copyright © 2017 Weatherdeck Books

3rd October 1991

The five-year-old child stared goggle-eyed at her birthday present. It was truly the most *beautiful* thing she had ever seen. After a rapt moment she clapped her hands and squealed with delight, ran up to it, touched its bright shiny handlebars, stroked its smooth pink and silver frame, ran both her hands over the saddle, pressing little fingers into its pliant softness. A whoop of sheer happiness welled up in her.

But never reached her lips.

The doctor said it was a narcoleptic episode, probably caused by overexcitement. The loss of motor function that followed was quite common in such cases. And it hadn't lasted more than a few minutes, a good sign. Just keep her calm for a few days.

But neither the doctor nor her parents would ever know what the little girl had seen in those frightful few moments before darkness had closed around her.

Part One

1

I looked up from the grey lino floor-tiles that for some unknowable reason had been the centre of my dulled attention, at the paper cup that had arrived at the table in front of me, and up at the blonde-haired police constable who'd delivered it; dolly-pretty, her smile unbearably kind.

"Tea, no sugar, okay Rosemary?"

"Thanks", I nodded vaguely, "it's Rosie by the way."

I gazed around for the first time at the small, magnolia-coloured room, cheery posters on the walls, wondering how long I'd been sitting here.

Waiting…

Nobody except Dad ever called me Rosemary.

I was distraught when I first discovered what rosemary was. It had been Granny who'd pointed it out to me one day in late summer in her rambling garden behind her rambling great house.

Though it wasn't until much later I discovered it *was* Granny's house. I'd always assumed the old place was ours, and Granny had come to live with us. It was mainly because of Granny that I'd been raised with an elevated sense of our family's social standing, and when the truth was revealed to me I was terrified my school friends would find out we were not the owners of our grand and rather charming country house.

I guess the rosemary thing was hubristic as well, but as an aspiring six-year-old it was a dreadful disappointment to find I'd been named after a rather dull and uninteresting shrub.

Eventually Mum had conceded Rose; no mere commonplace herb, but "a bloom of the most noble sort."

She was like that, my Mum; cultured and poetic, while Dad stuck doggedly with my given name.

'Course, in the Navy it soon became Rosie, which aristocratic Granny would have hated, had she lived.

Waiting…

At last the door squeaked open. A man lifted a chair over to sit facing me, pale, hairy hands resting motionless on denim knees, green surgical mask hanging loose around his neck. His hushed tones came down a long tunnel from somewhere in another universe…

Coming back from leave should be a breathless kind of reunion, catching up on gossip, swapping stories from home but glad to be back with your *real* mates.

But when it's *compassionate* leave you're back from, really?

Forget it.

Apart from the mumbled platitudes, nobody knows what to say. Sneaky looks to see how you're coping, sudden silence when you walk in the mess. You know they've been discussing you.

"Listen up," I said, shuffling my bum down amongst them, "Sympathy, as we all know, comes between 'shit' and 'syphilis' in the dictionary, right?"

I smirked at their gobsmacked faces.

"I'm over it, it's history, okay?"

Even Doc, with whom I'd had a quiet word earlier, looked shell-shocked.

"Spread the word, girls – I don't need pity, and don't fucking want it."

I left them to discuss me in the new light. Doc followed me out into the passageway and grabbed my arm.

"That was bullshit."

"Yeah," I said, pulling out of her grip, then grinned at her, "Good bullshit though, eh?"

She didn't even crack a smile, just gave me that funny squint of hers that, through her rimless glasses, made her look quite the nerd, despite her pale prettiness.

"Now you're just being a smart-arse," she snapped, "Trust me, the way you're handling this, you're heading for trouble."

"You finished, Doc?"

She stared at me a moment, then sighed and shook her head, "Don't know why I bothered," and strode back into the mess.

She was right though, I didn't feel nearly as sanguine as I was acting. Doc was my best friend and knew me better than anyone, maybe even myself.

My Div. Officer, Lieutenant Redfern, didn't think I was handling it well either. She sent for me later that morning to see her in her cabin.

"You don't think you've come back too early, Rosie?"

My hackles rose defensively. "What makes you say that, Ma'am?"

I shouldn't have been so obtuse, I know. She was a good egg, really, even came up for the funeral with Doc, bless her.

"Well, let's see," she said, meeting my hostility with infuriating calm, "it's only three days since you buried your mother, your father's still in hospital, and you've got another week's leave. Don't you think you should be at home?"

"My Dad's out of it," I grumbled, "solicitor's sorting out the paperwork, there's nothing for me to do until he's completed the probate, and nothing for me at home. Reckon I'm better off onboard, with my mates, you know?"

"All the same, Rosie..."

"Look at it this way, Ma'am, we're sailing in a few days for a work up, I've got my Board coming up next month, how would it look if I bunked off now?"

She paused, measuring me up, then said, "I'm sure the Board will be sympathetic..."

"I don't need sympathy, Ma'am, I need action. With the MarDet away I'll be needed on the boarding party. You know what the blokes will say if I skip this trip, the 'girls can't hack it' nonsense. You know what it's like."

She shook her head, "In these circumstances I'm sure..."

"Please, Ma'am, trust me on this, I need to be onboard."

The Padre had a go next, tea and sympathy in his cabin, that's all I needed. Not. At least I could tell him about Dad, and how I really felt about him, knowing it wouldn't go any further, and I guess that helped a bit.

That afternoon up on the fo'csle, me in overalls cleaning the guardrail bottle-screws with a wire brush and WD40, a couple of the guys came up to commiserate and give me a quick hug.

"Geroff me, yer wankers!" I said, laughing, "No Touching, remember?"

I woke up to the insistent blaring of the Tannoy Alert and the bunk-space lights flickering on. Yvonne was first out, dropping down from her top bunk and nearly catching Doc an ear-swipe as she clambered out of her middle one.

I looked at my watch and groaned, twenty-past five in the morning, barely an hour since I'd turned in after the Middle Watch. While Doc and Yvonne hauled out their action kit from their lockers, I waited in my pit to hear from the Tannoy what was up this time.

"Hands to Boarding Stations, Hands to Boarding Stations. Boarding Party muster outside the Armoury."

I groaned again and rolled out of bed while Doc and Yvonne grinned on sympathetically. There was no urgency for them now; their Boarding Station was in the Sick Bay, and wouldn't be needed till we got back, if at all.

We gathered at the armoury, eleven of us, me the coxswain, my two crew, and eight boarders, including the Boarding Officer, a freckly-faced twenty-year-old called Sub Lieutenant Francis, nicknamed 'Dick' behind his back, because he was; and his second-in-command, Petty Officer 'Dinger' Bell, the guy really in charge.

We were issued helmets and weapons, 9mm Glocks for the officer, PO, and boat's crew, SA80 Assault Rifles for the boarders. No ammo, of course, this was an exercise. Thus armed, we clattered noisily up ladders, the Boarding Officer to the Bridge for briefing, the rest of us to the boat deck to await further orders.

Reaching the boat deck lobby first, I unclipped the door and swung it open. It was wet and windy; spindrift swept across the deck in pulsing swathes. At least it wasn't raining. I stepped out and braced against the sudden wind and looked out at the grey waters of the Western Approaches, that wide strip of ocean between the Scilly Isles and France leading into the English Channel.

Four-foot waves lashed towards the starboard beam, their tops clipped to white manes of spume by the near-gale-force wind. Not yet too rough for the sea-boat, a sturdy 20-foot rigid-hulled inflatable that could hold its own in the roughest of seas.

Some of the younger guys in the boarding party looked a bit apprehensive, milling around and glancing up at the RHIB in its davits. They were a scratch crew, cobbled together from various departments to fill the gap left by the professionals, the

Royal Marine Detachment, who normally filled the role. The MarDet were currently away with their Commando Unit rolling in the snows of Norway. Me and my two crew, Able Seamen Tony Briggs, and Andy Rice, were Seaman Specialists. We'd worked together for the past year, including a stint in the Caribbean rescuing boats in trouble and intercepting drug-runners.

"Right chaps," shouted the officer, joining us from his briefing, "gather round. The target's a trawler suspected of gun-running, She's now six miles ahead. When she spotted us she turned north, making twelve knots. Our ETA alongside her is in one hour. We're to board and search and interview the four crew. Any questions?"

"Yes sir," I piped up, glancing out at the burgeoning seas, "best boarding points, amount of freeboard on the vessel?"

"Unknown, Carter, we'll have to assess her and decide on the way over. I'll tell you then what's required."

I bristled but said nothing.

"Granny to suck eggs," muttered Andy Rice from behind me. I turned and gave him a warning glance.

"Anything else?" asked the officer, a little flushed I thought, he must have heard Andy's comment despite the howling gale.

When nobody answered he rubbed his hands together and said, "Right then, Carter, get the boat ready to slip and…"

I held up a hand, barely keeping my temper, "Sir," I gritted, "I know my job, just make sure you know yours."

He reddened visibly, obvious to all, "Right, okay then," he blustered, "let's er… okay, right then, carry on, Cox'n." He turned and walked briskly to where the Boarding Party now sat huddled against the bulkhead.

I turned from him and came face to face with Dinger, the PO, frowning. "Watch it, Leading Hand," he growled, "you were sailing a bit close there."

I didn't answer, my hackles still high.

He pursed his lips and gave his head a sideways shake, "It's not like you to gob off at officers, Rosie. What's up?"

"Sorry, PO, but he's such a... okay, I'll keep it cool."

An hour later the target came into view on the starboard bow, an old steel-hulled MFV, a motor fishing vessel requisitioned by the navy in the sixties. At twelve knots into a gale, she was making heavy weather of it, battering into the troughs, green water breaking over the bow, then rearing up to expose her keel back to the pilothouse. I felt sorry for the crew, and even sorrier for us if we had to try a boarding. Thankfully, a short time later, the pipe came over the Tannoy.

"D'ya Hear There. Revert to Defence Stations. Boarding Party stand down – exercise cancelled due to adverse conditions."

After returning weapons I went to the mess and crawled back into my pit. I was on watch in three hours.

2

"I know it's been a while, Dad, but we've been on work-up – you remember those, eh? Playing at sea-battles and unlikely disaster scenarios; the Thursday War and all that crap?"

I gave his limp, shovel hand a little shake as if he would wake up. "You remember that stuff, don't you, Dad? All that running around in anti-flash gear, tripping over fire hoses. Same in your day, I expect, eh?"

They'd moved him to another room since the accident, light and airy, with pleasant pastel shades, chintzy curtains billowing inwards on the warm breeze.

Touching his lank grey hair, I made a note to ask the nurses when it was last washed.

I gave his forelock a little tug, *"You bastard!"*

I watched his blank face. Not a flicker.

"Mm, nice grapes. They're the big green seedless ones you like, really yummy.

"Anyway, I'm home for the weekend, and then, on Monday, guess what? I start my PO's course. Your daughter's going to be a Petty Officer. What do think of that, eh?"

I popped another grape.

"Mm, met some of your mates in the Dragon last night: Don, Eddie, and that black guy, Sherwin, is it? I was with Doc – you remember my run-ashore oppo, Doc Halliday, don't you? She's staying with me at the house. I reckon your mates think we're a pair of dykes – too polite to say so, of course.

Just those funny old-fashioned looks, you know? My generation, they'd just ask. Anyway, they all send their best.

"Mister Murchison, that's your quack, says your latest scan shows a faint glimmer of activity, only twenty percent of normal, but hey…" I tapped his brow, "looks like there's something going on in that moronic brain after all."

"So, if you *can* hear me, and the nurse reckons there's a good chance you can…"

I leaned in close and whispered, "*I fucking hate you!*"

I sat back, watching his face. One day, he was going to wake up. Would it happen slowly? A little trembling in the fingers, maybe a flickering eyelid, then a gradual return to consciousness? Or would his eyes suddenly fly open and stare crazily around?

Whatever, it wasn't going to happen during one of my visits. *Fuck!* If it did, he'd probably pretend to be still unconscious until this unpleasant person, previously known as his Rosemary, pissed off.

"I'm asking our solicitor about Power of Attorney, but he said it might take months to sort out. Until then, well, I'm in Limbo. If you were properly brain-dead I'd just tell them to turn you off."

3

"Can I help you, my love?"

My love?

I winced but didn't bite.

Gary Palmer had taken over as the new Boatyard Manager at Mullhaven a few months before I joined the Navy, so I'd only seen him around briefly – but I recognised him straight away. A big guy, overtight grey dungarees holding in a once-fit body now slackening towards middle-age. Rusty weathered face, salt 'n pepper beard, raddled hair, like he'd combed it with his banana fingers. I imagined him strumming a double-bass in a folk band.

"I'm Peter Carter's daughter," I said, locking up the jeep, "I emailed you."

"Ah, yes, Rosemary," he mumbled, "sorry to hear about yer mum."

"Thanks," I said, "and it's just *Rosie*, by the way." I scanned the forest of masts in the yard. "So, where is she, our old *Pasha*?"

"Come by the office, I'll get the key and walk you down."

From his office he led me through an assortment of chocked and cradled boats; some big and shiny, some being worked on, others neglected and lonely.

"So, how is he, your Dad?"

"Oh, you know, comfortable enough. They reckon he'll come round, but when?" I shrugged, "nobody knows." I flashed him a conciliatory smile, "Thanks for asking, by the way."

"Peter's a good man. 'ope he pulls through.

"Yeah," was all I could manage.

We walked in silence for a while, then he popped the big question. "What're you going to do about the boat? Do you know yet?"

I shook my head, "Not sure, I want to take a good look at her first."

"Well, there she is. Want me to put the ladder up for you?"

Without waiting a reply, he stooped under the hull of this grotty old tub and dragged out a long metal ladder. Then, to my astonishment, leaned it up against said grotty old tub.

I gaped. "That's *Pasha*?"

"Ah, she ain't in best condition, right enough,"

While he secured the ladder, I took a walk around her hull. The blue anti-foul had long-since gone, leaving a smooth but tired-looking gelcoat that in places showed tiny cracks in its surface. Lumps of rust had erupted on the keel, and part of the rudder was exposed down to bare, splintered plywood where an old filler repair had fallen away.

"Bit o work needed," Gary grunted, understating my thoughts, "unless you plan to sell her, then it'll be somebody else's problem." He glanced along the hull. "At least there's no sign of osmosis, and those spider-cracks?" He gave a reassuring grin, "not serious, just superficial."

He tapped the damaged rudder, causing another lump of filler to fall out. "Don't think you'll want to be repairing this again. Better off replacing it."

He checked his watch. "When you're done here, swing by the office and we'll talk options. And be careful up there, it's a long way to fall."

I gave him my brightest smile, covering the hopeless hole in my gut.

The cockpit was a mess; debris everywhere, teak strips on the sole and banquette, black and gungy. Down below was better; some slight mildew on the seat covers, but no bad smells, no sign of leaking windows or hatches. The sails were all bagged up neatly in the forepeak, along with the bedding in taped-up polythene bags.

I stopped by the chart table, the last chart we'd used still spread out there. I moved aside the logbook, protractor and a pair of dividers, and there was our pencilled track, *my* pencilled track.

Nearly six years ago that was; Weymouth Bay to St Catherine's Point to Mullhaven Harbour.

"Right, young lady," Dad had announced, as we motored out of Weymouth Harbour on a blustery sunny Sunday morning, "she's all yours. Take us home."

"Righty Ho!" I'd chirped, confidently taking the helm, as I'd done a hundred times before.

Clearing the Nothe Fort, I'd unfurled the big genoa to the brisk sou'westerly, killed the engine, and aimed at the distant cliffs of Purbeck. Beyond, stood the hazy outline that was the Isle of Wight.

"North or south of the Island?" I'd asked him.

"Dunno," a careless shrug, "you're the skipper," he stretched out on the banquette cushion and closed his eyes, "and by the way, you're all alone."

At that moment, all that was familiar had become suddenly strange and challenging. Inexplicably, all my hard-grown confidence deserted me – everything I'd learned just floated away on a terrifying tide of panic.

I grinned at the memory; Dad's attempts to be invisible; then, when I asked for help hoisting the main, he faked seasickness, pretending to honk over the side, then disappearing below groaning to lie down in the saloon.

I opened the logbook to the last entry.

1924: Tied up at Thornham Marina.
My first solo passage (Dad 'seasick' the whole way)

That was the last time we'd sailed *Pasha*. Two weeks later I went down to Plymouth to start my naval training.

Stowing away the instruments and chart, curiosity had me pull out a square sheet of plywood.

The coloured inks had faded, but the markings were still discernible. Dad's Uckers Board. The sixteen playing-pieces and two dice were there too, in a wooden domino box.

I slipped the board back under the pile of charts, making a note to rescue the set before the boat got sold.

If I sold her.

Up top, I unlashed the bagged-up dinghy on the foredeck and lowered it down to the concrete below, then flipped open the chain locker. The anchor chain was a heap of mouldering rust; probably still usable, but it would need laying out on the hard and cleaning with acid and oil.

What gave me most concern was the state of the standing rigging, the wire ropes that support the mast. I might not have noticed but for the rusty splinter that ripped into my middle finger when I caught hold of a shroud.

...unless you plan to sell her, then it'll be somebody else's problem.

"Yeah, Gary, I think you're bang on there. But..."

Sucking my bleeding digit, I swung down into the saloon to consult the first-aid kit.

"Good afternoon, how can I help?"

It was an open-plan office, three desks, two unoccupied, books and folders strewn around open laptops; the third, in contrast, as smart and tidy as the girl who'd spoken. Green-painted nails hovered mid-stroke above her keyboard as she waited to know who'd entered her domain. The wooden Toblerone on her desk told me her name was Sandra.

I breezed in and closed the door.

"Hi, I'm looking for Gary?"

Sandra arched a perfect, pencil-thin eyebrow. "And you are…?"

"Me? Well, I'm a customer."

Satisfaction at her crumpled dignity quickly turned to contrition – why was I such a bitch? I was never like this before…

"Rosie Carter," I said, smiling now, trying to warm the sudden chill, "my Dad owns *Pasha*. Is Gary about?"

"He's with a client," she gestured to two chairs by the door, "take a seat, he shouldn't be long."

Her eyes swung back to her monitor, resuming her rapid touch-typing, a skill I'd never mastered and had always envied. A local newspaper lay on the small table in front of me. The headline caught my attention:

MURDERED WOMAN WAS 'SEXUALLY ASSAULTED' SAY POLICE!
Possible connection with previous rape cases?

I picked up the paper and began reading.

> It was confirmed last night that the body of a woman found in Mullhaven on Thursday morning had been sexually assaulted before being strangled. Sources close to the investigation have revealed that Police have reasons to suspect a connection with this brutal murder and several

previous attacks on women in the town
going back almost twenty years.

I recalled as a teenager, Dad telling me not to wander out alone in the town. Before I'd got very far into the story the door next to me creaked open.

"Ah, Rosie," Gary said, "you all done?"

I folded the paper and dropped it back on the table.

"Yeah, for now, thanks," I said, standing and handing him the boat key, "I've got a lot to think about."

He walked across to one of the desks and picked up a folder, "PASHA" printed on the cover.

"I'm out to lunch, San, be an hour or so."

"Enjoy," Sandra said, somewhat dreamily, engaged in her monitor and rattling away.

Gary threw me a lopsidedly grin, opened the door and ushered me out.

"Fancy a spot of lunch?" he asked, as we walked across the carpark. He nodded towards a row of shopfronts on the street opposite. When I didn't answer straight away he added, "Don't worry, nothing fancy," he picked at his dungaree braces, "pub-lunch, just have a drink if you're not hungry."

"Pub-lunch sounds good," I said, "lead on."

Crossing the street, he led me through a gap between two shops; a loamy-smelling stone-walled alley that opened into a quaint little courtyard, ivy-covered walls, half a dozen rustic bench-tables. An overhead sign announced we were entering 'The Chandlery'. A double doorway led into the bar, but Gary chose an outside table for us.

"Hope you don't mind," he said, "I like a smoke."

"No problem," I assured him, "what can I get you to drink?

"Ooh, ta," he looked surprised, macho old-school, probably.

When I came back from the bar he was rolling a ciggy.

"I bet you came here with Dad," I said, putting our beers down, "this is just his sort of place."

"Yeah, many a Friday afternoon, him, me, and a couple of the riggers."

"How long ago was that, when he stopped coming, I mean?" he'd finished making his roll-up, and I reached over for his makings, "Do you mind?"

"Fill yer boots, my love."

He lit up his ciggy and pondered his beer sadly. "He quit coming 'bout three years ago. Happens all the time with weekenders – lose interest one reason or other. Usually it's the other 'alf that was never keen in the first place, ends up hating the boat like it was another woman."

He watched me making a roll-up, so now I was all thumbs and no fingers – I hadn't rolled one for years. Success, though. Fighting a triumphant grin, I reached for his lighter.

"Yeah," I said, blowing smoke at the sky, "maybe it was that. After I joined up she was pretty peed off about his weekend trips down here."

Sunday afternoons, before I drove back to Pompey. Mum's silent reproach, Dad settling down with a scotch and glowering sombrely at me over his glasses for not coming with him.

I said, "So when did you haul her out?"

But Gary was in rumination mode, not listening.

"I remember that last weekend he was here, when I lent a hand stowing the sails and awning. Peter seemed distant, thoughtful, like, you know? Course, I knew then he wouldn't bc down again for a while. Seen it too many times afore."

I waited for him to come down to earth, then asked again, "When did you haul her out?"

"About a week later," he said, "after that last time - he emailed. 'Lift her out,' he said, 'jet wash, then leave her on the hard till further notice.' Never said much else, 'ceptin' that you was away at sea and he wouldn't be sailing for a bit."

Yeah, I could've gone with him some of those weekends when my ship was in Pompey, but, leave Mum alone when every weekend was so precious? No way.

"The standing rigging's shot," I said, showing off my taped-up finger, "she'll need new stays and shrouds before she can sail."

He sucked his teeth, "Expensive! Look, Rosie, why don't you just hand her over to a broker, older Jeanneau's usually sell quite well…"

I shook my head. "Not while Dad's still alive."

He nodded, not very convincingly. "Can you afford to be sentimental?"

Call me superstitious, or whatever, but getting rid of her seemed like… well, like beginning to dismantle his life. It did cross my mind that that might not be a bad thing, but I just couldn't do it. Too many memories.

I sighed. "It's more than that… But, hey, you're right, I can't afford it, and if I was being purely practical…" I grinned through my dilemma, "I dunno. How about you run me through some options?"

"Well, let's assume you keep her," he said, flipping open *Pasha's* file but not looking at it, "Starting with the storage fee for the coming winter, can you pay that, if say, I offer you six months at a grand up front?"

I shook my head.

"Broke, eh?"

"Just about."

He sucked his teeth with a sideways head-flick, and said nothing more for a while, just smoked his fag and watched the ivy growing up the wall.

"Okay," he said, finally, "supposing I said two free months to get her in shape to lift in – then you could anchor her out – no mooring fees, see?"

He paused, and then "got an old rudder in the graveyard that'll fit your boat. A bit battered, but better condition than yours."

"Oh, that's very kind, thanks."

"No problem, been kickin' around for years, be glad to see the back on it."

"What else do I need to do before lift in?"

"Well, obviously you'll need to rub down the hull, de-rust and prime the keel, then antifoul. You'll need to service yer engine before you start her up; new filters, oil change, maybe new drive belts, load-test the starter battery. Er, I presume you know not to start the engine until she's in the water?"

"Yeah, yeah." I said. I did now.

"So when she's in you can take her straight out to anchor. Then the pressure's off, y'see – take as long as you like to get her fixed up without racking up more costs. So whadya think?"

"What I think, Gary," I said, picking up his empty glass, "is that you deserve another pint."

The next day, Saturday, I drove down to Mullhaven again, the back of the jeep packed with cleaning gear, and spent the day washing and scrubbing the deck and coach roof and blitzing the saloon, and afterwards took home all the seat and bunk covers.

While the first load was churning away in the washing machine, I made a start on going through Mum's bureau to sort out her paperwork for the family solicitor. She'd left no will, and with Dad out of it, the probate was apparently quite complicated.

Tucked away behind the bank statements and invoices I found a small address book with a photograph between its pages. The colours were a little faded, but I recognised *Pasha's* cockpit, taken from the companionway looking aft. She was at sea, and at the wheel was a girl in a red foully, blonde hair streaming behind her in the wind, a gleeful grin.

She was about my age, mid-twenties, and very attractive. I wondered who she was and when it was taken. On the back of the picture, a pencilled note:

GA, 1985

The year before I was born. The year *Pasha* was built. Odd that Mum had kept this picture; as far as I knew she'd never shown any interest in sailing, and had never been out on *Pasha*, so it must have been Dad who took the photo. Wow! Had Dad been caught playing way, and this was her way of reminding him of his misdeeds?

I looked again at the address book. The page the picture had been marking bore the same mysterious GA, and three Florida addresses, the first two scribbled out. The remaining one was in Miami.

I flicked through the rest of the pages, wishing I'd found this before the funeral. I decided to write a short generic letter to all the people I hadn't previously known about.

4

"Hey, Dad, s'mee."

I picked up his right hand. "Cor look at those talons. Well, I brought nail scissors, so stand by for the world's worst manicure – I'll try not to draw blood."

I stared at his closed eyes, his blank face, half expecting some comment or other.

"And you need a haircut. I'll see if they do that here. If not, I'll bring in some sheers next time. Can't have you looking like some tramp they found in the street, eh?"

I clipped away in silence for a while, pondering what he'd say to me if he could. When that hand was done I moved my chair to his other side.

"Passed my Board, by the way. Good marks too. Just got to wait for my B13 now – about three months, they reckon. Then it'll be Acting Petty Officer Carter, at your service. Then I can start preparing for the Officer Selection Board. Yes, Papa Dear, I'm on my way."

I paused to bask in his warm congratulations. It had been Dad's suggestion that I do a few years on the lower deck before becoming an officer, said it would save me the humiliation of being a midshipman and stand me in better stead with my troops.

"Can't quite believe I've actually done it, kept my focus, I mean, after everything, you killing Mum and that. Maybe grief helps concentrate the mind on other things. What do you reckon?"

pected my work and dropped his hand next to the other

Other news? Yeah. Well, they let us off early on Friday after our results, so guess what? I went to see *Pasha*. Boy, is she in a state – well, not so bad now. I spent Friday afternoon and all-day Saturday scrubbing out. Gary sends his regards by the way – says to stop lying around and get yer bum down to Mullhaven.

"Anyway, I'm going over there again next weekend to rub down the hull, ready for anti-foul before we put her in the water. Oh, and she's got a new rudder, well, a second hand one, anyway."

I stared at his face - he looked… sort of sad!

Not a single feature had changed, not a muscle had twitched. But he looked sad, when before, he'd looked neutral, restful even. Maybe it was me.

"I'm letting Doc use the house weekends while I'm working on the boat. She's got the hots for some bloke she met in the Dragon. I've banned her from taking him to ours, so she might have stayed at his, the little hussy. Well, that's my news. What's yours?"

I paused, giving him chance to speak.

"Oh, I know. You didn't have a stroke – Mister Murchison told me – they made a mistake with your first scan. It was a mild embolism that you had, caused by you hitting the back of your head on something solid, cos there was a bruise under your hair. Could've happened anytime between the scene and the hospital."

Another quiet moment while the accused laboured to respond.

"And now, they tell me, you've got something called 'Locked-in syndrome'."

I lifted his left eyelid. A blank Dad's eye stared back at me.

"Anybody in there? Well they tell me there is, cos 'Locked-in' means you can hear, and if your eyelids worked, or I pinned them open, you'd be able to see as well. Hi there. Now you've not only got me to answer to, the law are waiting for you to wake up, as well. Four times over the limit, you stupid…""

I let the lid drop, unable to entertain any longer the idea that Dad was seeing me with his conscious mind through that lifeless eye.

God!   How   I   hated   him   then.

5

Apart from one duty weekend onboard, I spent the rest of that summer's weekends working on *Pasha*.

Doc by now had got into a habit of going up by train to mine, or rather, Ron's, but my house was her base and refuge. I'd pick her up on Sunday afternoon, after my weekly talk with Dad. Bit of a round trip, but with Doc's mind dizzy in lust, I didn't really trust her with locking up properly.

By the end of my third weekend in Mullhaven *Pasha's* hull was looking much better. I'd scraped some resin into those unsightly spider-cracks, chipped and wire-brushed the rusty lumps off the keel, primed it, and slapped two coats of undercoat on the replaced rudder. She was now ready for antifoul.

"You'll need ten litres," Gary told me in the Chandlery one Saturday night, "two good coats, and I wouldn't skimp on the quality," he shook his shaggy head, "not worth it, not with anti-foul."

"How much?" I asked.

He did that annoying teeth-sucking thing again, "For the good stuff, 'bout ninety quid for a two-and-a-half litre tin."

"Jesus!" I grimaced. "That's nearly four-hundred pounds."

He nodded wisely, "Yachting's an expensive hobby, another reason people lose interest. What about that standing rigging, any ideas yet?"

Gary was giving me a reality check, I knew, but it felt like he was rubbing it in. He'd already priced up the wire rope for me; seventy-five metres came to nearly a grand, and that's before the rigger's bill for swaging on the end-fittings, the bits that connect it to the mast and the deck plates.

I put my head in my hands. "What am I gonna do, Gary?"

He was silent for a long while, then let out a resolved sigh, to which I looked up hopefully - his eyes bored into mine as he lowered his voice to a whisper, "I shouldn't say this, and if anybody asks, I'll deny it, but you work in a naval dockyard, don't you?"

I sat back and stared at him, stunned. He looked away and studied the wall.

"Can I buy a roll-up?" I said, reaching for his tobacco.

"I'm having a weekend off from the boat," I told Doc, meeting her at the mess door after my six-hour watch on the gangway, "we can drive up in my car, save fuel. You on?"

It was now mid-September and I'd run out of things to do on *Pasha* until she was relaunched.

"Yeah, great," Doc said, with a heroic grin, "let's have a girly weekend, I'll buy some wine. I'm on leave next week, so I'll go straight up to Mum's on Monday from yours. Got to dash, I'm already adrift."

I followed her out into the passageway and stopped her.

"No way, Doc, spend your weekend with Ron, don't let *me* cramp your style."

We kept silent while a couple of mates came out of the mess and passed us.

"*O-kay?*" I said, after they'd gone, "that's why you're going up isn't it, a steamy weekend with your pash?"

"No, actually. I was planning to go straight to Mum's on Friday, I'm on leave, remember?"

"Ah, big romance over, huh?"

She nodded. "He was a twat, I'll tell you later. And deffo *yes* to the weekend." She gave a little wave and turned the corner to go aft, to her job.

Doc was a Leading Writer and worked in the Ship's Office. Some said she had the cushiest number on HMS Windsor Castle. But I knew what she did; looking after the pay and paperwork for 183 people demanded long hours and diligent attention to detail.

After a fat-boy's breakfast and quick shower, I went forward to the Paint Shop, where the Painter was stirring a drum of boot-topping with a broom handle.

"Morning, Dicky," I said breezily, "how's it hanging?"

"Ah, you know, slack an' 'appy, as always." He lifted the stick, letting the slurpy black goo drain back into the drum, then wiped it clean with a rag.

"What can I get you?" he said, "The yellow chromate's on offer this week, an' it's a *cracking* vintage – he held an unopened paint can aloft, "Ah! Chateau d'Admiralty 1983, lovely bucket, like primroses in spring."

Dicky Doyle was imbued with a cynical acceptance that he'd never advance beyond AB, despite being almost forty. His value to me right now was his unique and long-fostered relationship with certain shady denizens of the dockyard.

"I don't need paint, Dicky, I need a favour," I tapped the clipboard hanging on the door, "this order ready for collection?"

His eyes narrowed, "Yeah," he said warily, "what's it to you?"

I scanned down the approved order, "Mm, twenty litres of grey topcoat, ten of interior white gloss. Er…" I gave him my sweetest smile, "want me to pick it up for you in my car? Save you lugging a trolley all that way."

He gave me a sly grin, "Madam, I detect ulterior motives 'ere," his scrawny face drew close, "what you up to, Rosie?"

"Actually, Dicky," I said, backing out of his face, "I need a *big* favour, strictly illegal, which I'll make worth your while."

Graeme, the Scots Canteen Manager, did little more than raise an eyebrow and say, "smoking a lot, aren't we, Rosie?" when I went for the fifth week in succession to buy my ration of two-hundred duty-free ciggies. I think he knew I'd stopped smoking a year back, though I was still registered onboard as one of the few remaining 'puffing pariahs'.

At morning Stand Easy, I bunked off ashore with my holdall, drove through the dockyard and parked by the pedestrian gate to Nelson Barracks. The Naval Clothing Store, commonly known as 'Slops', was just a short walk.

Returning to the car with my goodies, next call, Dockyard Stores, where I was to ask for a man called Bunny. By now my heart was racing like a demented road-drill.

Doc and I met at the gangway that Friday afternoon, glad-rags on, holdalls packed, ready for a chillout weekend in rural Surrey. It was summer, the sun was out, the breeze, warm. What could go wrong?

"Everything!" my pounding heart told me, as I ushered Doc into the jeep before stowing our holdalls in the boot.

I'd never once been stopped at the dockyard gates, and logic said it would be no different this time.

But a guilty conscience pays no attention to logic. All eyes watching, accusing, reading deceit in your every move. Legs forget how to walk, you go to the wrong door of your car, make numerous little errors in your desire to look normal, innocent.

"You okay?" Doc asked, after I picked up my dropped key and fumbled it into the ignition.

"Yeah, fine," I lied, "just keen to be away."

Crawling along in the Friday afternoon queue to leave the dockyard, the MoD-plod barely looked at us. The relief, gunning the jeep up Queen Street, was delicious.

We stopped at an out-of-town supermarket for Doc to go and forage for our weekend fodder. I stayed in the jeep and rolled a ciggy, irrationally nervous about the stuff in the boot. Forty minutes, and another roll-up later, she returned with two bulging carrier-bags, two bottles of Rioja poking out of one of them.

"Sorry, big queue at the checkout."

"Wedge them on the floor in the back," I told her.

She sniffed the air as she got in. "You started smoking again?"

I didn't reply, just blasted the air on full.

The trouble began when we got to mine, when, parking in the drive, Doc got to the boot before me and took out our holdalls.

"What's under the blanket?"

Before I could stop her, she whipped the rug off my goodies, stared at the stuff, then hissed out a long breath.

It was the cans of 'Antifoul (HM Yachts & Sailing Centres Only)' that gave it away, 'MoD Property' in big bold letters, casting suspicion immediately on the big shiny coil of wire rope and the box of stainless-steel brackets and bottle-screws.

"Jesus, Rosie, what've…"

"You shouldn't have done that, Doc," I said, trying to laugh it off, "now I'll have to kill you."

"It's not funny, Rosie!"

"Ah, cool it girl. It's just a few bits and bobs for the boat."

"Why didn't you tell me," she fumed. I could tell by her rising flush this wasn't going to end well.

"What," I said, "and have *both* of us crapping ourselves going through the gate?"

"No!" she fumed, "Cos I wouldn't have come, that's what. What the fuck were you thinking, you might have given up on your own career, but you'd no right to risk mine?"

Without waiting for my response – not that I had one - she picked up her bag and straight-legged it up to the house.

Had I *really* given up on my career? The thought shook me.

"Sorry," I said, as she moved aside to let me unlock the door, "wasn't thinking."

There was a stinging retort on her lips, but she kept them tightly shut, just glared at me.

For once, Doc didn't feel like cooking, so I got us a takeaway from the Indian in the village, and we ate it watching the usual Friday night drivel on the box. Despite the bottle of red we demolished, and my attempts to lighten things up, she stayed cool and distant, and went to bed early.

Coming downstairs next morning I found her in the hall, dressed and packed to go.

"Taking the train up to London," she explained, "'bout time I visited my Mum – been neglecting her lately."

"Alright," I said, "if that's how you feel, I'll drive you to the station."

"No thanks," she moved towards the door, "I'd rather walk."

"Listen, Doc," I began, reaching to touch her shoulder.

"Don't!" she slapped my hand away.

We stared at each other a moment, her brown, bespectacled eyes darkly unforgiving; me, probably looking needy and pathetic. Then she opened the door and, leaving, said, "See you a week on Monday, Rosie. Have fun."

"Yeah," I murmured, "bye, then."

8

Early next morning, I called Gary and asked him if he could give me a hand with the antifoul, if we could get it finished today and lift in tomorrow. I just wanted rid of the evidence. He was reluctant at first, but I charmed him round.

On Sunday morning I watched with a mixture of pride and trepidation as the guys adjusted the two slings around *Pasha's* glistening belly. Then she was clear of the cradle and moving toward the dock to the insistent sound of the traveller-crane's warning bleeper. I followed behind with the stern line in hand, on tenterhooks until her blue hull settled into the murky grey water.

When the deck was at dock-level I jumped aboard and went below to check the stern gland.

A dribble of water from the thick rubber skirt around the shaft was already filling up the small space beneath. Remembering what a smirking Gary had told me, I put my hand around it, squeezed hard, and, feeling a very slight give and a hiss of escaping air, released it. The leak stopped immediately, but I gave the gland a couple more squeezes for good measure.

The engine started at the third attempt, with an explosion of smoke and steam at the stern, before settling down to an uneven rumble, bringing water gushing sporadically from the exhaust, and a spontaneous round of applause from the guys on the dock; Gary with a smiling thumbs up, then asking if I needed a hand to anchor out.

"No, I'll be fine, thanks."

Memories of me and Dad came flooding back as I motored out into the sun-sparkled bay; the *gigglegurgle* from the engine exhaust. I must have been seven when I came up with that one. Dad laughed when I'd first said it, not because it was funny of itself, but because it described so accurately that peculiar sound of water spilling out astern, given a voice-like quality by the wavelets lapping over the pipe.

"Onomatopoeia," Mum had called it, when Dad told her later what I'd said. Mum, always the literary one. Mum, the poet.

"No," said Dad, "it was definitely '*gigglegurgle*'."

Mum just patted his cheek and smiled indulgently.

There were other words, too, the invention of a little girl's uncluttered mind, for the boat sounds. Like *demoncackle*; the weird combination of creaking from the rigging and the hull sliding through the water at speed; particularly evocative sitting alone in the cockpit during a night sail, with only the stars and your imagination for company.

I headed out to where three other yachts lay and dropped anchor in a muddy-bottomed four metres, three-hundred yards offshore, letting out twenty-five metres of my shiny new chain.

There was still much to do, but I took a moment to roll a ciggy and bask in the freedom of being on the water at last, free of mooring fees, all essential work completed. I tried not to think about the risks I'd taken to get her here.

I slept onboard that night, the first time in six years, set aside the guilt of missing Dad's Sunday visit, and drifted to sleep to the gentle, familiar rocking motion of the boat at anchor, feeling utterly relaxed and at home.

I woke to the sound of spraying water, drumming on the wet duvet, splashing cold on my face. In a wild panic I struggled to free myself from the tangle of bedding. Try as I might I couldn't move the cover off me. The duvet seemed jammed fast around me, like a straight-jacket, as if I'd rolled over and over in it. By now water was slopping over the bunk sill, seeping into the mattress and bedding. I screamed with frustration at my helplessness, but no sound came, just the slop and splash of rising water. I gave an almighty heave to free myself, to no avail.

Suddenly I was free, just like that. I was dry. The duvet moved aside easily when I kicked it aside. I got up and put my feet onto the dry carpet, then tumbled back onto the bunk laughing deliriously.

6

"Anyway, Doc left in a huff the next morning," I told Dad, finishing the story. "Now I've got a week-old fridgeful of food. And you know me and cooking."

I wondered whether he, in his unutterable thoughts, condemned my purloining of government stores, or approved of my resourcefulness. Assuming he could hear me, that is; I was still sceptical about this locked-in theory.

They'd given him a haircut, and his jim-jams smelled laundry-fresh.

"So now I'm a criminal, just like you, eh?"

No reaction.

"Though, in my case, of course, nobody died... 'cept I've probably lost my best friend."

I stood and went to the bottom of the bed, lifting the cover to check his feet. He'd been getting sores on his heels, and they'd put a rolled-up towel under his ankles to lift them clear.

"Ooh, nasty! Still, nurse reckons those pie-crusts will drop off soon, and you'll have bright new skin underneath, heels like a new-born baby, eh, Dad?"

If he ever got chance to use them.

I replaced the covers and resumed my seat.

"So, I decided to nip down to Mullhaven and make a start on the antifoul," I told him. "Actually, I got it finished – two coats, all done."

I got a flashback to Gary's face; a mixture of awe and brow-furrowed guilt for his complicity.

"Nothing to do with me, remember, not a word to anyone," he'd said, looking around furtively then picking up one of the glaringly incriminating tins. "You'll need to decant these into summat else – I'll bring you some empties down."

"And guess what, dear Papa, our old *Pasha's* back in the water.

…

"Had a good result from James, too, you know, the rigger at the boatyard? Didn't ask where the wire had come from, just said he'd take the surplus twenty-five metres in payment for making the shrouds and stays. Says to tell you it's your round when you next go down there.

"Ooh, and that reminds me, my Power of Attorney came through." I patted his cheek, "Turns out you're as broke as me. No insurance for Mum, just you. Very gallant, but you didn't die, did you?"

There was not quite five thousand pounds in his current account, his accumulated monthly pensions from Navy and State. No savings. So that was that. Even the wrecked car had only been third-party insured. I'd had no idea how financially challenged my parents had been in their retirement.

Mum's assets were still undergoing probate, the solicitor had said, but he didn't think there'd be much left after fees and the funeral expenses.

I slipped his patient record off the bed end and perused it for a while, put it back, then paused. I picked it up again.

"No! Not possible. They must have made a mistake with your blood group. And just so's you know, sweet Papa…"

The door swung open. I looked up, expecting to see the nurse on her hourly checks. Instead, I saw a ghost, and it was staring at Dad like he was another ghost. My brain threw a summersault. I jumped to my feet, knocking over the chair and staggering against the bed, head swimming, legs like willow-twigs.

"Huh! *Mum?*" I managed to croak through a suddenly dried-out throat.

She turned to me, a cruel apparition.

"No-no-no, Rosemary, it's alright," she soothed, rushing me with open arms.

I backed away, coming up hard against the wall. The thing coming towards me that was my mother, but couldn't be my mother, shimmered suddenly with colour, feathers sprouting out of those outspread arms, the kind oval face morphing into something hawk-like and predatory, sharp eyes glaring dispassionately either side of a grey raptor beak.

And spoke.

"I'm your Aunt Georgina, Margie's twin sister."

The arms that were now powerful, multi-hued wings, rose, and the creature soared overhead as my cheek slapped onto the cool, linoleum floor.

I want to scream, but my vocal chords refuse to co-operate. I want to get up but the muscles in my limbs will not respond. Disorientation; reality drifting away.

Where the hell am I?

Mum and Dad, turning silently together on the night among the stars, smiling into each other's eyes. They look like a couple in an old movie that Mum used to watch again and again. Except that old classic was filmed in black and white. Here the colours are as improbable as the scene itself; inexpressibly beautiful, unutterably surreal. A lurid sunrise grabs my attention briefly, then, turning back to where my parents had been dancing, a pair of silhouettes on the wing, flying towards the dying purple of the night.

Staff Nurse Julie Myers pokes her head into Mr Carter's private ward, sure she'd just heard a kerfuffle in there. Huh, nobody there, Rose must have left, or gone downstairs for a smoke. She breezes into the room.

"Hello, Peter, let's make you a bit more comfortable."

As she leans over the bed she sees the crumpled body on the other side, slumped against the radiator.

"Heavens!" she murmurs, pressing the red call button at the bedside, then hurrying around the bed.

I awoke lying on a hospital gurney, overhead strip-lights, the soft murmur of voices and the faint squeak of a nurse's crocks on the shiny floor, the alcohol whiff of hand-cleanser.

A face appeared above me. Julie, the daytime Staff Nurse.

"Ah, Rosie, you're awake. How are you feeling?"

I formed a reply that I was okay, but no words came out. My mouth remained motionless. I tried again, starting to panic. I couldn't move, anything. My brain was making the moves, but nothing was happening.

Julie frowned.

"Rosie. Blink for me?"

I blinked.

Fear rose up in me, a fear impossible to express, because, like Dad, I was paralysed. Did Locked-in run in families, like breast cancer and diabetes?

But I blinked, didn't I?

I blinked again, closed my eyes for longer, then opened them again. Julie must have seen the anxiety there. She stroked my brow and, smiling reassurance, said, "Don't worry, Rosie, I expect it's just a touch of sleep-paralysis. I'm sure you'll be fine in a few minutes, then we'll have a nice cuppa, okay?"

"So Margie never mentioned me, eh?" Aunt Georgina said over her teacup.

We'd gone down a floor to the coffee shop where we could talk; her idea, not mine. I was still too stunned to think clearly.

I shook my head, "Never any mention of a sister. Weird. And you *twins!* When did you last see Mum?"

"Ah, not for twenty-five years. We kind of… separated. I emigrated to the States shortly after you were born. Gosh, Rosemary, you don't half remind me of Margie, you've certainly got her looks."

I laughed, "So have you. You gave me quite a fright."

"Yeah, sorry about that. Shoulda been a bit more tactful, I guess, instead of just barging in on you like that," she chuckled, "even so, I didn't expect you to actually *faint away*. Thought that only happened in romantic novels."

"Me too," I said, trying to grin through my anxiety.

Narcolepsy, the nurse had explained. I'd just fallen asleep, probably due to emotional shock.

"Ever had an episode before?" Julie had asked.

"No," I'd lied, shaking my head. "What causes it?"

"We don't really know why it happens to some people, but it does. It might just be a one-off, or it could recur at any time. Would you like me to ask the Duty Houseman to come and have a word?"

"No!" I'd said, suddenly sitting up straight. "No doctors, please. I'd like to go now," forcing a grin, "and see an aunt I never knew I had."

She'd stared at me a moment; a frown creased her brow.

"You should at least go and see your GP, Rosie. There are treatments…"

"What, like there's a cure?"

"Well, no. but…"

"Okay, I'm out of here, see you next Sunday."

"Very well. Just one thing: please don't drive."

Yeah, right.

I looked pointedly now at my aunt.

"And you never contacted each other in all that time? No skyping, or email, even?"

She giggled, then reached over and patted my hand, "Our dispute started long before the Internet was invented, dear.

And the longer we were out of touch, the easier it was to let sleeping dogs lie."

I gave her the eyebrow. "Dispute?"

She stared at me, thoughtful, sad.

"It's a long story, Rosemary," she said at last, "can we leave it for another time, d'you mind?"

"Okay. It's Rosie, by the way."

When I'd first seen her, Aunt Georgina was the perfect image of Mum; same soft, brown eyes, auburn hair, in her case, worn short, like mine, and that pretty, oval face with cheek-dimples when she smiled. But, studying her now, she looked older, more wrinkles around the eyes, brow more furrowed. I could tell some of that was a natural humour and strong sunshine, and minimal makeup. But added to her speech and mannerisms, it all contributed to a mannish quality that I'd only now started to notice.

"So, you came alone?" I ventured.

"Yeah, my partner and I run a business, no way both of us could come."

I looked at her in silence for a long moment, then said, "Any cousins I should know about?"

She reddened slightly and shook her head. "Woulda been nice to have a kid, but not possible, I'm afraid."

"Mum was such a straight-lace, shame you couldn't make it up before… you know."

She sighed, "My partner's called Anna."

I smiled, "Don't worry, I'm not my Mum."

She gave me a crooked grin. "Talking of which, I fly home tomorrow, and I'd like to visit Margie's grave. Do think you could take me?"

"Course, we can go right now if you like. It's not far."

She frowned, "Don't you want to say goodbye to your Dad, first?"

"Nah, I'll see him next Sunday, that's soon enough for me?"

She gave me a puzzled glance but didn't pursue it. Instead she said: "In that case, do you mind if I go up and have a word?"

I grinned at that. "It'll be a bit one-sided – he's not very chatty but fill your boots."

"But he can hear everything, right?"

"So they tell me, just don't expect any reaction, that's all. I'll see you downstairs at the carpark entrance."

Outside, I found my hands were shaking so badly I could barely roll my ciggy. The memory of that odd little incident on my fifth birthday had faded into the years.

Until today.

7

After my smoke, I went back into the hospital florist and bought a bunch of white lilies, then brought the jeep round to the entrance. Aunt Georgina was already there; on her phone. She gave me a little wave, so I sat with the engine running until she'd finished.

"That was Anna," she explained, getting in the car, "wanted my flight details. Says hello, by the way, she's delighted I caught up with you."

"So how did you find me," I said, pulling away from the kerb, "I mean, how did you know which hospital?"

I wound down my window; the perfume of the lilies on the back seat was getting overpowering.

"Honey, you wrote to me, though it was obvious you didn't know who I was. It was a pretty impersonal letter."

I tried to recall who I'd written to.

"I came by your house this morning. Nobody home so I came to see Peter, and there you were."

"I was down at Mullhaven," I told her, "working on the boat. Didn't get back till noon, then I came straight here."

She went quiet, and when I glanced her way, she was staring ahead, but not seeing, her mind elsewhere.

"What?" I said.

"Just thinking about old *Pasha*"

It was my turn to gape. "You *know* her?"

"*Know* her?" She was my…"

She broke off and looked out of her window.

"I used to sail her," she finished, still looking away.

And then it suddenly dawned. I stopped for traffic lights, then turned to her.

"GA? Miami?"

She chuckled. "Our little cryptic codename, Georgie Anna. People weren't so liberal minded back in the eighties. Your Dad was an exception."

"Mum kept a photo, a blonde woman at the helm on *Pasha*. Would that be Anna?"

"Sure. Gee, they were good times."

Silence, until the lights changed, and I pulled away.

"You used to sail with Dad as well?"

"Sure. When Anna was away Peter stepped in to crew for me."

"So you knew him well, then, that's why you wanted to talk to him?"

She nodded. "We were good friends."

I concentrated on turning in through the narrow gap into the churchyard, and parked. Switching off the engine, I turned and looked at her pointedly.

"*How* good friends?"

She stared at me nonplussed, then snorted and swung open her door.

"Ha! The very thought!" she chimed, climbing out.

"Look, Rosie," she said after I'd locked the car and joined her, "My relationship was with Anna, not your Dad. Got the picture?"

I tried to imagine the alternative picture, and failing, smiled brightly and hooked my arm into hers.

"Mum's down this way."

We stood contemplating the headstone, Aunt Georgina weeping silent tears, my throat working furiously to hold mine back. Then my arm was under hers again and she pulled me in close, rubbing my hand.

"All those wasted years," she murmured, dabbing at her eyes with a tissue.

After a time, I disengaged myself and began tidying around the headstone.

"Hi Mum, fresh flowers for you…" I choked a bit, and shook away standing tears, "white lilies, your fave. Dad's still the same, but everyone's sure he'll wake up, one day."

I was talking for my own comfort. If I'd thought Mum was *up* there somewhere, listening, I would have asked her why the hell she'd let Dad drive with all that booze in him. Finishing, I stood back next to Aunt Georgina. The crisp new lilies stood proud and sombre against the black marble.

"So beautiful," my aunt whispered.

I squeezed her hand, sniffed back a single, miserable sob, and then wandered slowly back to the car to allow her a moment's privacy with her sister.

We drove back to mine in silence, where I squeaked the cork on Doc's second bottle of Rioja.

"So, Aunt Georgina," I said, handing her a glass of wine, "tell me about *Pasha*."

"Please, darling, just call me Georgie. 'Aunt Georgina' sounds so formal, don't you think?"

I flopped down beside her on the sofa, "Okay. Georgie it is." I took a slurp of wine, enjoying its sweet heaviness. Georgie sipped hers, then set the glass carefully down on the coffee table, but not before I'd noticed the slight wrinkling of her nose.

"You don't like Rioja," I said, "sorry, I should have asked."

She gave a sly grin, "I seem to remember Peter used to keep a fine stock of whisky…"

I laughed, standing up, "Highland or Island?"

"Oh, *Island*, every time," her beaming grin was delightful, "got a Laphroig, by any chance?"

"'Course, that was Mum's favourite tipple, too. Not that she drank much."

Pouring her scotch, I was struck once again how alike, and yet, how different this woman was to her twin. Georgie was a rougher, more 'lived in', less socially-conditioned version of her sister – Mum without the hang-ups. As much as I loved her, Mum had always been difficult to have a meaningful conversation with. My aunt, as I was learning, was transparent and open-hearted in a way Mum could never have been.

She took a generous sip of the golden spirit, and gave a deep, contented sigh. "Ooh, that's better. Now, you ready for some Brenton family history?"

I shuffled back comfortably into the sofa. "Go ahead, I'm all ears."

"My Dad," she began, "your Grandpa, whom you never knew because he died two years before you were born, left a covenant to make sure your Granny would be okay in her old age. In it, Margie and Peter were given a half share in the house in Guildford, on the proviso they moved in with Mum. You with me so far?"

I nodded, "Seems a bit unfair on you, but go on."

She went into a brief spell of ecstasy as she savoured her whisky.

"Oh, I was happy as a sandboy. I got *Spectre*, your Grandad's old boat, and a chunk of cash. And I had Anna – we'd been an item since '80. It was easier for us living aboard, especially back then."

I nodded.

She sipped her scotch and continued. "But Spectre was a shabby old boat, and we ended up selling her for a song then used some of Dad's money to buy *Pasha,* brand new off the blocks, in '85. Peter had already been out with us a few times on *Spectre*, so he was the logical choice to help us get the new boat commissioned and sea-trialled, you know, a man we could trust?"

"And Mum didn't mind him swanning off like that?"

"Not really. She had your Granny for company, and I'm sure you remember how famously they got along. You were what, twelve when she passed?"

I nodded, recalling how much like younger and older sister they'd seemed, rather than mother and daughter.

I gave a fond chuckle, "I loved growing up in that old house, all those wonky passageways and creaky floorboards, and the huge garden with its orchard. And the cellar where Granny used to make wine and jams and stuff – always used to smell of apples and fermenting fruit, all those huge jars bubbling away..."

"...Brenton Damson Wine," Georgie chimed in, "Brenton Raspberry Jam, Brenton's Ye Old Strong Cyder, with a 'Y'. People used to come from miles around to buy it at the door. And ha, I remember pasting labels on jars and bottles all day in the holidays," she snorted laughter, "it'd be child exploitation today; your Granny had quite a little earner, there."

"I was pretty pissed off when they sold it after I joined up," I complained, "they didn't even consult me, just upped and did it. Downsizing, they called it."

She patted my hand. "People sometimes have to make tough choices in retirement, when the income dries up. I grew up there too, remember, so I know how you feel. The upkeep of that old listed building was hideous, even in my day, more a liability than an asset."

The room was getting dark, so I jumped up and flicked on a light.

"You hungry?" I asked.

"Mm, I could manage a bite. What you got?"

I realised I hadn't a clue. Whatever Doc had loaded the fridge with, before she'd thrown one and buggered off.

I was sorting through the various packets, wondering what I could make them into, when Georgie slipped into the kitchen behind me.

"I thought maybe a sandwich?" I said, "we've got ham, and tomatoes, salad stuff…" I turned to her, "what do you think?"

"You don't cook, Rosie, do you?" she said, surveying the assortment of chilled packages piled randomly on the worktop.

"Never was my thing," I admitted, reddening, "we could go to the pub?"

We didn't go to the pub. Georgie took charge, chopping onions and grating carrots with a speed and skill I'd only seen on TV cookery shows, and soon the air was filled with the delicious aroma of frying onions and minced beef. I watched, fascinated, as she crushed garlic, chopped tomatoes and all the while rattling on about her life in Florida, as if talking incessantly was an intrinsic part of the food-preparation process.

Turns out her and Anna ran a software business, developing systems and online resources for merchant and investment banks across America and beyond.

"So you're a computer boffin?" I said, impressed, "started when it was new and exciting, I guess."

She laughed at that, without looking up from her work. "Yeah, it was exciting, and lucrative too, still is for some. But Anna's the geek in the partnership, she runs the technical team – I just look after the business end of things and count the beans."

I watched her smearing great dollops of garlic butter onto slices of French bread, made a mental note to offer Doc some money for the food and wine – might help to chill her out a bit.

Georgie wrapped the reconstructed French stick in foil and put it in the oven, then slipped a bunch of dried spaghetti sticks into a pan of boiling water. Everything she did seemed so highly organised, all coming together naturally; no fuss, no panic, tidying as she went. Even Doc wasn't that good, and *she* knew her way round the kitchen.

"There," she said, after checking the simmering meat sauce, "we eat in fifteen minutes." She waggled her empty glass, "Any chance of another nippy-sweetie? And then you can tell me all about life in the British Navy, and this friend of yours who buys a shedload of food and doesn't stay to eat it."

"Georgie," I said lining up my fork and spoon on my empty plate and trying to ignore the wreckage of bread crusts scattered on the table, "that was awesome. Thanks for cooking."

"Ah, don't mention it, sweetheart. Anyone can knock up a spag-bol."

I noticed her American accent thickening as the whisky mellowed her.

I threw her a wry grin. "Not quite everyone."

"Well, my dear, if you're set on cruising old *Pasha*, you're going to need to hone those culinary skills. Either that or get a crewmate that can cook."

I grimaced at the thought of sharing that small space with someone other than Dad – one of us would get pissed off pretty damn quick.

"Surprised your Dad didn't teach you," she continued, "all part of the same game, sailing and cooking. Can't live on cookies and snacks, you know."

"Oh, he tried to teach me, alright," I said, "believe me, he tried. Something about silk purses and pig's ears, I think."

"Yeah, not always the model of patience and tolerance, your Dad." She stood up and stacked our two plates. "Come on, I'll give you a few pointers while we're washing up."

- 49 -

9

"What puzzles me most, Papa dear, is not *why* you never told me about Aunt Georgie, I think I get that, but *how* you both kept it from me all those years."

I scooped up a dollop of moisturizer from the big heavy jar the nurse, Julie, had given me, and began smearing his feet. With those unsightly crusts gone from his heels; his feet looked as healthy as when he'd skipped about barefoot on *Pasha*. He still had good feet, for his age.

"I mean, all those sailing trips, when you could have told me without Mum knowing. You didn't trust me, did you, to keep our secret?"

I looked at his blank face.

"Nothing to say, huh? Well, you know what pisses me off more than anything else? You knew I went to Florida that time, didn't you? Knew I could easily have taken some station leave and visited her. Wow, Dad, what were you thinking?"

Five years ago, that was, on my first ship, we visited Fort Lauderdale and Mayport. The thought, and his maddening silence, was too much to bear. With a tightening knot in my stomach, I reached over and knocked on his forehead with my knuckles, hard enough to hurt.

"Hello! Anybody home?"

I bit my lip – shouldn't have done that.

I pulled the covers over his feet and went outside, stood for a minute taking deep breaths, then went downstairs for a smoke. This was my last visit with him until Christmas – I really ought to take charge of my emotions.

"Hi, I'm back," I said, breezing back in to his bedside.

But, I didn't feel any better disposed towards him, not really – scary thing was, I could easily imagine smothering him with his pillow.

"Got some great news to cheer you up. *Pasha's* in the water. Oh, I said last time, didn't I? Anyway, I took her for a quick sail around Mullhaven Harbour this morning – she goes like a dream. Can't wait to take her out properly."

The change of subject calmed me.

"But that won't be till December, we sail tomorrow for three months in the Eastern Med."

"Yeah, I know. You want to know who's looking after *Pasha*. Well, good old Gary to the rescue again. He's going to check her once a week, run the engine, keep the batteries charged. And he won't charge us unless he has to move her. Result eh?"

I rubbed his forehead where a hint of a bruise had appeared, and a great sob rushed up from my gut.

"Oh, Dad…"

How did I get like this?

"Everything alright in here, Rosie?"

It was Julie, the senior staff nurse, standing at the door, looking worried. I wondered if she suspected my spiteful abuse of her patient.

I wiped at my eyes. "Yeah, okay. Moisturizer jar slipped out of my hand." I drew my thumb over the mark that was now darkening on his forehead.

She didn't believe me, I could see in her eyes, suspicious, protective. She came to the bedside and examined the bruise.

"Maybe you should go now, Rosie," frostily assertive, "let him rest."

During the drive home I remembered something that had been bothering me, and when I got there, ran upstairs to where my parents kept the family documents. Both their Medical Cards where there.

And sure enough, they were both blood group 'O'.

Downstairs, stomach tight with anxiety, I logged on to Google and typed 'blood group genotypes' I chose the first entry, then held my breath as I waited to see if my assumption was wrong. When the page came up I scrolled down to the parents/offspring chart.

I stared uncomprehendingly, then my guts began to churn as a demon rose inside me.

The flimsy computer lid snaps shut with the sound of a closing vault. I try to stand but my legs won't support me; I sink to the carpet and fall onto my back, unable to move, and watch my laptop flapping around the room like a mechanical crow trapped in a place it doesn't want to be.

Grey clouds fold around me.

I came awake suddenly. Everything was back to normal in the room. It had been daylight when I'd collapsed, but now the room was in blue dimness, lit only by the glow of the computer screen.

And I couldn't move.

I tried to think through rising panic.

Both my parents were 'O', while my blood group on my naval ID card read 'AB Negative'. What could it mean? Had Mum had an affair that had got her pregnant? Did Dad know I wasn't really his daughter? Or was I adopted?

And did it matter?

What did matter right now, was that I was paralysed in an empty house, with no chance of help coming anytime soon. I was due back onboard on Monday morning. What time was it now?

I had no idea.

I closed my eyes and tried to sleep, tried to escape the reality that was threatening my sanity. But sleep eluded me as thoughts crowded in.

I began to count in my head: 1, 2, 3, 4, 5…

At fourteen thousand two hundred and forty-six, my legs twitched. I opened my eyes to the first grey light of dawn filtering through the sitting room curtains.

10

Far away to port, Portugal; the faint orange glow from several cities tingeing the far horizon, diminishing somewhat the rising figure of Orion and his surrounding retinue. To starboard the undimmed stars sparkled brightly against velvet black, neither Moon nor Venus yet present to sully a display so sharp and brilliant it hurt to look up for long.

Last half-hour of the Last Dogwatch as Lifebuoy Sentry. Half an hour alone on the quarterdeck, a wide space, open at the stern and sides beneath Windsor Castle's helicopter flight-deck. A calm evening, getting perceptibly warmer as our latitude decreased daily. As a leading hand I wasn't expected to do Lifebuoy Ghost, but with two of us in the watch, and nothing much else to occupy the time, we both chose to do a stint to spread the workload.

My prime job here was to watch for anyone falling overboard, an event so unlikely that in seven years of sea service I'd never heard of a single such incident. My other role was to act as Stern Lookout, but again, at twenty-two knots, it was rare for any vessel to close from astern. In short, there was little to do except gawk at the pitch-black sea.

Alone with my thoughts.

It was the third of October 2013, my 27th Birthday, and we were on passage to sunny Gibraltar and the Med for a two-month deployment in support of NATO forces in the Middle East.

I hadn't told anyone it was my Birthday for fear of what surprises my messmates would spring on me. Their crazy improvisations could be quite bizarre and in the light of my weird disorder, the thought of how I might respond scared me. Discovery would almost certainly get me *casevac*-ed ashore. Well, the day had passed without a mention; even my best friend, Doc, seemed to have overlooked the auspicious day.

Thoughts turned to Dad.

Yes, he was still my Dad, even if not biologically. If he didn't know, I certainly wasn't going to tell him.

I couldn't get out of my mind what I'd done at the hospital on my last visit. Guilt washed over me. I no longer blamed him for what happened. I just wanted him to wake up and hug me. I wanted to say sorry for how I'd treated him since the accident.

I guess I missed Mum too, but somehow that hurt burned less fiercely; it was as if I'd blanked out her memory, an intangible vacuum that left only a dull ache whenever I thought of her.

I thought too of *Pasha*. Doc had been right about me losing interest in my naval career. Yes, the sea still drew me, but I knew I'd rather be out here on *her*, slicing silently through the gently rolling swell, than thundering along on a steel juggernaut.

My relief, a spotty Ordinary Seaman whose day job was on the Top Part o' Ship, showed up at five-past-eight. I glared at him in the starlight but said nothing.

"Sorry," he mumbled as I handed him the binoculars.

Making my way below through the dimly-lit passageways, I reached the mess door, and listened. All quiet, good. I pushed open the door, stepped over the sill, and knew immediately something was up.

Oddly, it was dark; just a faint glow through the heavy curtain draped across the inner entrance. The lights were *never* switched off; the mess was in use twenty-four-seven at sea, people coming and going at all hours. Puzzled, I closed the door behind me and pulled aside the curtain.

A sea of faces flickering in the glow of a single candle. The lights came on, almost blinding me after my watch on the quarterdeck, accompanied by a cacophony of wild cheering, faces grinning and laughing, so many faces, not just the girls, but blokes as well; my boarding crew: Tony Briggs, and Andy Rice, Pincher Martin and a couple of other lads from the Focs'l Part o' Ship, Graeme, the NAAFI Manager, good mates all, but *men*. Men were officially banned from the female mess at sea.

Then, as my best friend Doc led the raucous uproar into a ragged chorus of "Happy Birthday…", a sudden blackness rose up inside me, and all the faces began to morph into leering caricatures, lurid shapes in fantastical colours closing in around me

"Oh, my God!" shouted someone.

"Grab her, she's falling," shouted another.

Inhuman, prehensile fingers reaching out to me, stretching, growing longer. I could hear, but couldn't move, the improbable images were all I could see, shards of intense light pierced my eyes. The last thing I remember was the sensation of floating, floating upwards to a sky of unearthly splendour, a million rainbows of impossible hues.

Vaguely I was aware of Doc's voice in my ear but couldn't understand her words; she might have been speaking Martian. The voices gradually faded into the background.

Silence

I am in another world, a world of incredible beauty, of alien colours, a world of perfect silence, resting on a bed of cool, fragrant flowers, their intense perfume filling my head. I could rest here forever. Faintly aware that this is not right. I am not right, but not caring. This is Heaven.

I am in Heaven.

…

After an eternity I began to be aware of reality once more. The grey criss-cross of bunk-springs above me, the perforated soundproofing in the deckhead, a strip light. A gabble of voices.

One said, "Her eyes just opened, Donna, she's back with us."

A face came into my line of vision, Donna, the Leading Medical Attendant. I felt my hand taken hold and lifted but could do nothing. Déjà vu all over again.

"Can you hear me, Rosie?"

I blinked but couldn't even move my eyeballs to look at her. Even though I'd been through this before, and knew it would pass eventually, it was still scary – I was starting to panic, felt like I was trapped in solid rock, held utterly motionless, claustrophobia with knobs on.

The fear must have shown in my paralysed eyeballs, at least, Donna must have seen it there, or sensed it perhaps.

"Stay with her, Doc," she said, back in a jiffy.

"Doc's worried face swam into view as Donna left."

"You okay, buddy? You gave me quite a fright there."

I blinked.

"Oh! Rosie, blink twice if you can hear me."

I blinked twice.

"Wow. Er, blink once for yes, twice for no, okay?"

I blinked.

"Are you in any pain, Rosie?"

I blinked twice.

Doc's face withdrew.

"What's that?" Doc's voice.

"Just a shot of Valium, to ease her anxiety. Then I'll get the Doc to look at her."

Donna's head reappeared over me.

I shook my head.

I shook my head.

"No!" I shouted, pushing her away. I sat up and dropped my feet to the deck.

"S'okay," I said to the stunned medic, "I'm okay now. Just give me a minute."

I looked up at the mess clock. Ten past eight. I'd only been out of it a few minutes.

Donna put the hypo on the table and sat down beside me. Doc's arm came around my shoulders from the other side and she pulled me in close. I looked around at the concerned faces of messmates and male visitors and, shaking off Doc's protective arm, laughed.

"Had you all there for a minute, eh? Just so's you know, I hate surprise parties."

I leaned over and blew out the single candle on the cake.

No one spoke, or cheered, or clapped.

"C'mon guys," I said, "any beer going for a thirsty Birthday girl?"

Later, as I was climbing into my pit, Doc, who was already turned in, whispered across to me, "What really happened to you? I know that wasn't a wind up and from the look on their faces when you tried to laugh it off, I doubt any of the others were fooled either."

"Just a funny turn, I'm okay now, so let's just forget it, eh? And you know the mess rule."

There was a poster over the bar in the mess square:

What you do here
What you see here
What you hear here
Let it stay here
When you leave here!

"And the lads won't say anything, they weren't even supposed to be here."

"Okay," Doc said doubtfully, "but if you want it kept quiet, I should have a word with Donna before she goes up to sickbay in the morning. She's bound to mention it to her boss."

"Don't worry about Donna, I had a quiet word earlier. She won't blab."

In truth it had been Donna who'd cornered *me*, followed me down the ladder when I'd skipped down to the heads.

"Has that ever happened to you before?"

Turning, I'd looked the medic in the eye.

And lied.

"Never. And please, keep this to yourself. Don't tell your boss, okay?"

She watched me for a moment then said, "we should get you checked over, Rosie. What you went through earlier... you just went totally limp and collapsed in a heap. That could be a form of epilepsy."

"Trust me on this, it's not epilepsy. If it happens again, I'll go and see the quack myself. Meanwhile, just keep shtum, alright?"

She shook her head, pursing her lips, unwilling to let it go.

So I'd added a sly addendum, "otherwise I might have to mention a certain beach party in St Lucia involving some black dudes and illicit substances."

She reddened, anger flaring, then turned and stomped back up the ladder. I'd made an enemy, but at least saved my career.

For now.

11

"Gangway!" I shouted, shouldering through the milling crowd of semi-drunken shipmates, clutching two bottles of chilled chardonnay and five glasses.

Friday night, first night in. The Angry Friar was our 'local' whenever we called into Gib, and Windy's lower-deckers tended to take over the place, sending expats and holidaymakers scurrying off in search of quieter places to drink.

It was at about this time (as I was later to learn from the Guardia Civil surveillance report), that a certain Juan Gonzales was readying his motorbike for his first contraband run of the night.

"What this then, Rosie?" called a bleary-eyed Pincher Martin, "vino-collapso? What's the occasion?"

I liked Pincher, but I think he fancied me a bit. It doesn't do to get too close to shipmates; there was the "No Touching" rule.

"Doc's B13 came through today," I shouted back across the din, "wanna join us?"

He shrugged, "Maybe later," he gazed lovingly at the half-drunk pint in his hand, "got a few more of these to sink first."

I grinned at him, "Yeah, well, in that case, consider yourself disinvited, pisshead."

I managed to sidestep a slosh of beer from someone getting over-animated telling some smutty joke to his giggling audience. Then a slurred voice, rather too close to my left ear.

"Ah, Rosy, and how's my favourite lady dabtoe?"

Dicky Doyle, the painter, letting me know I still owed him.

"I'm good, ta. Having a night with the girls."

"So I see. Deano's for din-dins later, is it?"

"Nah, not at Marina Bay prices," I said, brushing on past him, "we'll probably head across the border for tapas."

"Ooooh! *Tapas*," one of his mates sneered after me, "How *very* cosmo-fucking-politan."

"Wanker," I called over my shoulder, "why don't you give yer arse a chance?"

I finally made it to our table, where the girls offloaded me. Jo poured, and, with our glasses charged, I proposed the toast.

"To my bezzie oppo, *PO* Writer Joanna Halliday, Cheers Doc, and congrats. And... before anyone asks, no, I ain't jealous that you got yours before me..."

We chinked glasses and drank to Doc, before I added, "Jammy bitch!"

Snorts of laughter, that turned to helpless finger-pointing at Yvonne discharging snotty wine back into her glass.

We left the Angry Friar when the tuneless singing got too loud for us to hear each other. Karen and Jo declared tiredness through having been middle-watchmen the night before, and went back onboard, while the remaining three of us, Yvonne, Doc and I, walked up the hill to The Hole in the Wall.

Yvonne was new in our company, and I was surprised when she tagged along with us. She usually hung out with the guys. Curvaceous and leggy in high heels and a skimpy green dress, she'd unfastened her blonde hair to fall luxuriously around her bare shoulders.

"Friday night at Molly Blooms," she'd explained earlier, back in our shared bunk space, as if dressing to pull was a rarity for her, "all those tall, dark Spaniards, you never know, girls, I might get lucky."

Me and Doc had exchanged glances. When Yvonne was in pulling mode, it was rumoured, she rarely failed to score. She'd usually ambush her victim from the cover of a bunch of her male shipmates. It would be interesting to see how she operated in *our* company.

Reaching the bar in the crowded downstairs cellar, Doc demanded a round of tequila slammers with a panache I'd rarely seen in her. She'd taken off her specs, a sure sign she was going for it; looking her willowy best, wearing a silky white top that exposed her golden, sylph-like midriff, denim shorts and leather sandals decorated with coloured beads.

For me, with barely time to get a shower after securing the ship alongside, it was pink cotton shorts, baggy grey shirt, string sandals, a touch of mascara and lippy. My carelessly cool look.

We had a couple more shots in Casemates Square, then headed for the Frontier. A warm, blustery breeze buffeted us across the wide-open expanse of the airport runway; Doc and me with arms linked, Yvonne tottering alongside in her heels, Doc trying to lead us in some half-remembered matelot's song.

As the Frontier approached we shushed each other, then lapsed into muted giggling. The Spanish border guard waved us through with barely a glance at our passports, seemingly more interested in the surreptitious study of Yvonne's shapely, if slightly unsteady legs.

La Casa de la Esquina was in full swing, the serving staff miraculously keeping up with orders shouted with the undisciplined abandon that Brits often found so rude and intimidating. Shoving our way through this rowdy, but intrinsically good-natured crowd, we found jostle-space at the bar, and were at once recognised by a dishy Lothario in a blue-striped apron, who, unmindful of the intemperate protestations of the men whose orders he'd been taking, rushed over to serve us.

We ate perched on stools at the bar; a plate of bocarones and fries to share, a few odd individual tapas on the side, and three large glasses of *el vino tinto de casa* – which turned out to be a very passable Rioja.

While Doc and I joked and chatted, with occasional incursions from nameless but recognised frequenters of *La Casa*, Yvonne, clearly unhappy with our choice of venue, distracted herself by checking out the talent and engaging the few English-speakers in conversations of which they soon tired and wandered off, despite her appealing looks and blatant show of availability.

"This place sucks," she announced eventually, necking her wine before nabbing the last piece of bread to mop up gravy from her devoured meatballs, "let's find some *life*."

Wall-to-wall people packed Molly's, live rock music blasting from its flashing interior; the crowds spilling out onto the plaza, many of them blokes from our ship.

Yvonne volunteered to brave the crush to get our drinks, while Doc and I wandered over to where a bottle-walk challenge was underway between a bunch of our lads and some of the local honchos.

Pincher Martin was limbering up to beat the lengthy reach of a tall, proudly grinning Spaniard, to shouts of encouragement from our lot, and contemptuous jeering from the home opposition. Though much of the Spanish was lost on our guys, the taunting sentiments were painfully obvious. This was serious stuff – National Pride was at stake.

It was a big reach, and though I'd seen Pincher do better, as he began his walk - to a chanting of "Easy! - Easy! - Easy!" - I thought he looked a little unsteady.

An exultant cheer went up when his bottle outreached the other by a hair, but then wobbled and clinked against the target. A collective holding of breath, then a groan as both bottles fell over, and our champion collapsed in a heap of laughter and disappointment.

The opposition's cheering was frenzied and unrelenting, but their man, with a surprising show of chivalry, walked over and helped Pincher to his feet, patting his back in commiseration.

It was then that Pincher spotted me in the crowd. His eyes lit up, and he grinned.

It was well known that the bottle-walk was my party-piece, a legacy of my cycling youth and the intrinsic strength it had endowed to my thigh muscles. That and an almost obsessive need to excel at the game since first discovering it shortly after joining up by practicing my techniques in private whenever the opportunity arose. I was now at the age where I found it childish and a little embarrassing.

"C'mon," I said to Doc, urgently, "let's go find Yvonne."

"Uh huh," she grinned, putting out an arm to prevent my escape.

The inevitable chanting began, accompanied by a slow hand-clap, led by Pincher, and seconded now by Doc, who stood away to let me know she'd joined the conspiracy.

"Rose-y, Rose-y, Rose-y…" went the relentless chorus of my shipmates, until I had no choice but step up to the hockey.

As the ridiculous chanting grew louder and faster, the Spaniard eyed me with a puzzled, mildly amused expression. Tall, fit-looking and swarthy, with an unruly mop of black, curly hair, this guy, I thought, was quite something to look at.

"Technically," I said, smiling, "you've won. But the lads want me to have a go. Do you mind?"

"Please, señora," he said, beckoning me forward with a theatrical arm-sweep, "if you win, I buy you champagne."

"Done!" I said, reaching down and settling my palms onto the two empty Guinness bottles. With my legs straight, bum stuck up in the air, wishing I'd worn jeans instead of my skimpy pink shorts, I began walking the bottles out to the mark.

The chants of "Easy!" became deafening, a brief hiatus as one of my wrists wobbled, then I was out at full stretch, and all went quiet. The moment of truth. Transferring all my weight gingerly onto the bottle in my left hand, I reached out with my right, placing the other a good two inches beyond the target. I then snatched up the Spaniard's bottle, and walked myself safely back to the hockey.

The cheering, as I stood up, flushed with success, was noisily ecstatic, mates gathering round with much back-slapping and hearty congratulations. But my Spanish opponent was nowhere to be seen, which kind of spoiled my moment.

"He fucked off right after you won," Doc told me, slurring and laughing deliriously, "getting beaten by a *mere girl* too much for his ego. Bit dishy, though, wasn't he?"

"Dickhead!" I said. "So where's Yvonne?"

We found her at a table under the pub's outside awning, chatting up the band members on their break. They were young, long-haired and greasy-looking, and it was clear Yvonne's drunken charms were of little interest. We dragged up two more chairs.

"They're going back in for another session in a bit," she confided, passing us our drinks, "thought I'd grab this..."

She looked up and went gooey-eyed, as a big shiny ice-bucket arrived on the table in front of me.

"Ooh, hello?" she cooed.

"I apologise for it take so long," said the dishy Spaniard, with a smile that was just for me, placing two champagne glasses on the table, "It is only cava, I am afraid."

"No need to be afraid, Pedro," said Yvonne brashly, grabbing the bottle out of the ice and unwiring the cork, "all contributions gratefully accepted."

The poor guy just gave me a helpless grimace, and said, "This not the time, but I see you again, perhaps?"

Just then we were all startled by the sudden roar of a motorbike a couple of streets away, and when I looked back, the guy was gone.

Again.

"He left this," Doc said, picking a card out of one of the champagne glasses, then squinting to read it without her specs.

"Mateo Galindez, his mobile and email. Aww, how romantic is *that?*"

I snatched the card from her just as the cava cork popped, Yvonne now on her feet and off her head, whooping gloriously and showering the band boys with the sticky fizz, hastening their retreat inside.

"That got rid of them losers," she slurred, sitting down with a silly smirk on her booze-reddened face. "Now, where's that gorgeous waiter gone?"

"He wasn't…".Doc began.

"No, it's okay, Doc" I interrupted, patting her hand, "just leave it."

Shortly afterwards Pincher Martin came over to say he was heading back with some of the lads, and did we want to come.

"Yvonne?" said Doc, quite firmly, "you want to go with them?"

Yvonne got up, swaying a little so Pincher had to steady her. She peered down at us. "You two coming?"

"Nah," I said, catching Doc's miniscule head shake, "we'll hang on a bit longer, still got our drinks to finish."

With a sour look, she snatched up the cava bottle, took a defiant swig, which spilt down her nice party frock, and allowed Pincher to steer her away across the plaza, still clutching the bottle.

Doc and I exchanged looks, then fell about laughing.

Half an hour later, after several needless trips to the toilets in the hope of spotting my apparent admirer, the pair of us headed back to the Frontier, picking up a couple of kebabs to eat on the hoof.

On the way we post-mortem-ed the night's events. Doc made me laugh with her description of Mateo's face when I reached my bottle past his. And we giggled repeatedly at Yvonne's drunken antics and fruitless, but very funny attempts at scoring a shag.

At about the time we hung a left by the *Hotel de Azure* onto *Avenida Principe de Asturias*, Juan Gonzales was securing the last load of the night onto the back of his bike. *La Guardia Civil*, as I was later to learn, had been monitoring his movements, co-ordinating with a police helicopter and a patrol vessel offshore, so that both jet ski and motorbike riders could be apprehended simultaneously. Now, they were ready to spring their trap.

"Well," said Doc, a wicked grin spreading on her face, "are you going to get in touch with your cute Spanish beau?"

"I might, and then I might not."

"Don't be coy with me, Carter," she gave me a shove that sent me staggering towards the kerb, "you fancy him like fuck, don't you?"

She pulled me back in a giggling hug, "*Don't you?* Go on, admit it, you're wetting yourself for him."

"Behave yourself," I said. "Maybe I'll give Yvonne his card,"

"*Yvonne?* She wouldn't know what to do with a hunk like that. Come on, you do have the hots for him, don't you?"

We were passing the yacht marina on the opposite side of the wide dual carriageway. We took little notice of the roar of yet another unseen motorbike from that direction.

"Probably," I said.

"Probably? *Probably?* What kind of…"

Suddenly she released me and let out a terrified scream, backing away from a cockroach the size of a mouse that was scuttling across the sidewalk. Doc had a morbid phobia of large creepy-crawlies.

Then, without warning, two more motorbikes gunned out of the trees opposite and shot away with flashing blue lights towards the roundabout, where the first bike we'd heard was emerging, much too fast, from the marina approach road.

When I looked back at Doc, she was still freaking out at the oversized insect that seemed to be stalking her. She'd backed up against a big concrete planter that stood between her and the road.

I glanced worriedly at the roundabout, where the first guy had gone the wrong way around to escape the pursuing police bikes. They were all three racing towards us.

"Doc, it's only fucking cocky, pull yourself together, yer daft bint, there's a…"

She stepped around the planter and into the road before I could grab her.

"*Doc!*" I shrieked, "*get off the fucking road!*"

The smuggler would have seen her in time if he hadn't been looking back at his pursuers. When he did, he swerved to avoid her, but the bike went over onto its side, and parting with its rider, rolled sideways, barrelling over and over in its deadly trajectory in a cascade of sparks and screeching metal.

In the yellow glare of the streetlamps, I saw it all in horrifying slow-motion, my best friend staring in frozen terror at the big motorbike tumbling towards her, a thousand cigarette cartons flying behind like a flock of maddened gulls.

With a sickening crump the careering machine's underside slammed into her thighs, folding her pretty waist and sending her headlong onto the bike's solid frame. The dreadful pop of the steel pedal piercing her skull, the spurt of blood from her poor head, holding her impaled in a poisonous embrace with the bike as it rolled over and over, another twenty metres or more before screeching to a stop, leaving in its wake of scattered Malboro Lights a single foot, severed at the ankle, bloodied and twitching in its pretty sandal.

I was suddenly aware of a pain across my chest and the side of my face resting in cool, soft earth. Shouted Spanish and flashing blues filtered through a profusion of leaves and flowers.

Merciful sleep quickly followed.

12

The huge windows of the airport departure hall were like two-way mirrors.

Reflections of emptiness.

There stood I, staring back at myself, emotionally empty, insignificant against the towering massif beyond; The Rock, Levantine cloud floating over its ridge, like a white beret on a stone soldier's head.

Reflections of the past two miserable days; days haunted by sudden, unexpected flashbacks; the screeching of tortured metal and sparks, that look on Doc's face in her final moments, her poor broken head impaled on the pedal. It had all seemed so real. It still did.

Then the shock of waking up, once again in total paralysis, staring uncomprehendingly at the unharmed face of my best friend looking down at me with worried sympathy, cooing soothing words into my confused and disbelieving brain.

Reflection on the Medical Officer's recommendation to *casevac* me to UK – unfit for active service. My secret was now out – public knowledge. If only I'd come out of it before the ambulance arrived to take me to the hospital in Gibraltar.

Doc had tried, bless her, all the way back across the frontier; "she'll be okay in a minute, you'll see," she told the medics in the back of the swaying, windowless vehicle, then holding my hand and murmuring smiled reassurances, and using my blinked responses as proof that I was perfectly compos mentis inside that floppy exterior.

Doc and I had said our goodbyes, promising to stay in touch, both knowing full well I wouldn't be setting foot onboard HMS Windsor Castle again.

Windy had sailed this morning, off to the Eastern Med to support NATO in the messy Middle East.

A huge RAF C5 transporter, doubtless on its way back from supporting those same operations, domineered the military side of the airfield, dwarfing the two Tornado fighters parked beside it.

Behind me, my escort's reflection approached with our coffees; short, dumpily attractive with cropped blonde hair, sensible heels clipping on the shiny marble tiles. She was a sub-lieutenant from the Naval Base, like me, in civvies for travelling; drew the short straw because she was flying home on leave.

She looked about twenty and didn't know how she should act in charge of a traumatised and possibly psychotic junior rating; if I hadn't been so self-absorbed I might have felt sorry for her.

She didn't need to ask what had happened; it was all over yesterday's local news; one Gib paper had a picture on its front page; the wrecked motorbike, no blood or gore, no severed body parts, just packets of fags strewn over both carriageways, and the handcuffed Juan Gonzales being led away by two Guardia Civil officers:

Lucky Escape for Royal Navy Women in GC Motorbike Smuggling Bust

By now the story was buzzing around Facebook as well, so would certainly have attracted the attention of the UK press.

We'd been booked into cattle-class, but the airline, apparently having been briefed about me, upgraded us to Business. I slept fitfully for most of the three-hour flight and woke up groggy as the announcement came to fasten seatbelts for our approach to Gatwick.

We were met in the Arrivals Hall by a dark-haired stick-insect holding up a card with my name on it. She introduced herself as Nursing Officer Baxter, my onward custodian to Birmingham. My prior escort wished me all the best and scuttled off gratefully to her leave.

I'd assumed we'd travel up by train, but Baxter led me out onto the concourse where a naval staff car, complete with driver, awaited us. No expense spared, it seemed, for little wibbly wobbly me.

It was a damp, drizzly afternoon as our car filtered into the motorway traffic. Nobody had spoken since we'd left the airport. Once or twice I caught the driver watching me in his rear view. Baxter, next to me in the back, seemed content to travel in silence.

"So what happens now?" I asked her eventually.

She half turned in her seat to face me, her thin face drawn into a tight smile. I got a fleeting image of Cruella De Vil.

"Today, nothing much. The first thing is to get you settled into the Military Ward at QE."

"Military ward? What, like rows of beds full of injured war heroes?" I paused at her scolding look, and added, "Sorry, Ma'am, I didn't mean to sound so... so cynical, but I'm not ill you know? I don't need a hospital bed."

Her hard features softened, she chuckled gently.

"We're not a World War One field hospital, Rosie. You'll have your own private suite in the Women's Wing. It's all quite civilized. And tomorrow you'll see Doctor Hardy for your initial..."

"Are they going to kick me out?"

She gave a short sigh, "Our job is to assess your fitness for active service, with the aim of getting you back to your unit as soon as possible. My advice is to just focus on that."

And 'civilized', is exactly the impression I got on my arrival at the Queen Elizabeth RCDM – The Royal Centre for Defence Medicine. The huge, modern, rambling complex, I learned from my thick wad of Joining Instructions, had been opened only a few months previously, replacing the outgrown facility down the road at Selly Oak.

My third-floor room was spacious, carpeted in powder blue; pine bedframe with sprung mattress under crisp, white sheets and an anchor-patterned bedspread; a small desk, complete with Internet socket; bathroom with shower *and* bath.

A big picture-window looked out onto the University Campus. I tried the opener, it yielded to let in faint traffic sounds. At least they didn't have me down as a jumper.

My home for the next… fuck knows how long.

After unpacking, I plugged in my laptop, logged into Facebook, then sat staring at my profile picture, Doc's happy, grinning face pressed close to mine.

"Why do you think you're here, Rosie?" Gently assertive, a hint of a Scots accent. Doctor John Hardy was a hawkish-looking man, around mid-forties, reddish hair turning silver at the sides, piercing pale blue eyes.

It was the next day, and I was in the 'Psychiatrist's Chair', not a place I'd ever imagined myself.

"I was hoping you could tell *me*," I said, feeling inexplicably hostile.

I expected a rebuke or something, but he was unfazed, even smiled good-humouredly, and said nothing. He seemed to have all the time in the world, not in the least disturbed by the silence, a silence I soon began to find excruciating.

Finally, I said, "Three nights ago, I saw my best mate mashed up by a motorbike. But it never happened, it was all in my head. When I woke up I was paralysed, stayed that way for about three hours. Similar things have happened a few times, but I was dealing with it."

"Mm, and how, exactly, were you dealing with it?"

"I've got a lid on my emotions," I said, carelessly, "if I do that, it doesn't happen."

"But the other night, when you thought your friend was going to die?"

"Yeah, well…"

He let the silence drift around us while I fidgeted and avoided his penetrating gaze, those pale blue eyes that seemed to know everything.

"Is that how you dealt with your mother's death," he said eventually, "by keeping your emotions under control?"

I didn't reply. A defensive wall was rising up inside me, and though I suspected it would be unhelpful, there was nothing I could do to prevent it. Once again, that long space of silence. I realised my right knee was trammelling under his intent gaze; motionless as a spider, he could wait an eternity for my response.

With a determined effort, I got my twitchy knee under control, and caved in with a humourless chuckle.

"Wailed like a baby when they told me." I expelled a big sigh. "It was only later, when I saw her lying there… I just felt cold then, kind of numb, you know?"

He nodded slowly. "Not an uncommon response. Tell me about your father – he remains in a coma, I understand."

Stabbing guilt suddenly waded in, pricking the backs of my eyes.

"You find it painful to talk about him?"

I tried to organise a response. "No, no not really. Sorry. It's just that…" I tailed off, not really knowing where I was going with it. Not knowing where to start.

I had decided at some point to stop punishing Dad for Mum's death; if he really was cognisant he'd be hating himself more than I ever could.

But the way I'd treated him...

"It's complicated," I said, finally.

"Alright, Rosie," he said, "we'll deal with that another time. Just take a moment, then, in your own words, talk us through what happened last Friday night."

I told it cold, describing the false vision I'd had in all its gory detail. He didn't interrupt, just let me ramble on in my dull monotone, occasionally making notes. When I finished he let that deafening silence settle on us once more, assessing me now, staring intently.

"Are we done?" I said at last.

"Try to relax for the rest of the day," he said, unfolding from his chair, suddenly business-like, "read a book, use the common room, meet some of the other patients. Take a walk, but stay on the campus. No alcohol. I'll see you again at ten am tomorrow." He opened the door.

"Thanks," I mumbled, fleeing past him.

I was in that place for three weeks.

13

Even though the nurse had warned me before I went in, it was a real shock to see Dad with his eyes open, just staring ahead, blank. He couldn't blink. They dropped gel into them every hour, and closed them at night, like curtains

They'd moved in a TV on a tall trolley into his line of sight; some nature programme was on, bats in Borneo, the sound turned down, but audible. I switched it off and pulled a chair to his bedside.

"Hi Dad, s'mee." I kissed his forehead, "back from the funny farm."

The bed was different too; high tech, electric controls to change position, and a feature to set it slowly undulating to prevent bed sores.

His eyes disturbed me. But for the steady rise and fall of his chest, the softly beeping heart monitor, he could have been a corpse.

I told him everything, haltingly, choking back sobs, longing to see those rigid eyes turn to me and soften. I wanted him to tell me it would be alright. I wanted a hug. I *know*; wallowing in self-pity, feeling about twelve.

But somehow, spilling it all out like that calmed my screwed-up emotions – or let them ride out. Anyway, I felt suddenly chirpier.

"Clinical Depression, can you believe that? Good news is, they've moved me to a rehab centre not far from here. Quite a laidback place, really - I go to counselling sessions twice a week, and the rest of the time's my own.

"Bad news is, I'm probably for the chop. Medical discharge with a small pension and resettlement grant. Then I'm supposed to sign up with an NHS psychiatrist and apply for disability allowance.

"Well sod that for a game of soldiers. Want to hear *my* plan?"

I imagined him nodding sagely, saying: "Go on then, Rosemary, let's hear it."

"I'm going to pay your sister-in-law a surprise visit."

I stopped to let that sink in; processing might be hard work for him.

"I'm going soon, Dad, but I won't get there till Easter. Can you guess why?"

I gave him a full minute, then put my grinning face in the way of those dead eyes.

"Yup, I'm going to get *Pasha* ready to cross the Atlantic, I'm sailing her to Florida just as soon as I get my discharge. Got it all nicely planned out."

Perhaps it was cruel to tell him, but how much crueller to stop visiting him without explanation? I pictured his reaction, were he able. The furthest I'd sailed was Alderney. With him, ten years ago; I'd never sailed out alone.

Until yesterday.

"I know you want to talk me out of it, but if you knew how much I want this…" I stroked his brow, "how much I *need* this…"

I'd decided last night, out in the Channel on *Pasha*. It was only out there, alone under the bright stars, that I came face-to-face with myself, and my demons. It seemed that *Pasha* had done for me what the shrinks could not. Having a plan was cathartic.

"We can still have our Sunday chats while I'm away, cos I've arranged with the nurses to have my emails read out to you. It won't be every Sunday, obviously, I'll be mostly at sea. But whenever I can, you know?"

I gave his hand a stroke, "okay, Dad? And I was thinking you could come to Florida as well, when you... when you're better. I know Georgie would love that. Hey, you might even be there waiting when I get there – now there's a thought."

14

The following Saturday, first weekend in December, I drove back down to Mullhaven to take *Pasha* out for her final sea-trial before departure.

Gary intercepted me in the carpark.

"Got a minute, Rosie, something to show you."

I followed him into the boatshed behind his office.

"There," he said, stopping in front of a pile of junk, "came off an old wooden yawl – if yer still set on this big adventure, that is."

I stared nonplussed at the heap of rusty metal struts and wire cables.

"Oh, and this," he said, adding a wooden, paddle-like object, "the business end o things."

"Er, a self-steering vane?" I guessed.

"A bit weatherworn, granted, but strong and serviceable; she'll fit your boat nicely."

"How much?" I'd looked at self-steering gear online and decided even second-hand ones were way out of my pocket.

"Two-hundred, fitted and set up."

I whistled. "Okay, Gary, what's the catch?"

A mischievous twinkle, "Didn't your old man tell you never look a gift-horse in the mouth?"

I pretended to think a moment, then shook my head, "No, he'd be more likely to say: 'always check astern before you start a turn.'"

He chuckled. "Equally good advice, I'd say. Nah, trust me, this one's all kosher. Cost me nothing, so I'm just charging labour."

We shook hands on the deal, and I agreed to bring *Pasha* to the pontoon after my sail, so he could get to work on it next week.

"Oh, and I dug you out a set of charts and pilots to see you to the Florida coast. They're a few years out of date, but better than spending a grand on new ones, eh?"

"Thanks, Gary, what would I do without you?"

His grin was almost wolfish. He seemed to thrive on pleasing me, which I have to admit, in my desperation, I rather exploited.

The bay, as I paddled the dinghy out to *Pasha*, was grey and overcast, but a throaty breeze blew from the west, a scattering of whitecaps dotted the water beyond the harbour entrance. The forecast promised clouds clearing in the afternoon. It was just the sort of day for a good workout under sail. The sort of day that would have had Dad rubbing his hands with anticipation.

I hoisted the dinghy up on the stern gantry, thinking I would need a different arrangement once the steering vane was fitted. For the oceanic passage I planned to deflate the dinghy and stow it in the forepeak cabin. For shorter trips I would need either to tow it or stow it on deck forward of the mast.

The anchor came up caked in thick, black ooze, so I let it trail in the water for the first few hundred yards, then kicked in the autopilot while I stepped forward to stow it, all clean and shiny once more.

The mainsail slid smoothly up the mast on sliders I'd dry-lubricated this morning at anchor. I'd also shaken out the reef that I'd used to shorten the sail on my previous trip; today I wanted a full load trial, her first serious work with the new rigging. Likewise, I let out the genoa, the big headsail furled around the forestay, to its full extent, simultaneously pulling in on the sheet around the winch, and gave an involuntary whoop as she heeled over sharply to leeward, the wind at ninety degrees on the starboard beam; a beam reach.

Clearing the wide harbour entrance, I killed the engine then just sat there, enjoying the sensation of racing along in relative silence, *Pasha* slicing effortlessly through the short, choppy sea; imagining I could almost hear her rejoice in that blissful whisper of wind and water.

Clearing land, and avoiding a ship mooring buoy - placed there for vessels awaiting instructions from their owners - I eased her gradually downwind, knowing I'd have a serious beat back upwind later. I'd been a bit slow on changing tack on previous trips and wanted to up my game before the passage south.

Meanwhile, it was time to practice sailing goose-winged; a downwind technique I would need for my Atlantic crossing. This involved having the mainsail on one side and the headsail on the other, the latter held out with a metal spinnaker pole clipped onto the mast. With Dad, it had been relatively easy, but for a novice single hander, it was a real challenge. It would also be necessary to attach a preventer rope to the mainsail boom to stop it swinging violently to the other side if the wind suddenly shifted – or I screwed up.

Attaching a preventer to the boom was quite straightforward – I'd got it ready before sailing. The tricky part was bearing out the genoa on the spinnaker pole. Especially tricky because I'd forgotten to get the pole ready for deployment before leaving – I should have had it attached to the mast, instead of fastened in its stowage along the toe-rail.

So I furled away the genoa and went forward. Maybe I should have worn a harness but imagined getting tangled in the complicated array of ropes needed to control the spinnaker pole. Considering the risk minimal, I decided to work free and unencumbered.

Before long I was lost in the complexities of fore-guy, after-guy, and topping lift, getting the right line through the correct block, following the lead through the fairlead and back inboard over the guardrails, imagining how it would deploy when I pulled on this rope or that, twice getting it hopelessly wrong and starting again.

Dad, where are you when I need you?

And all the while casting about anxiously for shipping and fishing floats. The work took twenty frustrating minutes, but I got it right eventually, cursing my ineptitude as finally I locked the leeward genoa sheet into the end of the pole.

The out-rig deployed like a dream; the sun came out, and I sat rolling a congratulatory ciggy as we coasted past dazzling white cliffs at a blistering ten knots.

Early lunch was a cheese and salad sandwich, an apple, and a cup of tea. Cooking, which I was gradually getting the hang of, was for evening meals only, I'd decided.

At noon I unrigged the pole and preventer, then began the long haul back to Mullhaven.

Beating upwind: zigzagging in long legs either side of the wind, turning through the wind at the end of each leg, letting go the one genoa sheet while hauling in on the other. Get it right it goes like clockwork, get it wrong it's a mad, exhausting scramble. I needed the practice.

Four hours and a gruelling sixteen tacks later, with the sun lowering over the port bow, I was within sight of the harbour entrance. I switched to autopilot and sat down to roll a ciggy.

Close-hauled with a genoa that reaches back almost to the cockpit, there is a massive blind spot to leeward. Dad had always warned me about this; reminding me to keep checking beneath the sail for unseen dangers ahead. It must have been the elation of a successful trip, the euphoria of achievement, that distracted me in those critical minutes. Bad seamanship, and bad luck.

There was a shout, close to my ear, shockingly close. *"Leeeewaaard!"*

I stood up, confused, dropped my makings, loose tobacco flying around the cockpit.

I was suddenly thrown against the wheel, an awful juddering crunch from forward. I grabbed onto the backstay as *Pasha* tacked and slewed beam on, dipping her rail deep into the waves. A swirl of cold green water washed into the cockpit. Then a shriek of tortured fibreglass as the big ship mooring buoy disengaged from *Pasha's* shattered bow, scraping along the hull before falling clear astern.

15

Miraculously, Pasha had hove to, the genoa backed against the wind, keeping her heeled over to port so the damaged starboard bow was mostly clear of the water. With a sinking heart I rushed below.

Water gushed up through the saloon sole and slopped from side to side as the boat rolled on the swell. The bilge pump had kicked in, its urgent whirring deadened by total immersion, hopeless against the deluge that had flooded in from forward.

I stared horrified at the devastation in the forepeak. The bed-cushions dislodged and torn among the melee of shattered woodwork, pushed away from the impact on the starboard side, where daylight alternated with the inrush of green water through a ragged, football-sized hole.

I found a pillow among the wreckage and stuffed it into the hole. For the moment, the inflow of water was stemmed, but I could see it wouldn't last long. That sodden pillow would wash out as soon as I tried to get underway.

What would Dad do? I didn't know – we'd never had a collision.

I looked across the saloon at the VHF radio – it had an emergency button. If I activated it, an automatic distress signal would go out with my position and boat details. The coastguard would respond quickly, take me off the boat, try to tow her in. I imagined her slowly sinking, and finally being abandoned.

"Sorry love, we couldn't save your boat."

No way!

I had been well trained in damage control and knew the principles of repairing a breached hull. I thought of the racks of timber, adjustable steel props, and splinter-boxes kept on a warship for that very purpose. I would need to improvise.

I began by clearing away the wreckage from the forepeak; I needed room to work, and time to think of a solution. A flat piece of wood was what I needed, something strong but bendy. There were of course the bedding boards in the forepeak, but those that remained unbroken were either too small to cover the splintered hole, or too big to fit snugly in the space around it.

While I worked, my thoughts kept wandering back to Dad. From nowhere, a memory popped up; a sunny day in East Cowes, me and Dad playing Uckers in the cockpit.

Uckers... of course! I still had Dad's Uckers board; a sixty-centimetre square of polished marine-ply. Perfect.

I remembered also there was a felt carpet under my bunk mattresses. I dragged it out and cut out a square of about a metre. This, placed between the wood and the splintered fibreglass, would help seal the hole.

In the Lazarette I found two suitable pieces of two-by-two and got to work cutting them to length, then, with much grunting and straining in the tight space, managed a fair job of plugging up the hole.

I stood back and admired my handiwork; Dad's Uckers board with its felt backing securely held by the two props jammed into the V of the hull.

The next problem was the water; I'd shipped enough by now to make the boat wallow heavily. It was up to my ankles in the saloon, and spilling over the sill of the engine bay. And the bilge pump had stopped. If water got to the batteries under my bunk, I'd be screwed.

By now soaked to the skin and shivering with cold, I set to work cranking the hand pump – it took three exhausting hours, stopping occasionally to check my position and look out for shipping, but eventually I had the worst of it overboard; still a fair amount slapping under the sole boards, but good enough for now. Good enough for government work; one of Dad's frequent aphorisms.

I suddenly felt weak, exhausted, and had a pounding headache. Dehydration and low blood sugar, I realised. I gulped down a cup of water then scrambled up to the cockpit with a cereal bar crammed into my mouth.

I hadn't moved a great deal in the four or so hours hove to; the red and green lights of the harbour entrance winked enticingly on the starboard quarter. The wind had dropped to a light breeze, the sea black and calm.

I released the genoa sheet and furled it, allowing Pasha to sail off on a starboard tack. Once she had way on, I tacked and pointed at the harbour entrance. Now the damaged section was under water, and I went down to check for leaks, pleased to hear the bilge pump had kicked in again. There was a little seepage around the repair, but nothing to worry about.

I returned to the cockpit and cranked up the engine, full of myself for a disaster averted by prompt and effective action. Ignoring for the time being the complacency and poor seamanship that had got me into this mess, that had probably wrecked my plans for a great trans-Atlantic adventure.

Rolling a ciggy, I was reminded of the strange voice I'd heard just before we hit the buoy. Was it some kind of premonition that had conjured up a vocal warning? Or was I *really* on the verge of madness?

16

"Six Grand? Really?"

Gary looked at me apologetically across his desk. Sandra was tapping away at her keyboard, but I could tell she was listening, could almost hear her self-satisfied gloating.

"Plus VAT," he reminded me. "Obviously that includes haul out and lift in, full repair of the hull, forepeak rebuilt, stained and varnished, with all work guaranteed. Your insurance should cover it."

"She's only insured Third Party," I told him.

He sucked in softly, shaking his head. "Sorry, not much else I can say."

"And supposing I found the cash, how long would it take?"

He did that sucking thing through his teeth. "We're quite busy just now, what with Christmas, and all the…"

"Gary! How long?"

His brow darkened; he sat smouldering a moment, then said, "End of January. Sorry, best I can do."

That evening, three days after my argument with the mooring buoy, I emailed Georgina from home. I didn't exactly ask her for the money, just told her about my encounter with a mooring buoy in the Channel, trying (not very successfully) to make it a funny story, and explained my predicament.

But I secretly hoped she'd come through for me. I hated doing it, but I had nowhere else to turn.

And because I'd kept her in the dark about Doc's death, my so-called mental breakdown and discharge from the Mob, and my plan to sail to Florida, I filled her in on all that too. I didn't want to pile on the agony, but she had to know now.

Next morning her reply was waiting.

> Gosh, Rosie, I don't know where to start.
> Why on earth did you let me believe you were okay, still on your ship somewhere in the Med? When you were going through all that stuff? Didn't I say I'd ALWAYS be there for you? Christ, sweetheart, what were you thinking? Don't EVER do that to me again – if I was there right now, I'd give you a good slap.

The screen blurred; I brushed at my eyes, sniffed, then read on.

> Your account of the collision with a buoy made me laugh, but I can tell you're beating yourself up over it. I've nearly come a cropper myself with that great big genoa, often thought of getting it shortened so you can see under it. Maybe you should consider that. You'll lose a bit of power, but hey, better than what happened???
> And don't worry. Everything will come good. You'll see.
> Now, stay in touch and keep me up to date.
> Much Love
> Georgie

I spent Christmas Day with Dad. The nurses had arranged a dinner party in his room. Santa hats, balloons and crackers. And a miniature Christmas tree. Roast beef and Yorkshire pudding, and plum duff with brandy sauce. And a feeding-tube up the nose for the guest of honour.

I told him all about my mishap in the Channel, imagined him wincing, then a lecture about keeping lookout, and later, a joke about it. The nurses all listened goggle-eyed, a novel kind of Christmas story for them.

It was quite bizarre, but I did enjoy those few hours among the chatty nurses and staff, comforted by their devotion to their silently staring patient, comforted in the knowledge that he'd be well looked after in my long absence.

If I managed to get *Pasha* repaired.

I had about fifteen hundred pounds in my bank account. I needed five thousand more to get Gary started on the work. At least she was hauled out in the boatyard, so I didn't need to worry about her sinking at anchor.

On New Year's Eve I drove down to Pompey to catch up with some of my old shipmates. Windy had got back from deployment in mid-December and most of the girls were on leave, including Doc. We'd exchanged a few emails and she'd promised to drop by at the house for a weekend catch-up early in the New Year.

But the some of the lads I knew were still around; those who were detailed or had volunteered to stay aboard during the leave period, and those sad buggers who simply had nowhere else to go.

I got there just after seven, checked into the Royal Home Club, then walked down to The Hard to meet up in the Ship Anson, our ship's regular haunt just outside the dockyard gate.

A cheer went up when I walked in – as usual, our lot had taken over most of the little pub. They found me a seat, and a pint quickly arrived in front of me. It was great to be there, among those familiar faces, and for a few brief hours, I was one of them again.

Only one thing marred the evening for me. Dicky Doyle, the curmudgeonly ship's painter, came out while I was having a ciggy outside and took me aside.

"MoD plod been onboard, asking questions," he murmured, looking furtively round, "apparently one of the dockyard stores bods has been arrested. Could be something to do with the stuff you er... acquired, shall we say."

"Shit! How much do they know, do you reckon?"

"Not much. Don't think it's anything to worry about. Just thought you ought to know."

"So, they questioned you?"

He chuckled. "Yeah, put on me best cherubic look. Don't worry, your name didn't come up."

When I got home there was an email from Lester Granville, our solicitor, asking me to call at his office in Hazelmere next morning.

The office was in the High Street, a short walk from a supermarket car park where I'd parked. The unobtrusive door was hemmed between a barbershop and a florist. A small brass plaque read simply: Granville & Finningwold, Solicitors.

Lester Granville, seventy-something, urbane and immaculate as always in his three-piece pinstripe, was talking to the receptionist.

"Rosie, my dear!" he said, peering over his ancient half-moon glasses, "come on through."

Lester had been the family's solicitor for as long as anyone could remember; he'd known me all my life, had been a close friend of Granny's when we'd lived in the old house in Guildford.

His office was as urbane and old-fashioned as the man himself. Oak panels adorned with paintings, mainly of racehorses, a sprawling walnut desk fronted by two comfortable chairs upholstered in shiny red leather.

"Take a seat, dear. Tea?"

"Thanks, but no," I said, eager to know why I was here, but too awed to ask.

"Righty ho, then, let's get down to business. We've now completed probate for your late mother's estate. These are the documents," he handed me a thin buff folder, "read them at your leisure, but please keep them in a safe place – we have to charge you if you ever need duplicates produced."

He smiled over his glasses, grey eyes that matched his hair. Was that it, a folder he could just have posted?

"I'll just fill you in in some of the detail. First there's this," he slid a cheque across his desk to me, "the balance of your mother's estate, minus our fee and the outstanding bills and invoices you've kindly sent in."

I looked at the cheque; £879.69p.

"You'll find a full financial breakdown in the file. But there's something else. Your mother opened a Trust Fund shortly after you were born. It would appear she made regular payments into this fund until about eleven years ago. It'll take a week or so to get the funds transferred, but the balance of the account is quite substantial."

My throat went dry.

"How much?"

"Something in the region of thirty-five thousand pounds."

I emailed Gary the minute I got home.

A week later, after yet another counselling session with my outpatient consultant, I went down to check on the work on *Pasha*.

Locking up the car, I noticed a police car in the carpark, nobody inside. I wouldn't normally have given it another thought, but Dicky's news had left me edgy.

They'd un-stepped Pasha's mast and moved her into the boatshed. There was scaffolding around the bow; the damaged section had been cut out, leaving a big square hole.

"What's happening, Gary? I'd have thought they'd have at least started on the fibre-glassing by now."

"Got staff problems," he said, then gave a derisive snort, "man-flu."

He saw my glum look and softened his tone.

"Paul should be back tomorrow, then we'll get started. She'll be ready end of the month, promise."

"So what do the cops want?" I said.

"Oh, them. They're still trawling for witnesses for that murder back in the summer. They're talking to some of the younger lads that might've been out on the town the night it happened, askin' if they saw anything. Bit late if you ask me."

He must have noticed my relief.

"Don't worry, Rosie, you ain't on their radar."

As far as you know, I thought. The sooner I sailed away, the   better.

17

Gary was true to his word; by the beginning of February *Pasha* was back in the water, restored to her beautiful self, with the addition of the reconditioned self-steering vane bolted onto the transom.

I spent the following week ferrying bags of food and clothing from home down to Mullhaven, and by Sunday, with every nook and cranny filled with tinned food and bottles of water, fuelled up and fired up, I was ready to go.

I made one final drive home, popped in to say goodbye to Dad on the way, locked the car in the garage and secured the house. Then I took the train to Chichester, and a taxi to Mullhaven, and slept onboard overnight, ready for an early departure in the morning.

I was just preparing to slip from the pontoon next morning, when Gary Palmer came running along the jetty, calling to me. He was carrying a large holdall.

"Look, Rosie, I been thinking. You've never used a steering vane before - they can be tricky if you don't know how to set 'em up. So why don't I come with you as far as Lisbon, and I'll teach you how it works?"

The out-of-the-blue offer stunned me – he'd had all the past week to mention this, and anyway, I felt a little put out by his assumption that I'd want him along. It also felt a little patronising – the vane gear didn't look complicated; it couldn't be rocket-science. Besides, I wanted to do this alone.

"I don't know, Gary, I'm not really prepared for a two-hander. You know, food, water; and I've only got one lifejacket, one set of foul-weather gear."

He gave me a worried frown.

"I got all my own gear," he said, "an' we can always pop in at La Corunna if we get short o provisions." He nodded at the vane on the stern, "That stuff ain't as simple as it looks, you know, and getting it wrong could get you in all sorts o trouble. Now, you got a nice new bunk in the v-berth, what say I break it in for you, eh?"

"But what about your work? Aren't you needed here?"

"Oh, Sandra can manage without me for a couple o weeks, she practically runs the place anyway. I been thinking about a holiday; a nice cruise and a week in the Algarve sounds just perfect."

I tried to find other objections, but in the end, I caved in. I threw him a cheerful smile.

"All right, Gary, you're on. Climb aboard."

There was an odd moment after he swung his bag over the rail and made to grab the shroud; the boat suddenly healed over away from him and he almost lost his balance. He got safely aboard, however, and grinned sheepishly.

"Whew, that could've ended badly, must've been a bit o ground swell."

I looked out onto the bay – a force five, easterly was forecast for later, but right now, it was a millpond.

After we cleared the harbour, a light breeze sprang up. We set full sails to run before it and killed the engine.

"Cup of tea?" I asked Gary, who'd taken the helm while I'd trimmed the sails.

"Lovely!"

While I was waiting for the kettle, I started the log with the initial entry:

8th February 2013
Crew: Rosie Carter (Capt), Gary Palmer
0745: Departed Mullhaven bound for Lisbon, Portugal.

From now on I would log our Position, Course & Speed roughly every four hours.

Coming up to the cockpit with the tea, I was grateful for my heavy-duty salopette and seaboots. It was a chilly morning, still overcast, with occasional flurries of snow blowing into the cockpit from the stiffening easterly. Gary, who'd pulled on his foul-weather jacket, flicked on the autopilot, sat down and took a slurp of his tea.

"Ahh, that's just what I needed," he said.

He'd seemed quite tense as we'd crossed the harbour, but now appeared more relaxed. Like me, I thought; most at home out on the water. We both began rolling cigarettes. I'd made a New Year Resolution to only smoke with a drink. Tea counted.

"Right," said Gary, putting down his empty mug, "let's have a go at that steering vane, eh?"

His sudden assertiveness irritated me – I was skipper, after all. But I let it go for now.

He hitched himself up onto the stern counter and patted a seat beside him. "Hop up here and we'll get started with your intro to self-steering."

I shuffled down beside him.

"Now, this is called a servo-pendulum system, or SPS. It's purely mechanical, no drain on yer batteries, see. Once set up, it'll always sail to the wind, never to a course. That means, if the wind changes, your course changes. All clear so far?"

I nodded. "Go on."

"Now, this here at the top is the windvane, same principle as that un on yer wind turbine. This wooden bit at the bottom is the steering oar, it reacts to movement of the windvane by turning its angle. When that happens, the pressure moves the oar to one side or other, see?"

"Yup, all clear so far."

"Now, you'll see I've bolted a drum to the front of your wheel. That's where these lines go, and I'll show you how in a minute. The most important thing to learn, is that if yer sails ain't balanced, this rig won't work properly, and running downwind like this, especially now the wind's getting up, we probably need to reduce sail."

It took an hour to explain, but I got it. It was more complicated than I'd assumed, and there were quite a few little traps and idiosyncrasies to take in, but I got it.

1203: 50 28.3N 00 57.8W Co 260M Sp 8.
Wind E 18 kts Px 1014MB
Sailing: 2 Reefs & Shortened Genoa.
Self-Steering Rig working well

I was pleased as punch with my new rig, and Gary seemed equally chuffed with himself that I'd picked it up so quickly.

I didn't have the heart to tell him I'd been reading up online and watching YouTube videos on how to do it.

Ungrateful, I know, but now I'd mastered the windvane, I didn't really want him onboard anymore. It felt like he was trying to take over, and I'd had to assert my authority as skipper more than once during the day.

Like when we'd reefed the main, earlier.

"Take the halliard, Gary, I'll go to the mast."

"No, my dear, let me go forward, that sea's getting' a bit boisterous."

"Gary! Take the fucking halliard!"

He reacted with that surly look I was growing to hate, his eyeballs casting to the sky.

"Alright, have it your way," he muttered, "just take care up there."

That evening I boiled some rice and heated up a pot of Thai curried chicken. Yeah, I'd been practicing my culinary skills, with tips and tricks from Georgie in her emails. I'd knocked up batches of curries, stews, and bolognaise sauce at home and portioned them into sealable plastic tubs. Enough to last me to Gib, or at least it would have been when there was only me to feed.

"Right, I'm going to get some shuteye," Gary declared after dinner, "call me when you want a relief."

"I'll call you at eight, Gary," I said, coldly, "four-hour watches. You do the first, I'll do the middle, you do the morning. *If* that's alright with you?"

I couldn't see his face in the darkness but sensed his anger. "Too bad if it ain't by the sounds of it," he said, then stomped below.

I shouted down after him, "Just remember whose skipper here, Gary, and we'll get along just fine."

"Doubt it," he muttered, slamming the forepeak cabin door behind him.

This was going to be the voyage from hell.

I couldn't do it.

Fifteen miles to the northwest was Portland Bill; I could see its loom on the horizon. In the morning, I decided right then, I would drop him off somewhere convenient for the train.

The wind was gradually backing, and I made incremental adjustments to the vane until I was forced to gybe. Then I took the lines off the windvane and engaged the autopilot. I would need to tell Gary tonight of my change of plan.

1945: 50 28.3N 02 31.7W Co 275M Sp 5.
Wind NNE 14 kts Px 1014MB

At eight, I went below and knocked on his door. "Gary," I said quietly, "eight-o-clock, you awake?"

"Yeah," he grunted, "be there in a jiffy."

I picked up my phone from the chart table and checked for a signal – I could at least check his train times for him.

The saloon light came on. Gary looked at the phone in my hand, then at the chart plotter.

"Why we headin' for Torbay, Rosie?"

"This isn't working, Gary, for either of us. I'm going to drop you in Brixham. You can get the train home from there."

He became very still, his expression wolf-like. He shook his head, sadly. "Can't let you do that, my dear."

"I'm sorry, Gary, but I'm not arguing about it. I'm very grateful for…"

He came up close, his face livid. I stood my ground. I wasn't about to be bullied by this man.

"I *said*," he slapped the phone out of my hand, sending it clattering onto the sole boards, "I can't let you do that. This boat goes to Portugal."

I took a step backwards to get out of his face, fighting for clear thoughts through rising panic. In a flash of inspiration, I shot my arm out to the VHF to hit the distress button, but he was quicker; pushed me aside and turned off the radio, then swung back towards me.

"Big mistake, darling."

His huge backhand slammed against my cheek bone, sending me sprawling into the galley space. Swooning from fear and dizziness, I tried to scramble to my feet, but now he dropped his full weight down on me, groping for my throat. I managed to get my legs up under him, my feet on his chest, and with a strength fuelled by terror, sprung my legs out straight.

He staggered back across the saloon, caught the table edge, and fell onto the sole boards with a thundering crash.

While he struggled to extricate his big frame from between banquette and mess-table I swept up my phone from the deck and leapt up into the cockpit.

I fumbled in the dark, trying to get the phone dial-pad up on screen, aware of his huge shadow rising out of the companionway, me hitting all the wrong buttons in my terror. I'd entered the second nine of 999, when the phone was dashed out of my hands and sent spinning over the guardrail.

He grabbed the front of my salopette and heaved me up and backwards, grabbing my wrists and arching my back over the cockpit table, his body pressed tightly against me. I tried desperately to get a knee into his groin, but to no avail. I was helpless under his deadening weight.

"Feisty girl, aintcha?" he grunted, his face close to mine, leering, drooling spittle. "Strong thighs too, I likes that in a girl, I really do."

He released one of my wrists and began pulling down the zipper of my salopette. I beat my clenched fist against his head, the only part I could reach with my free hand but could find no purchase to give my blows any strength.

By now he had the zipper down below my waist, and his big hand began to explore inside, pushing down towards my panties.

Suddenly, my thoughts cleared. I stopped resisting, and arched further back, reaching my arms backwards in an act of total submission.

"That's right my dear," he breathed, "lie back and think of England. Much better for both on us that way."

His hand was now deep down there – fighting revulsion, I parted my legs as if to welcome his big, probing fingers, felt his hot breath heavy and urgent on my face.

I felt like puking, imagined throwing up spew into that leering face. Instead I concentrated on my fingers, reaching, reaching. I let out a moan as one huge finger pressed crudely against my lily, trying to penetrate.

At long last my fingertips brushed against the PVC pocket I'd been searching for. I moved them upwards until I felt the cold handle inside. I parted my thighs wider, making him delirious with desire, then grabbed the winch handle and swung it down on his head with all the strength I could muster.

He fell back onto the seating, stunned, but clearly still conscious. I should have hit him again then, but by now my thoughts were far from ordered. Instead, I scrabbled away from him to the other side of the cockpit, zipped up my salopette, and sat on the counter, watching him, the winch handle still in my hand.

Gary sat slumped, lowered head shaking slowly from side to side. In the light from the saloon I could see I'd caught him on the left temple; his hair on that side glistened with blood, dark lines of it ran down his cheek and jaw.

I had to think fast. I couldn't bring myself to finish the job, not in cold blood. That'd be murder, wouldn't it? Or justifiable homicide. Was there such a thing?

The radio, of course!

I shimmied toward the companionway. But I'd left it too late. Gary staggered to his feet and blocked my way, glowering at me with seething hatred.

"Look, Gary, you need help. Let me call the coastguard and I promise I won't mention any of this. I'll say you had a fall, let them take you ashore, eh? Get you fixed up?"

He wasn't listening, stood there snorting like a bull, intent on revenge. With a snarl he sprang at me. I leapt up onto the counter, backs of my thighs hard up against the top guardrail, hanging onto the bimini frame. As he bore down on me I swung the winch handle, but he blocked it with his arm.

Just then, inexplicably, *Pasha* lost her wind and lurched to starboard. Gary groped the air, made a grab for me, and toppled over the guardrail.

There was an anguished cry from somewhere, and for a nanosecond I thought it was over. But I was jerked backwards and realised he'd caught hold of the back of my salopette; I lost my grip on the wet slippery frame and plunged into an icy sea.

18

A big silvery moon had come out from behind the clouds; shimmering and wobbling on the surface far above me, it guided me back up through the freezing, swirling confusion. I broke surface, gasping with cold-shock. Icy water had flooded the lining of my salopette. Somewhere close by, Gary was spluttering and crying out incoherently.

I took a deep breath and let myself slip under again as I struggled to kick off my seaboots. I'd practiced sea-survival countless times in the Navy and knew the rules by heart. Estimated survival time in these waters, good swimmer without lifejacket, ten minutes.

Lifted on a wave crest, I glimpsed *Pasha's* stern light as she sailed away into the night. Then, falling back into the trough, I heard a shout close by, and a great weight descended on me, pushing me deep down again. I surfaced to find Gary flailing hopelessly, gasping and spluttering between cries for help, trying to grab onto me.

"I can't... swim," he gasped, "please... help me."

He reached out for me again, but I kicked away from him. I had no intention of dying in his foul embrace – better to drown alone.

After a short while I couldn't hear him anymore.

Oddly, I felt no fear. Just a weird kind of detachment, a calm acceptance of the fate that had determined, here was my end. Deep sadness, yes, regrets, yes. But no fear.

Most of all, I wanted my Dad.

A wave lifted me, and I saw a light. A green light. A ship! Next wave, I saw it again. And again. It seemed stationary, a trawler, perhaps, pulling in nets, and not too far. Hoping against hope, I began to swim towards it.

It was slow, hard work to swim in that choppy, windblown sea. The cold was already seeping into my joints, making them ache, weakening my efforts. Once it got to my core, it would be game over.

But hope pushed me on, slow, steady strokes, don't overwork, conserve energy. Energy is life.

I kept losing sight of that green light in the troughs, but rising on each crest, I saw it again, adjusting my direction, keeping my focus on one simple objective – to reach that light, to survive.

But inevitably, the deadly cold was working its way into my core and my waterlogged salopette was dragging heavily, draining the last of my reserves.

I lost track of time; everything became dreamlike. I knew the end was close. I hadn't seen the light for some time now. Hope faded. I couldn't swim another stroke. I was numb and exhausted. I was finished.

I turned onto my back, and let my head slip beneath the water, looking up at that big silvery moon for the last time.

I was about to let the cold, soothing sea into my tortured lungs with a last, fatal inhalation, when something butted against my head. I struggled upright, ran my hands disbelievingly over the smooth white surface. From somewhere I found the strength to swim on my back, along the sleek hull to find a way to climb aboard. Reaching the stern, I saw the name on the transom, and thought I must have died after all. And there was my way aboard; the self-steering rig.

I don't think climbing Everest could have been harder than dragging my exhausted body up that rig, it took every ounce of my being, every atom of willpower.

A long time afterwards, I sat dazed and shivering in the saloon, a duvet around me, cradling a cup of hot chocolate in my numbed fingers.

Pasha's autopilot had somehow disengaged itself, and she had naturally hove to. I didn't ponder on my unbelievable luck, had other things to get my sluggish mind around.

Namely, what to do now.

"Call it in, Rosemary."

I sat up, suddenly alert, and a little frightened.

"Who said that?" I said, feeling immediately stupid for having done so. Okay, so I was hallucinating, hearing voices. That was understandable for someone in hypothermic shock. Wasn't it?

But whether or not I'd imagined it, it was the right thing to do. I should call in a mayday.

I struggled to my feet, stiff and creaking like an old woman, and switched on the VHF. As soon as it powered up, I pushed in the Distress button, checked our position on the chart plotter, and unclipped the mic.

Mayday, Mayday, Mayday
This is sailing yacht Pasha,
My position, three-one miles east of Berry Head, I say again, three-one miles east of Berry Head.
I have a man overboard, I say again, man overboard.
Have been unable to locate my lost crewmember. Please send assistance.
This is sailing yacht Pasha, over.

The reply came instantly.

Pasha, this is Falmouth Coastguard,
Copied your Mayday. Rescue services have been alerted.
What is your present course and speed, the time of your man overboard, and your best estimate of the man-overboard position?

I thought a moment, then said.

This is Pasha,
I am currently hove to, making zero decimal two knots on a track of two zero zero. The incident happened within the past two hours, and my best estimate is within one mile of me, possibly to the north, over.

Thank you, Pasha, now please report the size of your vessel, and number of souls remaining onboard.

This is Pasha, I am a thirty-two-foot sloop, with one person remaining onboard, over.

This is Falmouth Coastguard, Roger that, Pasha. Please remain in your current location. Helicopter, callsign Rescue 56 has been scrambled, and should be with you shortly. Out
All Stations, All Stations, All Stations. This is Falmouth Coastguard, Search and Rescue operations in progress in Lyme Bay. One person reported missing. All vessels in the area are requested to keep good lookout and report any sightings. Stations not involved are requested to minimise traffic on Channel Sixteen until further notice, Falmouth Coastguard, out.

I slumped back down and rolled a ciggy. Ten minutes later, Rescue 56 came on the radio, ordering me to sail to Dartmouth and await further instructions.

I was in a semi-trance at the wheel some hours later when the report came through that a body had been recovered.

19

I woke to a knocking on the side of the boat.

"Hello, anyone aboard?"

"Just a minute," I croaked, climbing stiffly out of bed. There was a throbbing on the side of my face. I glanced in the mirror; a dark bruise on my cheekbone from Gary's club of a hand. Pulling on jeans and sweater, I poked my head out of the companionway.

A man and a woman were standing on the quayside. He was smartly-dressed in suit and tie, briefcase and a grim face; she in dark trousers and blue jersey with Coastguard epaulettes, apologetic smile.

"Hi," I said.

"Are you the captain of this vessel, Madam?" It was the woman that spoke. She was fortyish with a lived-in face and short, dark hair.

"Yes, I was told to wait here until someone came to see me – er, I guess that's you?"

The man stepped forward, "May we come aboard?" making it clear that I had no choice in the matter. He stepped over the guardrail, and the woman followed. I led them down the ladder, and offered them tea, which they declined.

She sat next to me on the banquette, he took a seat opposite, opened his briefcase on the table in front of him.

"My name is Karen," she said, wincing slightly as she caught sight of my bruised face, "and I'm from the Maritime Coastguard Agency."

"Rosie," I said, shaking hands, "Rosie Carter."

"And this gentleman is Mark Bland, from the Marine Accident Investigation Branch."

"Hello," I nodded across the table.

A curt return nod, still sorting out papers from his briefcase.

"I'm so sorry your crewman didn't survive," Karen said, a hand tentatively on my shoulder, "but after so long in the water..." she grimaced and shrugged.

I nodded.

"Was he a relative?"

I shook my head. "He was a... someone I knew. I'd intended to go solo, but he offered to crew for me as far as Portugal."

She gave a slow nod, relieved, probably, that she wasn't dealing with a grieving daughter or niece. "And how are you feeling, now, Rosie?" she said, crooningly, "Are you up to answering to a few questions?"

I nodded.

The man from the MAIB lifted his briefcase onto the seat next to him, leaving two official-looking forms on the table. He took a pen from his inside pocket, and clicked it, efficient and business-like.

"Now, Rosie" he said, "I've been sent to investigate a fatality at sea – a standard procedure, and nothing sinister. My job is not to apportion blame or responsibility, but to determine the facts of the accident and submit them for Branch Review. After the necessary form filling, I'll need to see your boat registration, ship's log and take photographs of your current navigation chart. Then you'll need to show me exactly what happened last night. I'll take a look around the boat and may snap off a more few pictures. Alright?"

I nodded again, thinking furiously. If I told it how it was, I'd be stuck here forever; police enquiries were bound to follow, endless questions and interviews. Fuck! I might not even be believed – what then?

The lengthy form-filling at least gave me chance to get the story straight in my head. I apologised that I hadn't filled in the logbook since the incident.

"Quite the usual thing," he said, "understandable under the circumstances – in shock and alone, looking for your lost crew– last thing one thinks about is keeping a record, eh? Now, let's go up top and you can show me exactly what happened."

Up in the cockpit, he said, "Now take your time and think carefully, just before the accident, describe the situation for me."

I sat down next to the wheel on the starboard side.

"I was sitting just here. We were on a beam reach, starboard tack, heading about due west, six knots. Two reefs in the main, three quarters of the genoa out. Sailing on autopilot. There was a biggish sea from the starboard quarter. Gary was coming up the ladder to relieve me."

"Any shipping about at that time?" he asked.

"Could just about make out the lights of Torbay ahead. We'd passed some fishing boats about half an hour earlier, but there was nothing else since."

"And what happened next?"

"The autopilot had been struggling a bit – I'd had to take her in hand a couple of times." I shook my head, "Gary stood up on the counter to look out over the sprayhood. Just then, a big wave slewed her round to port, and the autopilot lost it. Before I could do anything, she broached and the mains'l gybed – it all happened in an instant; that boom whipped across so fast… then… Gary wasn't… wasn't there anymore."

I put my head in my hands and looked down at my feet, felt Karen's arm go around my shoulder.

"Take your time, Rosie," she murmured. "Go on when you're ready."

"Er, before you do," Mark said, "just to be clear, neither of you were wearing lifejackets or harnesses, is that correct?"

"I know we should have been. But... no, we weren't."

"Very well," he said, "what happened next?"

"*Pasha* was head to wind, rolling like a pig, sails flogging like crazy... no wait a minute, that's not right."

I paused, felt my face reddening, trapped in my erroneous fabrication.

"No," I said, finally, "we were downwind. That's right. The main was filled, and the genoa was flogging a bit on the lee. I turned to port and heaved in on the mainsheet until she hove to. Yeah, that was it."

I looked at Karen, "It was a confusing situation, sorry."

"I understand," she said, but there was a look in her eyes. Unsure of me, now.

Mark was staring but said nothing.

I hurried on. "I thought I couldn't have gone very far since he went over. If I tried to sail off to turn and search for him I'd have wasted time and maybe miss the chance of him swimming back to the boat. So I stayed hove to and called in the Mayday."

"Mm," he said, "under the circumstances, heaving to was probably the right call. It's always a difficult one, that. So what time was it, when you got chance to look?"

"Not sure, but you'll know when I called it in. Couldn't have been more than a few minutes after he went over."

"The call was logged at 2214," Mark said, "so, shall we say, five minutes before that?"

I nodded, "that'd be about right, sorry."

By now I was burning with guilt and wishing I'd told the truth. I'd added two hours to the actual time of Gary dragging us both over. Would they be able to tell how long he'd been in the water? Would they even bother to check?

Either way, too late now – I was stuck with my lies.

Mark was studying the lifebuoy in its stowage, the polyester lifeline dry and neatly stowed in its net. He stepped across and examined it.

"You didn't think to deploy this" he said, "to help Mister Palmer get back if he could have?" He seemed incredulous, justifiably so.

I shook my head, sadly. "Never thought," was all I could think of.

Stepping back to the starboard banquette, he touched his polished shoe against the empty pocket by the winch.

"You're missing a winch handle," he said.

"Yeah, lost it overboard a while back."

Only partly true; it had gone overboard last night.

"That's a nasty bruise," he said, studying my face, "how did you come by it?"

"Oh, that," I said, padding fingers gingerly over my swollen cheek, "when she gybed the mainsheet whipped across my face."

He sucked his teeth. "Nasty!"

They'd been gone less than an hour when the police car pulled   up   on   the   quay.

20

I was on the coach roof stowing the mainsail when they pulled up. My heart sank. Two uniforms emerged from the car, one, the driver, a woman. These were followed by a man in jeans and a black waterproof.

"Rosemary Carter, is it?" said the latter.

"That's right, but I go by Rosie. How can I help?"

"I'm Detective Sergeant Yardley. You lost a crew member last night. We need a statement."

He was craggy and square, like a rugby player, a diffident manner overlaid with strong west-country. A statement. That didn't sound too ominous. But why three of them? And why a detective?

"Okay," I said brightly, "be right with you."

They all three stood watching me tug the lazy-bag zipper along the length of the boom. Finishing, I jumped down into the cockpit.

"Come aboard." I said, smiling.

"Er, no, Rosie, it doesn't work like that. We need you to come with us to the police station."

"Oh, okay. I'll just lock up the boat then."

"There'll be no need for that, Constable Davies here will stay with your boat. She'll be quite safe."

The woman went to the car and opened the rear door for me. I thought for a bad moment she was going to put a hand on my head like they do in films, but she just hovered until I was safely inside, then closed the door. Yardley got in the front passenger seat. Nobody spoke during the short drive.

I was shown to a dreary interview room, a humming strip-light and a whiff of disinfectant. A table lay against one wall, three moulded plastic chairs, an angle poise lamp and a recording machine.

Yardley followed me in and ushered me to the single chair, then took one of the two opposite, dropping a blue file cover on the table. The female uniform entered with a plastic cup, which she placed in front of me.

"It's tea," she said, the first time she'd spoken, "hope that's okay. No sugar I'm afraid. We're out." She smiled an apology.

"Don't worry," I smiled back, "I'm sweet enough."

They both grinned at that, but not for long.

Yardley switched on the recorder.

"Interview with Rosemary Carter, Wednesday 13th of February 2013, officers present: Detective Sergeant Paul Yardley, and Constable June Agutter. The time now is 1536."

He turned his face to me.

"Now, Rosie, we're investigating the death of Gary Palmer. Before we begin, I have to caution you. You do not have to say anything. But it may harm your defence if you do not mention when questioned something which you later rely on in Court. Anything you do say may be given in evidence. Do you understand?"

I stared, gobsmacked. "Am I under arrest, then?"

"Don't worry, Rosie," said the woman, Agutter, "it's just a formality. You're not being accused of anything at this stage. Fatalities at sea have to be investigated."

"I know that," I said, "I've already given a statement today. A guy from MAIB came to see me earlier."

"Yeah, we know," said Yardley, "we have a copy of Mister Bland's report. There are a few things we're puzzled about, a few things we need to clear up."

Heat crept up into my face. I felt trapped. I sat back and tried to relax.

"Okay," I said, "fire away."

They made me go through the whole thing again, and I tried my best to keep the story consistent. When I'd finished, they looked at me in silence for a moment."

"What!" I said, "you don't believe me? Why the f... why on earth would I lie?"

A good question, one I was now asking myself.

Yardley opened the folder and took something out. "For the record," he said, "I'm now showing Ms Carter a post-mortem photograph of Gary Palmer."

The picture he placed in front of me was a close-up of Gary's dead face, ashen grey, eyes mercifully closed. Wet matted hair had been lifted away from his right temple, exposing the now washed out open wound where I'd hit him.

Yardley said, "Rosie, can you explain the wound to Mister Palmer's head?"

"I can only guess that the boom hit him there when it knocked him over. I didn't see it happen. We'd broached in heavy weather, and I was busy dealing with the boat."

"Well, see, Rosie, that's something that don't quite add up with me, being a sailor myself. The wind was from the north, fifteen to twenty knots according to the Coastguard reports, with a sea running sou'westerly. A broach in they conditions would've spun your bow to windward. You couldn't have gybed. You see my problem?"

I sat glaring at him. He was right, of course. In my confusion I'd given the wrong story to Bland, having changed it from the one that would've worked.

"Even if you had gybed," he continued, "which I see from your expression, you know is improbable, you'd know you had a crewmember in harm's way. You're an experienced yachtswoman, he'd be your first priority, not so?"

I studied my trainers under the table, trying to think clearly.

"For the recording, Ms Carter looks down and declines to comment. Now, Rosie, look closely at the wound on Mister Palmer's temple. You see those, what look like teeth marks around it? Can you explain them for me?"

I let out a horselaugh, stupid, I know, but I said, "I didn't bite him to death, if that's what you mean."

Agutter drew a sharp breath and looked up at the ceiling.

"No, you didn't bite him," said Yardley, clearly irritated at my flippancy, "but those marks are consistent with a blow from the business end of…"

"Okay, okay. There was no broach. I whacked him with the winch-handle. He attacked me - it was self-defence."

Agutter looked shocked.

Yardley sat back with a satisfied smirk. After a moment he said, "Interview suspended at 1611," and switched off the machine.

"At this stage, Rosie," his voice now softer, a friendly smile, "you might want to consider having a legal representative present. We can arrange one for you, or you might want to appoint your own. Do you have a solicitor?"

I shook my head. "Not down here, he's based in Surrey."

Agutter said, "We can let you phone him, if you like?"

"No, it's okay. Please get me someone."

Just then, the door opened; a man poked his head in. "Sorry, Paul. I need a word. Somethings come up."

They left me stewing alone, and gradually, those dark clouds of guilt gave way to the liberation of a truth about to be told. I'd behaved like a fool; I was the victim here, after all.

I began to go over the real events of last night, reliving the horror, but intent on accuracy in the inevitable next interview. Then I was struck by an appalling notion; what if the incident with Gary had been one of my turns? Had I simply conjured up his violent assault and reacted in imaginary self-defence, stunning him with the winch handle and shoving him overboard?

But I'd been in the water too, my wet clothes and salopette hanging in the head this morning was proof of that; the MAIB guy had commented on it. I touched my tender cheek. And how did...

Yardley entered the room. He was alone, carrying a cup of tea. He smiled and put it in front of me, china cup this time, not a machine-brew.

"No sugar," he grinned, "cuz you're sweet enough?"

He sat down opposite but didn't switch on the recorder.

He looked at me a moment, then said, "Tell me about Gary Palmer. How long have you known him?"

I paused, thinking.

"I first met him properly in around August last year, when I started refitting *Pasha*, my boat, well, my Dad's boat actually. Look, what's going on?"

"You say that was when you met him properly. You knew him before that?"

"Yes, about nine years ago, when I used to go sailing with my Dad. He'd only been there a few weeks then though. The Manager was a different guy before that. I think he died, and Gary came and took over."

"Did Mr Palmer ever tell you where he'd worked before he came to Mullhaven?"

"No, why would he? And what's this all about?"

"He never mentioned Penlaggen, in Cornwall?"

"No!" I was getting really irritated by now.

"Or that he'd worked in Mullhaven before, as a rigger, in the 1980's?"

"No, I didn't know that. Look, are you going to arrest me, or can I go now?"

"I don't want to arrest you, Rosie, but it would be better for both of us if you stayed here a while longer. All I can tell you just now is that you are helping us with our enquiries in a murder investigation."

"Murder? But I…"

"We're not investigating you, Rosie, otherwise this interview would have been recorded. Suffice to say, were Gary Palmer still alive, he would right now be being interviewed under caution."

Later that evening, after a meal of fish and chips, courtesy of Devon & Cornwall Police, I gave them the statement I should have from the first, leaving out nothing; not even my abandonment of Gary in the water, for which I felt justified. Off the record, Yardley agreed, though I would now have to tell that to the coroner's inquest.

After that, I was free to go, but told to be in nearby Totnes for the inquest the following Monday. When I got back to *Pasha* later that evening, the copper they'd left in charge was removing blue and white tape from her guardrails. For a horrible few hours, my boat had been a designated crime scene.

As I sank into my bunk a great weight lifted from my shoulders.

21

Next morning, I moved *Pasha* across the river and took a berth at the marina, a chance to top up my fuel and water tanks, and keep the batteries charged on shore power.

And Internet access. As soon as I got connected I wrote Georgie a long email about what happened. Then I used a pay-phone ashore to call the hospital to check on Dad. There'd been no change – he was 'comfortable'.

I waited another half an hour for a reply from Georgie, but none came, so I decided to take a long walk to clear my head.

It was a sunny but bitingly cold morning as I struck out along the clifftop from Kingswear, following the coast around towards Berry Head. The wind had shifted back to the east, bringing an ear-pinching chill that made me wish I'd brought my beany-hat and gloves.

I upped my pace and forged on, taking in the gorgeous coastal scenery and steely-blue seascape beyond, and quite soon the effort of climbing and descending the rugged coastal path pumped heat into those extremities and lifted my spirits.

Around mid-afternoon, getting thirsty, having long-since emptied my water bottle, and not to mention a mite peckish, I struck inland. An hour later I found a pub on the Brixham road and sat down to a crab sandwich and a pint of local cider. Afterwards, I caught the bus back to Kingswear.

Back at the marina, I took a long, hot shower in the washrooms, then, as a chill darkness fell on the late afternoon, I dug out Dad's old fan-heater and plugged it into the mains socket – one of the many benefits of shore-power. As the saloon grew warm and cosy, I settled down with my Kindle to read Joshua Slocum's *Sailing Alone Around the World,* one of Georgie's recommendations.

I was soon lost in the extraordinary tale of this nineteenth-century sailor, the first ever single-handed circumnavigation. It was after midnight when I finally crawled into my bunk.

That night I dreamt of sparkling jewels exploding upwards from the bow and cascading down on me in the open cockpit, diamond necklaces thrown up then split asunder in a shower of gems. The dream turned dark, however, when a faceless shadow emerged out of the companionway and lunged at me. I tried to get away, but my limbs refused to move; I tried to scream, as two great banana hands reached out towards my throat, but no sound came.

I jerked awake, feet kicking, stubbing a knee painfully on the headlining. Then I forgot the dream as a vicious cramp locked my right calf. I jumped out of bed and stamped my foot on the deck until the muscle relaxed.

My own stupid fault; after yesterday's unaccustomed exertions, I should've done some stretching exercises before turning in. It was five-thirty, too late to hope for more sleep. I made tea, rolled a ciggy, and went back to my reading, awaiting the hunger that would signal breakfast.

Friday and Saturday passed uneventfully. I spent the time reading, lunching at a little pub in the village, and wandering the gift shops; it was dead of Winter, and there were few people about. As the weekend dragged by, I grew increasingly anxious about the coming inquest. And puzzled that Georgie hadn't replied to my email.

On Sunday, I motored *Pasha* up the Dart, winding my careful way up the picture-book river to Totnes, and found a space to tie up at the Steamer Quay.

The inquest was at ten-o-clock next morning at the Civic Hall. I got there early and took a seat at the back. Yardley was already there, stood talking to a couple of uniformed officers up near the raised bench; he nodded to me as I entered but didn't come over. On the bench above, the Coroner was fussing over some paperwork with a clerk. Press photographers and reporters milled around in little groups. There were a few curious glances as I took my seat, but I avoided eye contact. They would know who I was soon enough.

It turned out a bit of an anti-climax. Yardley was first to give evidence, and after giving the name of the deceased, read out the statement I'd given. I was then called, and asked if the statement was accurate, if there was anything I wished to add. I said no.

Someone from the Crown Prosecution was called and told the court there was compelling evidence that Palmer had been the perpetrator of a brutal murder in Mullhaven and the rape of several young women over the past twenty years. He had been about to be apprehended by Sussex Police when he made his escape, deceiving Ms Carter into helping him abscond abroad.

He also mentioned that Gary's holdall, which I'd handed over to Police last week, had contained a large quantity of cash which he'd embezzled from the Boatyard. For a shameful, but fleeting moment I regretted making that Mayday call.

The cause of death was drowning. The blow to the head was not considered a contributing factor. The verdict: Death by Misadventure.

When it was over, the press people made a hurried and untidy exit. I was about to follow when Yardley intercepted me.

"Not that way, Rosie, unless you want they morons firing questions and flash bulbs in your face."

He led me to a door in the back of the hall, and down a corridor to a side entrance.

"Can I give you a lift down to Dartmouth?" he said as we emerged onto a small carpark at the back.

"Thanks, but my boat's here. Motored up yesterday."

"Oh, okay then. I'd keep your head down for a few days. You'll be front-page headlines tomorrow, my dear. Then the world and his brother'll be after you for interviews and pictures."

I thanked him and scurried away back to *Pasha*. I intended to be at sea by tomorrow afternoon.

22

I emerged next morning to find two men on the quay sniffing around the boat. They both wore suits and ties.

"Can I help you?" I said.

"Er, Miss Carter?"

"If you're from the papers, I'm not…"

"We're not press, Miss. Can you confirm that you are Rosemary Carter?"

The speaker was around thirty, short-cropped hair and shiny brown shoes.

"That's me," I said, warily, "*Rosie* Carter. So, who are you?"

"Sergeant Walker," he flashed me an ID card, "Ministry of Defence Police, and this is my colleague, Sergeant Trimble."

For a moment, I was stunned, just stared back at him. Then I said, "I'm not in the Navy anymore. I was discharged two weeks ago."

"We know that, Miss," said the second man, sauntering up from where he'd been studying *Pasha's* bow, "we'd like to ask you some questions. Would you mind stepping ashore?"

I stayed were I was. "Why, what's this about?"

"Look, Miss," said the first guy, Walker, "we can make this hard or easy. Please just step ashore and come with us to the Police Station just up the road. Otherwise we'll need to have you arrested by the local plod. I'm sure you don't want that."

By now my heart pounded furiously. I knew what this was about.

"Just give me a minute, I'll get a coat." I stepped down to the saloon, mind in turmoil. For a brief second, I forgot what I came down for, then snatched my light waterproof from its hook and pulled on my beany hat. I paused a moment on the ladder, trying to breathe normally, then stepped up into the cockpit. I slotted in the wash boards and locked them, then stepped ashore.

The interview room was similar to the one in Dartmouth, but grubbier.

"I'll come straight to the point, Miss Carter," said Walker, pulling up a chair opposite while his colleague remained standing, "we're investigation the theft of certain naval stores items from Portsmouth Naval Base, and have reason to believe you may have been involved while serving onboard HMS Windsor Castle."

I kept quiet, looking him in the eye, aware of the other staring from over his shoulder.

"As you probably know, we have no powers of arrest over you as a civilian, away from Crown Property. At this stage we are merely fact-finding. You are not under caution, and anything you tell us will be strictly between us. However, I must advise you that if there seems sufficient prima facie evidence of your involvement then we will be obliged to hand the matter over to the appropriate authorities. Do you understand?"

"So, I don't have to speak, I'm not under arrest, and you can't detain me. Why don't I just walk?"

"In theory, that's true," conceded Walker, "but I advise against it until you've heard what we have to say. It's in your own interests to know how much evidence we already have. And I would add that the local police are co-operating closely with our investigation, hence the use of this facility."

"And these er, 'appropriate authorities'?"

"That would be the Hampshire Constabulary and the Crown Prosecutor's Office."

I slumped back and blew out a breath. "Okay, what've you got?"

He pulled a brown envelope from an inside pocket and shook out several photographs face down onto the desk. He shuffled through them and selected one, which he placed in front of me.

"During a search of the work-premises of Gary Palmer in Mullhaven, Sussex Police came across these in a boatshed. Do you know what they are?"

Shit! That bastard was supposed to have got rid of those.

"Obviously," I said, "empty paint cans."

"Anything special about them, the markings?"

I picked up the photo and studied it, but I knew anyway.

"Yacht antifoul, MoD Property," I said, tonelessly.

"And what do you suppose they were doing in a civilian boatyard, Rosemary?"

"It's Rosie. How should I know?"

"Well, Rosie, I can tell you that these four tins were in the category V&A, Valuable and Attractive. Therefore they have to be accounted for at a monthly audit. These four went missing from Portsmouth Dockyard Stores sometime during September last year. Ring any bells?"

I shook my head.

"You were working on your boat in Mullhaven around then, is that right?"

"That doesn't mean I nicked that antifoul," I blurted out.

He nodded slowly, then selected another picture and put it on top of the first.

"This picture is from a security camera outside the store from where the paint went missing. It was taken on September the twelfth. Can you explain why you were there on that day?"

I picked up the picture of my Suzuki Jeep, the front registration number clearly legible.

"I was collecting paint for the ship, doing a favour for a friend, really."

"And that friend would be Able Seaman Doyle, is that correct?"

"The ship's painter, yes." I said. It felt like I was driving downhill with no brakes.

"And this picture, taken earlier the same day, your vehicle again, this time outside the pedestrian gate to Naval Barracks. You went to the Naval Clothing Store and bought four woollen jersey's, size, extra-large. Now, I would guess your size as small to medium, Rosie, is that about right?"

My headlong rush downhill increased, a brick wall coming up ahead.

"Medium," I whispered.

"Oh, and these are all male jersey's, according to the receipt. Who were they for?"

I didn't say anything.

"Were they for the dockyard storeman, Rosie, to exchange for the paint you smuggled out of the dockyard?"

I kept silent.

Walker looked up at his mate. Trimble nodded. "Yeah, I'm happy if you are."

Walker gathered up the pictures and stood to leave.

"What, that's it?" I said.

"Unless there's any more you want to tell us, Rosie?" said Trimble.

I shook my head, and they filed out of the room, no thank you or goodbyes, not even a backward glance. They left the door open, and a minute later a uniformed policeman stepped in, and behind him, a female officer. It was she who spoke.

"Rosemary Carter, I am Inspector Connelly from Hampshire Constabulary. I'm arresting you on suspicion of theft of Crown property from Her Majesty's Naval Base, Portsmouth. You don't have to say anything but…etcetera, etcetera, etcetera."

I would know that caution by heart soon.

23

They escorted me back to the boat to pack a bag.

"Will she be okay here?" I asked, handing the inspector my keys, "only you're not supposed to stay more than forty-eight hours."

"Don't worry," she said, "the local police will look after it until the delivery crew arrive."

"Delivery crew?" I said, uneasily.

"Your boat's evidence," she said, coldly, "it'll be taken to Gosport and impounded there."

Nobody spoke during the three-hour drive to Portsmouth, which gave me plenty of time, sitting alone in the back, to contemplate the string of misfortunes that had culminated in this final humiliation.

I could see no way out of my predicament. My plan to sail to Florida lay in ruins. Instead of Easter with Georgie, I would spend it languishing in some dreary prison cell.

Yet another interview room, where I was formally charged. They took my passport, then released me on police bail to appear before the Crown Court on Thursday. No fixed time; I should be at the court from nine am and wait my turn to be called.

I took the train home, called our family solicitor, and got an appointment for next morning.

There was an email from Georgie, sent twelve hours ago:

Hi Rosie,
I'm coming over.

Suddenly I didn't feel quite so lost and alone. My aunt was flying all that way just to be with me after my ordeal with Gary. Who would have thought?

And she knew Gary? How weird was that?

Of course, she didn't know how much crap I'd landed in.

I tapped out a reply, telling her I'd be here at home tomorrow night, and she should come straight here. I told her I'd lost my phone overboard. I'd had the house landline disconnected, so there was no point giving her the number.

The big story on the BBC News was the demise of what they were calling the Mullhaven Mauler, interviews with locals of their relief that the twenty-year horror was at an end.

There was a pencil sketch of me giving evidence at the inquest, and an apologetic reporter at the scene about how he'd failed to track down the 'woman who'd foiled his latest attack' for an interview. There was also a clip where they'd found *Pasha* at the quay in Totnes, a police sentry who refused to answer questions and told them to move away. My whereabouts was an intriguing mystery that would enthral them for days to come.

There was a newspaper on Lester's desk, one of the national broadsheets. And there was my picture, on the front page, the same sketch they'd shown on TV last night.

'Sailing Heroine Foils Mullhaven Mauler', read the headline. Lester saw me looking and turned the paper over.

"Rather disconcerting, I imagine," he said, "seeing yourself in newsprint. No photos though, so you've managed to slip their net, eh?"

"So far," I said, "until somebody that knows me tips them off."

"And how are you, Rosie. Can't imagine what you went through last week. Must have been terrifying."

I nodded, biting my lip to stop it quivering.

Charlene came through with two coffees, softly touched my shoulder, and left again without speaking.

"Want to talk about it?" he said when she'd closed the door.

I shook my head, gulped, and pulled myself together.

"Lester, I'm in big trouble, *really* big trouble."

He leaned back and took off his spectacles, pursed his lips.

"Rosie, if this is about you leaving that animal to drown, I don't think…"

"No, no, nothing like that."

I paused, took a sip of coffee, wondering how much I could safely tell him without prejudicing my case and putting him in an awkward position. It all hung on whether I was going to come clean or try to wing it on a denial, a decision I was still struggling with.

"I've been charged with stealing some stuff from the dockyard, back in September. I have to appear at Portsmouth Crown Court tomorrow."

He started forward, made an O with his mouth, genuinely shocked.

"And did you?" he held up a hand. "No, don't answer that. For now, just tell me whether you're denying the charge."

"I haven't said anything, at least, not officially."

"What does that mean, exactly, 'not officially'?"

I told him about the two MoD plods talking to me off the record, what they'd shown me, telling me what they knew.

"But you made no admission of guilt, Rosie? Think carefully, this is important. You said nothing by way of admission to either the police or the MoD investigators?"

I shook my head. "I'm sure I didn't"

"Good. Now, as you're aware, I'm not a criminal lawyer. I'll have to hand you off to one of my colleagues, a barrister. If you're happy for me to appoint him, I'll call him right now."

I nodded, and he pressed the buzzer on his intercom:

"Charlene, get me Mr O'Sullivan on the phone, please."

"Yes, Mr Granville."

I sipped my coffee. My hand was shaking. I wanted a ciggy.

"So, Rosie, how's your Dad?"

I'd been thinking a lot about Dad. Should I go and see him? If I did I'd only end up blurting out the whole sorry mess. Would that be fair on him?

"I haven't seen him since Sunday before last," I said, "but they tell me he's comfortable."

"No sign of him coming out of this Locked-in thing?"

I shook my head. "No change. He just sits watching telly all day. The nurses are great though, they talk to him all the time as if he was just, you know, normal…"

The intercom clicked, "Mr O'Sullivan on line two."

Lester picked up.

"Kieran, how's your workload?"

…

"Good, because I've got a young lady due to appear before Portsmouth Crown Court tomorrow. Are you free to take the case?"

…

"Theft from Her Majesty's Dockyard."

…

"Yes, she's here with me now."

…

"Just outside Hazelmere, I'll have Charlene mail you her home address…" he put a hand over the mouthpiece, "if that's alright with you, Rosie?"

I nodded.

...

"Rosie Carter."

...

"Yes, *that* Rosemary Carter, it seems the Mullhaven Police turned up something during their search of Palmer's workshops."

...

"Hang on, I'll ask her."

"Can he come to your home at two this afternoon?"

I nodded again.

"Yes, that's fine, Kieran."

...

"Yes, I'll tell her. Cheerio, old chap, and thanks."

He hung up.

"Now, Rosie, this is important: between now and your hearing, say nothing to anyone about this. Got that?"

"Don't worry," I said, getting up, "I won't."

He stood up and opened the door for me, smiling warmly. "O'Sullivan's one of the best," he said, as I shuffled out, "he'll do whatever he can for you. And good luck for tomorrow. Any problems, just give me a tinkle, alright?"

Outside on the street, I stopped, thinking. Something I'd told Lester had been niggling. Then it came to me.

Oh shit!

I ran furiously to the car, cursing my stupidity. Arriving at the hospital in eye-watering time, I left the car unlocked and badly parked, sprinted through reception and up the stairs to Dad's ward.

"Rosie?" said the nurse at the desk, "We thought..."

"Has my Dad been watching telly? Has he seen the news?"

"No, Rosie, he hasn't," she came around to the front and put her hands on my shoulders. "We all heard about that... that... what you went through. We didn't open his eyes this morning, and his telly's been taken out."

"Thank you," I said, taking her hands from my shoulders and holding them, "Thank you, I really mean it."

I went in to see Dad, not to talk, just to look at him. I stood quietly by his bed, wanting desperately to touch him, to say I loved him.

The barrister rang the doorbell promptly at two-o-clock.

"Rosie, is it? I'm Kieran O'Sullivan." A soft, almost melodious voice, with a faint Irish brogue.

"Hi, Kieran, come on in," I said, "and thanks for coming."

He was short; mid-forties, slim, holiday-tan, dark-suited, and carried an old-style leather briefcase that bulged at the sides. I showed him into the dining-room where I had a fresh pot of tea waiting.

"Now, Rosie," he began, taking a file from his case and placing it in front of him, "first thing to say is that I've talked to the Clerk of the Court and managed to get a time for your hearing – ten-thirty tomorrow morning, okay?"

"Oh, that's better," I said, pouring the tea, "thought I'd just be waiting around all day, not knowing."

"They invariably run a little late though, so it'll probably be closer to eleven. We should be out well before noon, anyway."

I gaped. "You reckon it'll be that quick? Surely not."

"Ah! You thought you were having your trial tomorrow. Well, no, Rosie. Tomorrow's only a Plea and Trial-preparation Hearing. The charges will be read out to you, you'll be asked whether you plead Guilty, or Not Guilty, and depending on your plea, you'll be sent either for trial, or for sentencing."

"And how long before that happens, either way?"

"In the case of a Not Guilty plea, it'll be up to the Crown Prosecutors, based on how long they need to complete their investigations. Most likely they'll give you a fixed date within two weeks of the Hearing. Should we decide to plead Guilty, then the Court will decide on a date for sentencing."

I bit my lip as the implications of what was happening to me, and the likely outcome, finally sank in.

He watched me a moment, and his brown eyes softened. "It's all somewhat daunting, I know. But try not to get too anxious. Okay?"

I nodded.

"Let's start with what happened in Totnes, when you were first questioned about these allegations. Walk me through the sequence of events, who said what to whom, as far as you can recall, and where you were at the time."

He scribbled notes while I talked, page after page of them, stopping me once or twice to clarify this point or that. Afterwards, he sat back and finished his by now lukewarm tea. I offered him a fresh cup, but he shook his head.

"And that was the only evidence they presented to you: the empty paint cans and your car outside the store where they originated?"

"That, and the receipt for what I'd bought at slops"

"Slops?"

"The Naval Clothing Store in Nelson Barracks."

"Oh, okay, that was the jerseys they claim you bought to exchange for the paint."

"Correct."

"And how much would you say the paint was worth, if say, you popped down to B&Q for it?"

"They wouldn't have it in B&Q," I said, "it was copper-based antifoul – you'd need to buy it from a chandlery. Just short of four-hundred pounds, I'd say."

He stared at me.

"Whew, that's some paint. And a poor deal for four woolly jerseys, wouldn't you say?"

"And a thousand duty-free fags." I said, instantly regretting it.

He frowned. "There was no mention of cigarettes in the prosecution's evidence, so we'll forget you said that, okay?"

"Sorry."

"As your counsel, I'm not obliged to volunteer anything to the other side that might prejudice our case. But if they suspect I know something specific, they can compel me to reveal it. That's something to bear in mind if we decide to plead Not Guilty. Is that clear?"

"Is that what you're suggesting, that I should plead Not Guilty?"

He shook his head, "No, Rosie, I am not, not at this stage, anyway. When they get your boat to Gosport, they'll go over it with the proverbial fine-toothed comb. At the moment their evidence is fairly flimsy and circumstantial. I'm sure they can't positively identify paint that's already been used, so which way I advise you depends on what else they might turn up."

He raised a quizzical eyebrow.

I gave a big, resigned sigh. There was only one way this could go.

"If I plead Guilty, what will I get, d'you think?"

He studied my face, then said, "Let's be clear, Rosie, what are they going to find on your boat? I need to know if I'm to defend your case."

I shrugged, and said flatly, "Oh, just four heavy-duty marine batteries, fifty metres of galvanized anchor-chain, and all my standing rigging."

He sucked in hard through his teeth. "All identifiable as Crown Property?"

I nodded.

"Oh, except maybe the wire rope. Not sure how they'd tell it was nicked."

"And that's it, Rosie? You're sure there's nothing else?"

"Nah, that's the lot. I needed to fix Pasha up for sea, and I was stony broke. Seemed a good idea at the time. Stupid, now, looking back. So what will I get?"

He pursed his lips. "Recent military service, no criminal record till now, lay it on thick, a saint who slipped by the wayside... we've got a reasonable judge who's usually reluctant to send people down. Victor Mumbles."

I couldn't help a grin. "Does he really?"

He ignored the quip, probably heard it a hundred times.

24

My Brief was right, we were in court no more than twenty minutes. The charges were read out, I pleaded Guilty, with other offences to be taken into account; Kieran handed the Judge a list of all the stuff I'd illegally procured during August and September last year: the four batteries, the anchor chain, and the wire rope and swage-fittings. The case was referred for Sentencing the following Friday. My bail application was not opposed.

Kieran, still in his silks and wig, caught up with me as I left the Courts.

"Rosie, we need a chat. Give me five minutes, then I'll meet you in the café across the square. That okay?"

By the time I'd rolled and smoked my ciggy, he joined me, and we went in together. I found a table in a quiet corner while Kieran went for the coffees.

"I managed to find out about your boat," he said, placing two oversized quirky green mugs on the table, "she arrived in Gosport this morning, and they'll lift her out this afternoon."

"Oh, that's all right then," I said, "any more good news?"

He looked hurt by the irony but smiled anyway. "It's always better to know the worst early, more opportunity to prepare a defence."

"Ha! That shouldn't take long. And what was all that Discovery stuff the Judge was on about? Confused the hell out of me."

"I'll be straight with you, Rosie, it doesn't look good. The best we can try for is mitigating circumstances for a lenient sentence. Anything I plan to bring up in the way of evidence to support a case for leniency must be shared with the Prosecution beforehand. That's what the Judge meant by 'Discovery'."

"What mitigating circumstances?"

He sighed. "That's up to you, Rosie, whatever you can tell me; your state of mind when you did it, anyone who might have encouraged you to do it, though I realise it might be difficult for you to implicate a friend."

I sat thinking a moment, then shook my head.

"You're sure there's nothing? Nothing at all I can use?"

I pulled a straight mouth and shook my head again. I didn't intend to discuss my state of mind with anyone. And saying that a dead man had sparked the original idea seemed too convenient, such an obvious scapegoat. I didn't need a lawyer to tell me such a claim would be highly suspect.

"Okay, fair enough." He pushed a business card across the table. "If you think of anything, give me a call, or email. There's still another angle we can look at, but I'll need to do some research."

"Another angle?"

He leaned forward. "Corruption in dockyard services that make these crimes so easy, tempting otherwise honest people to break the law."

"Now I can see why barristers get paid so much."

He winked a grin, then grew serious.

"Rosie, just one more thing." He checked over his shoulder for eavesdroppers, then leaned in, "there was at least one press reporter in court today. Normally a case like this wouldn't arouse much interest, but sooner or later someone is bound to make the connection with the Rosemary Carter that ended Palmer's murderous career. It might harm your case if you talk to them, so best say nothing, no matter what they offer for your story. Just until our case is concluded. Agreed?"

"Suits me just fine," I said.

I saw them as soon as I turned into our street; I pulled into the kerb and sat with the engine running. Half a dozen of them, men and women, loitering outside our drive, some with cameras, others wired up with microphones, looking up at the house for signs of life. I toyed with the idea of turning around, maybe drive down to London and stay with Ivy, Doc's mum, for a while.

But no. I had to be at home for Georgie; she could show up anytime. Besides, I wasn't going to be driven from my own home.

Oh, fuck it!

I slammed into gear and gunned it, and with horn blaring, spun recklessly into the drive, scattering the panicked paparazzi, and squealed to a halt inches from the garage door.

A flash in my face as I threw open the Jeep door, a barrage of shouted questions, more camera flashes. Someone barred my way to the door, a young woman, "Just an interview, Rosemary, five minutes, that's all. We'll make it..."

"Get out of my fucking way!" I snarled in her face.

She paled, and stepped aside, but others were now crowding in behind, clicking away, firing questions. I unlocked the door and slammed it behind me, leaning against it, breathing hard.

The clamour outside continued, like some zombie horror movie. Someone pushed in the letterbox flap, "Just a few words, Miss Carter, please?"

I snapped it down with the heel of my hand, rewarded with a yelp of pain from beyond the door. They didn't try it again.

I went around pulling closed all the downstairs curtains, then made a sandwich and settled down to watch TV, the volume turned up to drown out the wheedling from outside. An hour later, it was quiet, and when I twitched aside the sitting-room curtain the street was empty.

It wasn't until darkness fell, and the bloodhounds hadn't returned, that I finally began to relax. Shortly after seven, a taxi pulled up outside. It was my aunt.

25

I cooked us a meal, much to Georgie's approval. She hovered in the kitchen, watching me work, but didn't interfere; just chatted on about the difficulties of getting a last-minute flight in the high season.

"Not the recommended way of doing it, but shit, Sweetie, I was desperate. You shouldn't have to go through this nightmare alone."

She didn't know the worst of it yet.

"There's something else I have to tell you, and you're not going to like it."

Georgie listened grim-faced as I told her what I'd done to get Pasha to sea, her eyes growing wider with each new revelation. I told her about my arrest, and afterwards she just sat staring at me in disbelief.

"Well, say something," I said at last.

"What do you want me to say, Rosie? You're a stupid bloody fool? But I guess you already know that. I'm sure things'll work out? But that'd be a bloody lie. Truth is, the only thing that'll work out is a spell in gaol."

"I… I thought you'd understand why…"

"Understand? *Understand?* What I understand is: you turned yourself into a damned criminal."

"It was only bad luck I got caught. If Gary had got rid of those tins like he was supposed…"

"Rosie, can you hear yourself? You stole from your own *government*. That's like... like treason, for Christ's sake. A crime against Society. In the States, that'd get you..."

But I couldn't listen to any more. Stung by my aunt's shocking betrayal, I dashed into the kitchen, grabbed my makings, and went out into the garden. I was shaking so badly I couldn't roll my ciggy.

The kitchen door creaked softly behind me.

"Here, let me," Georgie said, gently taking the train-crash of paper and tobacco from my fingers. In seconds she handed me back a perfectly made cigarette.

I spluttered a laugh. "Where did you learn to do that? I didn't know you even smoked."

"Ah, there's a lot you don't know about your Aunt Georgie," her eyes glinted through the dark chill of night, "full of hidden depths, that's me."

I lit up and took a deep drag, blowing smoke into the bare branches of the old apple tree. After a while, I said, "I've let you down, Georgie, I know that. After all you've done for me. I'm so sorry."

"Well, sweetie, to be fair, you didn't even know I existed when you did that stuff. So it wasn't *me* you let down..." She left the rest unsaid.

Next morning there was an email from Kieran; could he come to see me on Wednesday morning to discuss our defence. I agreed.

Around mid-morning a couple of yesterday's news hounds reappeared; one came up to the door and tried the bell, but I'd disconnected it. When he started hammering at the door, Georgie stuck her head out of the window.

"She's got nothing to say, so piss off and stop harassing her."

She slammed the window on his protested 'rights to represent the Public Interest'. Next time I looked out, they were both gone.

"They'll be back, I know it." I grumbled.

"Then why don't we both take off somewhere?" Georgie suggested.

The thought of venturing out gave me the collywobbles. Maybe I was being paranoid, but I feared being recognised from pictures taken during yesterday's paparazzi frenzy. And for once in my life, I didn't want to be by the sea, as if it were somehow to blame for, or at least, a constant reminder of, all my woes.

In the end, we got out the road atlas, and soon settled on a suitable destination; as secluded a place I could think of within a hundred-miles - we reckoned there'd be few hill-walkers about in February.

By noon, we were on the road, and under the balm of Georgie's lively chatter, the awful dread of my uncertain future began to ease into the background. We were heading diagonally across-country to Worcestershire.

We booked into a little B&B in Great Malvern and whiled away the remainder of the day walking around the quant little town. At one of the classier arts & craft shops, Georgie bought a beautiful jade bracelet and matching earrings to take home for Anna.

"How long will you stay?" I asked her as we left the shop.

She grinned. "Fed up with me already?"

"Of course not," I hooked my arm into hers, "just want to know how long I've got you for."

She patted my hand. "Let's just get next Friday over, then we'll see."

We paused outside the Festival Theatre, Georgie was gazing up at the billboard; tonight's performance was a production of The Media.

"I love Greek Tragedy," she said.

I said, "I've never seen one."

"C'mon, let's get tickets, broaden your education. You'll love The Media, Sweetie," she screwed up her face, "loads of murder and revenge."

"Lovely!" I said. "Oh, go on then, you've won me over."

It was two hours before the show, so we found a pub nearby for dinner. It was crowded with diners, probably doing the same as us, but we found a free table.

"Didn't she kill her own children?" I said, as we sat down with our drinks.

Georgie looked impressed, then a little disappointed. "I thought you hadn't seen it?"

"I remember reading it at Uni, it's a story that's hard to forget."

"You went to University? I didn't know that."

"No, I know, how would you? I signed up for Humanities at Bristol, dropped out of year two to join the Navy."

She studied my face intently, then said, "Sounds like the kind of impetuous move I might have made. Any regrets?"

I shook my head. "Best thing I ever did. I loved the Mob, loved the travel, loved being at..."

It crept up out of nowhere. One second I was fine, the next, I was weeping like a kid whose toys had been kicked away. And people were looking.

Georgie took my hands in hers. "C'mon, Sweetie, let's pop outside for a minute, you can have a smoke and tell your Aunt Georgie all about it."

I gave an involuntary laugh through snuffles and nodded.

There was a beer garden out back, a few bench-tables on weed-pocked flag-stones. We were the only ones braving the sharp evening air. Georgie had brought along our coats, which we shuffled into before sitting down. I took out my makings.

"This time last year," I said, "I was in the Caribbean - West Indies Guardship, you know? I was having the time of my life, stopping off for days at a time at these amazing islands, beach parties, swimming and snorkelling, all that stuff that most civvies only ever dream about. At sea we used to intercept drug-runners and hand them over to the US Coastguard, rescue yachts and motorboats that had got into trouble, there was so much to do, so much to keep us busy."

Georgie watched me with an intensity I hadn't seen before. She didn't say a word, just waited for me to go on.

"And, I had the best mates in the world, comrades, you know? We put our lives on the line for each other - not for the Queen, or the Country, or any of that bullshit. We were there to watch each other's backs, and we did.

"I was on a roll, back then, a good career ahead, PO's Course coming up in August, a great service record, and looking forward to my Officer's Board and at least another fifteen years."

I paused to light my ciggy, then looked at it.

"Didn't smoke then, either. I *had* done for a short while but packed up after the previous Christmas.

"What I'm trying to say Georgie, in the frame of mind I was then, I would never have dreamt of doing what I did, nicking all that gear. In fact, I would probably have shopped anyone I caught doing it. What a hypocrite!"

She raised her eyebrows, and nodded agreement. "We're all of us hypocrites at one time or other, Sweetie, me included."

"It all started to unravel after Mum... you know, after the accident. At first, I thought I had it all under control, I *really* did. Get over it, I kept telling myself, these things happen, but you're still in control. Do you know what I'm saying? I was in control alright; in control of what though? Stealing from the Navy I loved, and piling the guilt on my helpless Dad for killing my Mum?"

I noticed Georgie was shivering, and it dawned on me that twenty-four hours ago she'd been in the sweltering tropics. I stubbed out and we went back inside to the warm.

Despite it's dark and disturbing plot, I loved The Media. The story was told as a dream by a young American man, a tourist who'd fallen asleep among the ruins of ancient Corinth after a row with his girlfriend. As the haunting voices of the chorus grew, and grey shapes closed around the sleeping form, I was wafted back to the time of legend, and the gods. For three hours I was in another place, where magic was real and jealousy invariably lethal; my knowledge of the horrific conclusion did nothing to lessen its shocking impact.

On Saturday morning we struck up into the hills and spent the whole day walking the ridgeway footpath, warmed by our exertions and undeterred by the occasional flurries of wintery rain. It was strange to see Georgie in her sister's walking gear, and once, I almost called her 'Mum'.

There is a break halfway, where the path dips down to a roadway that cuts through the ridge. We stopped here for lunch, at an attractive little pub by the roadside, then mounted the next section for the final leg, which culminated in an iron-age fort. We reached it just as the sun made its first appearance of the day, low on the horizon, winking goodnight from beneath a huddle of crimson cloud.

There was a bus back to Great Malvern.

"When did you last see your Dad?" Georgie suddenly asked as we drove home the next day.

"Not since Christmas," I said.

I explained about not wanting him panicking in his locked-in mind, to have him content in the illusion that everything had gone according to plan.

"It was bad enough me turning up at Christmas and telling him about the collision, but if I drop in and I tell him what happened afterwards… He doesn't need to know that, does he? To have all that worry, and frustration cos he can't do anything? I'm scared what that might do to him."

Georgie said, "What if I went to see him?"

"And say what? That his daughter's somewhere in mid-Atlantic, but you came to England anyway. Not plausible, Georgie, he'd suspect something was wrong."

"Could say I'm over here on business?"

"Well… yes you could. Hey, I hadn't thought of that."

I thought about it now, and after a moment, said, "Go on then, Georgie, make his day, just be careful what you say."

"Very poetic, Sweetie, just like Margie."

"I'll take that as a compliment," I said, flashing her a grin.

26

Wednesday Morning. We'd just cleared away the breakfast things when Kieran showed up. We sat at the dining-room table again, on opposite sides.

"I got a look at the Prosecution's evidence this morning, Rosie. The stuff they took from your boat."

Georgie came through and perched herself at the head of the table.

"Just pretend I'm not here," she said.

I threw her a smile and turned back to Kieran. "But why do they need evidence if I've already pleaded Guilty?"

"Costs, I expect," Georgie said.

I glared at her.

"Sorry, dear. Just ignore me."

Kieran said, "They need to know the value, as it may be of relevance to the sentence they ask for. But more importantly from the Prosecution's point of view, they'll be immediately ready for trial if you change your plea at any time."

He leaned in.

"Now, Rosie, is there *anything*, anything at all I can use to mitigate your case? Think carefully, this might be our last chance, our *only* chance, to avoid you going to prison."

I shook my head.

"Of *course* there is!" Georgie chimed in, "go on, Rosie, tell him. Or I will."

I glared at her, while a bewildered Kieran stared at me.

Red-faced and livid, she said, "If you think I'm going to sit here quietly while you throw away a chance to stay out of gaol, my girl, you can think again. Now pull yourself together and don't be so fucking spineless. *Tell* him!"

Trial Day.

Kieran met me at the entrance. Once through Security he led me to a table in the big hall under the lawcourts. All around us people sat in huddled conversation with their briefs, indistinct whisperings echoing in the high vaulted ceiling.

"Last day of freedom," I murmured, looking around the crowded hall.

"Not necessarily, Rosie. Mumbles can be a bit of a tyrant, but he's always fair, and doesn't like sending people down if he can avoid it."

"Doesn't he have to follow certain rules, I mean, sentencing guidelines?"

"Only if the case is straightforward. From what you told me on Wednesday, and what I've discovered since, I think we've got a reasonable chance."

I sat up straight. "*What* have you discovered?"

He reached into his battered briefcase and pulled out a file, a blue folder.

"I've managed to acquire a copy of your Service Record."

I stared at him. "Really? How on earth…?"

"Let's just say, from someone who wants to help. The original will be sent to you anyway, in due course."

I leaned in. "You know, Kieran, stealing from the Navy can get you into big trouble."

My flippancy won a hard stare that quickly dissolved into a chuckle. He held up the folder.

"What I read in here is very interesting, Rosie. Why didn't you tell me about your break in Good Conduct in August last year, about your, let's see," he flipped the file open and read,

'Often erratic behaviour and lack of concentration at work'. And, 'A disappointing lapse after six years of sparkling performance.'"

He raised a quizzical eyebrow.

"I'm not exactly proud of it."

"Depression is not something to be ashamed of, Rosie. It's well understood these days and goes a long way to explain why you acted out of character in doing what you did. Listen to what your Captain wrote about your promotion to Petty Officer:

'Stood over for six months pending improvement in conduct. This *otherwise exemplary* rating was recently bereaved of her mother in an accident which left her father in a semi-comatose state. Since she has declined the offer of indefinite compassionate leave, we should expect her to settle down again in due course. In the meantime she should be handled with some sensitivity.'"

"You're asking me to say I was having a breakdown, and that's why I stole the stuff for my boat?"

"Not quite, Rosie. All I want you to do is stand in the witness box and answer my questions. I won't ask you to give an opinion about your state of mind, I promise, just the facts. The important thing is, just answer openly and truthfully. You'll be cross-examined by the Prosecution, almost certainly, but it's nothing to worry about, just stay calm and answer the questions. If you don't lie or try to cover up, they can't trap you."

We were called up to Court Three at ten-thirty, where I was left waiting alone in the corridor for another anxious half-hour.

Then I was through those imposing double doors, being led by the Usher. The room felt crowded and confused; the only face I saw in focus was Georgie's, smiling encouragement from the Public Gallery.

Once up in the dock I felt less exposed and began to match my surroundings to what Kieran had briefed me about the court setup.

There was a surprising lot of chatter, mostly from the dozen or so people up where Georgie was. I wondered who they all were; when I looked the question at my aunt she just shrugged and gave a little shake of her head.

I focussed on one face staring at me, and suddenly realised she was the reporter I'd pissed off last week outside the house. My heart sank when I realised they were all probably newshounds hoping for a bit of drama.

Kieran, sitting alone at a table just below me, turned and nodded with a half-smile that looked distinctly nervous and went back to flicking through his paperwork, grey wig bobbing up and down as he read, reminding me of an actor unsure of his lines as the play was about to start. It didn't exactly fill me with confidence.

In contrast, the Prosecutor, a slinky creature in pristine robe, immaculate wig and professionally applied make-up, stood calmly chatting and chuckling with a couple of male colleagues. Her name, Kieran had told me, was Leonora Markham and I shouldn't be taken in by her softly-spoken appeal – she was as ruthless as she was stunningly gorgeous.

Then came a stentorian "Silence in Court, all rise.". A hush descended, a door opened behind the bench, and through it walked Judge Victor Mumbles, QC.

He strolled to his seat and slumped down, an elderly man with heavy jowls that framed his double chin and seemed to drag his eyes into a houndlike expression, an image enhanced by the flaps of his ancient grey wig.

He glanced glumly around the room, studied me briefly over his glasses, then said, "Please, sit down everybody."

He nodded down at the Clerk, who stood and turned to face me.

"The Defendant will stand."

I stood.

"State your name, and address, for the court."

As I did, I caught Georgie's eye. She winked, and for a moment, I was transported back to the Malvern Hills.

Then I became aware of someone talking down at the front, and everyone but me listening. I tuned in, and realised it was my charges being read out.

"Do you understand the charges?"

"Y... yes."

"And do you stand by your plea of Guilty?"

"Yes, Yes I do"

"The defendant may sit," said Judge Victor Mumbles, QC.

I sank down onto the bench.

"Ms Markham," said Judge Victor Mumbles, QC, "I understand you wish to oppose the Pre-sentencing Report."

The woman stood up, flashed a pointed glance at Kieran, then answered the judge, "Yes, Your Honour. The plaintiff is concerned that the Basis of Plea, if allowed, would suggest that the Ministry of Defence had failed in it's duty of care to Miss Carter during part of her active service, an allegation it strongly refutes."

She plonked herself down and Kieran immediately bobbed up.

"Your Honour, my client has admitted her crimes and stands by her plea of Guilty. Prosecution's only motive for contesting Basis of Plea is to avoid future claims against the MoD by my client. Protection against possible future litigation cannot be valid grounds for..."

A furious-looking Markham jumped up, "Your Honour, if my learned friend is sugg..."

"Enough!" said a clearly irritated Judge Victor Mumbles, QC, holding out a palm to each of the pair and then beckoning them forward, "Counsels will approach the Bench."

I watched the two lawyers arguing their points sotto voce amid much head-shaking and gesticulating, while Judge Victor Mumbles, QC, looked from one to the other with almost avuncular indulgence. He finally shut them both up with a gesture, gave his opinion, or whatever, and sent them back to their respective places. I hadn't heard a word of the exchange, but the self-satisfied smirk on the woman's face, and Kieran's grimace as he glanced up at me, filled me with dread.

Once both had taken their seats, Judge Victor Mumbles, QC, beamed his rheumy eyes around the court before they finally came to rest on me.

"Now, Ms Carter, the reminder of these proceedings will take the form of a Newton hearing, meaning that your counsel will call witnesses who may then be cross-examined by the counsel for the prosecution. It is important that you understand this is not a trial, though it may at times feel like one, merely a hearing to petition the court for a more lenient sentence. The final decision is mine, and mine alone, and though it might not be the result you may have wished for, my conclusion will be fair and unbiased. Do you understand?"

I nodded. "Y-yes," and gave him my sweetest little-girl smile.

He lowered his gaze to Kieran.

"Mr O'Sullivan, are all your witnesses present at my court?"

Kieran bobbed up, "They are, Your Honour."

"Ms Markham?"

"We are ready to proceed, Your Honour."

"Very well, let us get started. Mr O'Sullivan?"

"I call Lieutenant Megan Redfern, Royal Navy."

I watched my ex-DO as she entered the court in uniform and walked smartly to the witness box, sat down and removed her cap which she placed tidily in her lap.

The clerk swore her in and Kieran took the floor.

"Good morning Lieutenant, would you please start by telling the court your role in relation to my client, Rosemary Carter while she served aboard HMS Windsor Castle."

"Certainly. I was Leading Seaman Carter's Divisional Officer, responsible for all aspects of her welfare and conduct, the maintenance of her Service Record, and, in consultation with her line manager, oversight of her work performance."

"And how long were you Ms Carter's Divisional Officer?"

"Well basically, from when she first joined the ship until she left it. We both joined her in January 2010 when the ship was first commissioned. Carter left us in October last year whilst in Gibraltar."

"So you knew Ms Carter for almost two years, and would I be right in assuming you had unique knowledge of both her career development and personal circumstances?"

"Yes, but of course, her personal life would be limited to what she was willing to divulge to me. We only take an interest in personal issues where they affect professional performance."

"Yes, we'll come to that in due course. How would you summarise Ms Carter's professional conduct during the period you first became acquainted until the summer of last year?"

"I would say she was exemplary, as she had been, according to her service record, on her previous two ships. She showed herself a skilled and dedicated seaman, often outperforming many of her male colleagues, and setting a fine example to junior members of her Part of Ship."

I was by now cringing with embarrassment. Was that really me she was talking about?

"And I understand she was due for promotion, is that right?"

Redfern nodded.

"Yes. She was recommended for Petty Officer early in 2012. Unfortunately, the ship was too operationally committed at the time to release her, but she eventually sat her PO's Board in August. She passed with better than average points, which was surprising, considering what she'd recently been through."

She glanced up at me with a frown, as if she thought I might crack up at her reference to the accident.

"I assume you mean the events of seventeenth of June. Would you please tell the court what happened?"

"Yes, of course. It was a Sunday. The ship was alongside in Portsmouth and I was away on weekend leave. At around 2215 that night the quartermaster on watch received a phone call from the Surrey police. The Duty Officer was sent for to take the call and was told there had been a road traffic accident involving Leading Seaman Carter's parents. No details were available, except that they had been taken to a hospital near Hazelmere. Carter herself had been on duty over the weekend, so she was onboard. The Duty Officer informed her of the accident and released her from duty.

Redfern cleared her throat before continuing. She looked genuinely distraught but soldiered on. I felt her pain in telling the tale, and my own eyes began to fill up as I relived that dreadful night.

"The Duty Officer called me at home to brief me on events. The following morning, I received a call from Carter. She told me her mother had died and her father was in Intensive Care, apparently in a coma."

She paused and took a shaky breath, before continuing. By now tears were streaming down my cheeks.

"I granted her compassionate leave for two weeks and told her to call if she needed longer."

Kieran looked over at me, then up at the bench

"We'll take a fifteen-minute recess," rumbled Judge Victor Mumbles, QC.

27

"Kind of brought it all home to me," said Georgie, as we met in the corridor outside the Courtroom, "what you went through that night."

I was still too emotional to speak. I was desperate for a smoke but there wasn't time to get through Security and back again.

"Where's Kieran," she said, casting around at the milling groups outside the other courtrooms. The other witnesses were sitting together on a bench down the corridor, Redfern now with them. I would have loved to go down and chat, but my brief had warned me to stay apart until... until afterwards.

If I wasn't taken down, was the unspoken caveat.

"The judge called both counsels to his chambers," I said, "not sure what that's about. Chummy drinks and a chat, I expect. They're all mates behind all that theatrical posing."

Georgie laughed. "You watch too many courtroom dramas, Sweetie. Mind you, that lady on the other side could be straight out of one of 'em. No, it'll be some technical issue, maybe the old duffer wants to speed things up."

"Did you notice how my old DO remembered all that stuff and rattled it off without notes?"

"Yeah, she was pretty good, alright. Must have practiced that talk all night. My word, she certainly heaped the praise on you. Makes me wonder why they didn't try harder to keep you in."

I gave her a sour grin, "I expect you're about to find out."

"Now, Lieutenant," Kieran began after we'd resumed our places, "how did Ms Carter's performance and attitude hold up after this tragic accident?"

"Well, to be frank, it didn't, really. She came back from leave only a couple of days after her mother's funeral. I urged her to go home and stay away for at least another week."

"Oh? Why was that?"

"When I was told she was back onboard, naturally I sent for her to come and see me in my cabin straightaway. I found her unusually cold and distant, uncommunicative. I'd always found her a gregarious and cheerful rating. Now she seemed sullen, like a different person. I knew she wasn't ready to come back, needed more time to get herself together, so to speak."

"You told her you thought she wasn't ready to come back?"

"I did. But she wouldn't hear of it, insisted she would be better off among her friends onboard. Under the circumstances it would have been inappropriate to *order* her ashore. I did, however, review her case with the Captain and the ship's Chaplain, and we concluded it would be best she returned her to her duties, her friends and colleagues, and relative normality, and where we could keep a close eye on her."

"And during those first few days after her return, did anyone else in authority talk to her in relation to her bereavement and personal circumstances?"

"Yes, I understand the Chaplain spoke to her, although of course, any conversation between them would have been in strict confidence."

"Yes, of course. Now, Lieutenant, was Ms Carter at any point in the days following her return, offered bereavement counselling?"

"Objection, Your Honour," said Markham, jumping to her feet, "witness has already explained she could not know what advice the Chaplain had offered, therefor cannot say whether counselling was offered."

Before the Judge could intervene, Kieran said, "very well, I'll rephrase the question, Lieutenant, *to the best of your knowledge*, was Ms Carter at any point in the days following her return, offered bereavement counselling?"

"To the best of my knowledge, no."

"And as her Divisional Officer, and I quote from your own testimony, 'responsible for all aspects of her welfare', would it have been within your own remit to ensure that such counselling was offered?"

"Well, yes, of course. But it's a matter of judgement. Everyone reacts differently to family bereavement, and sometimes such advice is seen by ratings as interference in their private affairs."

"And in your judgement at the time, an offer of counselling was not justified in my client's case?"

"At the time, no. With the benefit of hindsight? Well, it was probably the wrong call."

She glanced up at me again, looking a little beleaguered, I thought. I was beginning to feel sorry for her and wished Kieran would back off a little. She'd done her best for me, after all.

"Probably the wrong call," echoed Kieran, unnecessarily. "Let us now turn to…"

Markham was on her feet again. "Your Honour, I object to my learned friend's tone. Witness has provided open and frank testimony on behalf of the Plaintiff, and, I would remind the court, is not the guilty party here and should not be harassed in this way."

"I agree," growled Judge Victor Mumbles, QC, "Mr O'Sullivan, turn down the rhetoric. This is a mitigation hearing, not a jury trial."

"Very well, Your Honour," said Kieran, his holiday tan turning puce. "Lieutenant Redfern, let us now turn to the period late June to early October 2012. I understand the ship remained in Portsmouth during that time?"

"There were five days at sea, twenty-fifth to thirtieth of June, in support of ships on Operational Workup, but after that, yes, we were in DED, preparing for a deployment to the Eastern Mediterranean in the Autumn."

"DED?"

"Sorry. Docking and Essential Defects. We spent a week in dry dock in late July, then returned to Northwest Wall until early October, when we sailed for the Med."

"And the five days at sea, what was the ship doing during that week?"

"It was pretty intensive. Three warships and a Fleet Auxiliary were working up in the Western Approaches prior to a Middle East Deployment. We were part of a five-ship flotilla in support of their training, anti-aircraft and anti-submarine operations, replenishments at sea, fuelling, helicopter transfers, naval gunfire support and support of amphibious operations."

"And what duties would the then Leading Seaman Carter, be expected to perform during these operations?"

"Mainly seamanship and replenishment evolutions, coxswain of the seaboat when required, as well as watch on deck duties throughout night watches. Her main day duty was Leading Hand of the Forecastle Part of Ship where she supervised maintenance, anchoring and berthing operations."

"Quite a full and varied list of roles. And how well did she perform during that week, would you say?"

"Generally, she performed her duties adequately, but I have to say, there were one or two problems, a number of adverse reports that gave me some concern. Her attitude to superiors was frequently described as surly and uncooperative, bordering at times on insubordination."

"And what action, if any, was taken to correct this lapse in Ms Carter's good conduct?"

"Allowances were made. She was given a warning."

"Allowances were made, presumably because she'd only buried her mother the previous week, and her father lay in hospital in a ..."

"Objection!" cried Markham, on her feet and clearly furious, "Counsel is once again attempting to badger the witness into implied criticism of her employers."

"Overruled," rumbled Judge Victor Mumbles, QC, "I find the question pertinent. The witness will answer it. And I remind you, Ms Markham, there is no jury here. I am quite capable of reaching my own judicial conclusions without your assistance."

The beauteous barrister blushed prettily, nodded and sat down.

"Well, Lieutenant?" preened Kieran.

"Yes."

"And just one final question, in the three months following that week at sea, was there any marked improvement in Ms Carter's performance and behaviour?"

"Well, yes, and no. She worked hard at her PO's Board, and as I pointed out earlier, passed with unusually high points. But I'm afraid that wasn't reflected in her work onboard subsequently. She became sloppy and careless, argumentative with superiors, and seemed to lose interest in her career. I was deeply disappointed, especially since she was earmarked for Officer Selection, and reprimanded her several times.

"So she worked hard for her promotion, excelled with flying colours, even expressed a wish to become an officer, then, inexplicably, seemed to just, what, lose interest?"

"To be frank, she seemed more interested in working on her father's boat and spent all her free weekends there. When her Form B13 (that is, her promotion to PO) arrived in September the Captain declined to endorse it on several recommendations, from myself and fellow officers, and it was sent back."

"Thank you, Lieutenant. No further questions, but please remain seated. Counsel for the prosecution may wish to cross-examine."

"Ms Markham?" said Judge Victor Mumbles, QC.

"Yes, Your Honour, just a couple of questions."

She smiled sweetly at Redfern. "Lieutenant, how long have you been carrying out the duties of Divisional Officer?"

"Oh, about Six and a half years now, on Windsor Castle and two previous ships."

"Presumably you had both men and women in your division?"

"Yes. The navy treats men and women equally, except of course in the matter of sleeping accommodation."

"And during your time as a Divisional Officer, roughly speaking, how many of your junior ratings have suffered family bereavement, would you say?"

Her head jigged minutely from side to side and she did a mental recount.

"Around eight, I would say, maybe more."

"Around eight. And of those eight, how many would you say had their naval careers blighted in the way you've just described?"

"Well, none that I can think of. Most go through a rough patch for a day or two, sometimes a week or two, but then bounce right back into normal shipboard life."

Kieran, at his table below me, stared down at his notes, shaking his head as he listened to the beauteous barrister win back his hard-fought points.

"So, in general, ratings suffering bereavement are not offered counselling, indeed, don't need it."

"I would go further and say that many would actively resent it."

Markham looked across at my brief, the gleam of victory in her eyes, but he didn't look up.

She turned back to the officer who'd praised me as a hero - 'a skilled and dedicated seaman', *an exemplar, for fuck's sake* - then in the next breath downgraded me to sulky insubordinate who couldn't take orders.

And a sad spineless wimp, to boot.

"Thank you, Lieutenant. You may leave the court."

She didn't look up as she walked stiffly beneath, her face shielded by the peak of her cap.

28

"I call Doctor John Hardy."

The tall Scotsman took his time walking across the courtroom floor, tweed jacket unbuttoned, collar-length sandy-red hair turning a distinguished grey at the back and sides, looking characteristically calm and relaxed, even gave me a finger-waggle as he passed beneath, piercing blue eyes that looked into your soul, just the hint of a smile, stepped lightly into the witness box, sat quietly down, and looked patiently at Kieran as if time was a meaningless concept.

I'd been terrified at my first consultation with him, but in later sessions had begun to find him quite attractive. He was fifty-something and married, out of bounds in my book. Not that he'd give me a second glance outside his professional role.

"Thank you for coming, Doctor Hardy," said Kieran, "please briefly introduce yourself to the court?"

"Yes, my name is John Hardy, and I'm the Senior Clinical Psychologist at The Royal Centre for Defence Medicine in Birmingham. I work primarily with service personnel that have been exposed to psychological trauma, assess their capacity for continued active service, and, where necessary, triage them for the most appropriate treatment to aid their recovery."

A curious flutter from some of the press folks in the gallery was quickly silenced by a withering look from Judge Victor Mumbles, QC.

"Thank you, Doctor. Now, my client, then Leading Seaman, Rosemary Carter, was referred to you in October 2012, is that correct?"

"Yes, it is. The eleventh of October, to be precise."

"And could you outline for us the circumstances of that referral?"

"I could indeed. Rosie suffered a major psychotic episode whilst on her ship in Gibraltar. The breakdown presented in a particularly unusual way, which prompted the ship's Medical Officer to set up a conference call with staff at RCDM. I was summoned to advise on the case."

Judge Victor Mumbles, QC, harrumphed and leaned over towards the witness box.

"Assuming that psychological breakdowns don't occur every day in the Royal Navy, Doctor, can you elaborate on what you mean by 'unusual' in this context?"

"Certainly, Your Honour. The subject suffered a narcoleptic attack whilst on shore leave from her ship and, on waking, underwent severe and prolonged cataplexy. Put simply, she was totally paralysed while fully awake for almost three hours."

Judge Victor Mumbles, QC, turned his rheumy eyes on me, "How dreadful!"

I absorbed his gruff sympathy with an emotional chin-wobble.

"So," Kieran said, "there was a video conference to decide what to do. What was the conclusion?"

"First indications suggested a straightforward case of Narcolepsy with associative Sleep Paralysis. I recommended her immediate evacuation to Birmingham. She was admitted to RCDM the following day."

"You used the word 'straightforward' just now. Am I to take it this is a common disorder?"

"The condition affects about one in two-thousand of the general population at one time in their lives and can be a chronic recurring disorder in a small minority of cases. As this case had presented several times in the recent past, the latter was a distinct possibility."

"You say this had happened before, Doctor. Why was it only after this last event that action was taken?"

"A good question, and an internal matter for the ship concerned. Not really my place to comment, except to say that Rosie herself was, shall we say, resourceful, in concealing her condition."

"And I'm sure if I ask you to comment further on that last remark, you'll decline to elaborate on grounds of patient confidentiality."

"That would be correct."

"But your subsequent session with my client did reveal to you the history of her illness, is that correct?"

"Yes."

"And would you be willing to share your discoveries and clinical analysis with the court? And you can take it as read that my client has given her consent."

"With Rosie's consent, I would."

Kieran glanced up at the Bench.

"Ms Carter," boomed Judge Victor Mumbles, QC, "has your counsel discussed this with you?"

I nodded, "Yes, Sir."

"Nevertheless, I will not have members of the press in my court during the remainder of this witness's testimony. Clear the public gallery!"

The disgruntled paparazzi filed out, leaving a defiant Georgie sitting there alone. But nobody challenged her.

"Mr O'Sullivan, you may proceed."

"Thank you, Your Honour. Doctor Hardy, how long was my client under your care?"

"About a month, during which we had once, sometimes twice daily sessions."

"And without going into too much detail of her treatment, what did you conclude about her condition?"

"Rosie suffers from an exotic form of narcolepsy, caused by a chemical imbalance occurring during moments of extreme emotional reaction to external events.

"She presents none of the usual symptoms associated with the disorder, such as persistent tiredness and spontaneous sleep events, however.

"When something triggers in her a strong emotional reaction, she enters a hypnagogic hallucinatory state where bizarre and improbable images manifest as if real. At the same time, she suffers catastrophic cataplexy, a total loss of muscle control. Sleep soon follows, during which vivid dreams often continue. On waking she invariably remains in cataplexy which can last minutes or hours."

"You say it is an exotic disorder. Have you ever come across this particular form of it before?"

"Not directly. But I worked as a Research Fellow for three years at the Sleep Research Centre at MIT, Massachusetts, and came across several peer-reviewed case studies that presented close similarities, some virtually identical, in fact. My case notes from that time proved a useful background supplement in my assessment of Rosie's symptoms."

"And these case studies in the United States, were there any identifiable underlying causes that might have triggered the disorder?"

"The causal evidence is inconclusive, and often anecdotal, though in my view, quite compelling as far as it goes. But yes, in the cases I reviewed, most had undergone significant and persisting emotional stress prior to the onset of the condition. Sufferers often had lost close relatives. Soldiers missing in war, husbands or children that had vanished without trace.

Enduring guilt was a consistent theme. Lack of closure was another."

"Thank you, Doctor. Now, turning back to my client, when did her condition first present itself?" he glanced at the beauteous barrister who'd jumped up to intervene, and quickly added, "as far as you are aware, that is."

She sat down again, disappointed.

"As far as I could ascertain, the first event coincided with the appearance at her father's hospital bedside of someone who closely resembled her recently deceased mother."

"And such a shocking…"

"Mr O'Sullivan," growled Judge Victor Mumbles, QC, "I am quite capable of grasping your point. Kindly move on."

Kieran paused, thrown out of his stride for a moment, but then rallied.

"Now, aside from these disturbing attacks, how would you describe her psychological well-being when she arrived under your care?"

"Initially I found Rosie a, shall we say, challenging patient," he threw me a rueful grin, "resistant to probing, tending to shut down when faced with difficult but necessary questions, and quite rude at times. Uncommunicative behaviour can be indicative of some underlying problem; anxiety, guilt, morbidity, or other stress factors which can ultimately lead to various depressive disorders. Eventually we got to the essentials of the matter when she agreed to undergo hypnosis."

"So, you put her to sleep?"

The Scotsman stared at Kieran as if he'd lost his mind.

"On the contrary. Hypnosis puts the subject into a state of hyper-awareness. The technique is well understood by mental health practitioners and is extremely useful in the analysis and treatment of psychological disorders."

"Forgive my ignorance, Doctor, please continue - what did you discover?"

I held my breath. This was crunch time. I glanced over at Georgie who had her eyes fixed on Doctor Hardy. She didn't know what was coming.

"Rosie had subjected her father to a degree of verbal abuse during her early visits, berating him quite mercilessly for the death of her mother."

I couldn't meet her eyes, but knew she was staring at me.

Doctor Hardy was still talking.

"… came to regret her unkindness; her remorse turning to guilt and self-loathing. Outwardly she became uncharacteristically morose, lost interest in her career, and at times became rather unpleasant in her dealings with colleagues and superiors. She also admitted to an obsession with renovating her father's boat to atone for her behaviour."

"Finally, Doctor Hardy, you will be aware that my client has been indicted for the theft of naval stores in the pursuit of that obsession with her father's boat. In your *professional opinion*," Kieran glanced round at the beauteous barrister before continuing, "…could her state of mind at the time have contributed to her committing those offences?"

The beauteous barrister remained seated.

"Difficult to say for certain, but her past record would suggest she acted out of character, and certainly in a stressed emotional state and altered priorities, her moral compass could certainly have gone askew."

"Thank you, Doctor. No further questions."

As Kieran returned to his seat Judge Victor Mumbles, QC, looked down at the beauteous barrister, "Ms Markham, do you wish to cross-examine?"

"No, Your Honour."

She was keeping her powder dry for little old me.

"In that case, we'll adjourn for lunch." He looked up at the clock, "It is now one-fifteen, the court will reconvene at two-o-clock. And Mr O'Sullivan, I want to see an end to this today."

With that, Judge Victor Mumbles, QC, banged his gavel and left the room.

29

"I call the Defendant, Rosemary Carter."

Passing close to Kieran on my way to the witness box, I whispered, "No you don't, you call me Rosie."

Kieran winced, and the Clerk scowled, but Judge Victor Mumbles, QC, seemed not to notice.

I'd just scuppered two quick voddies across the road during my excursion outside the court for a smoke and was feeling inappropriately flippant.

"Might be my last booze for a couple of years," I'd told a furious Aunt Georgie who'd been waiting in the entrance hall for my return.

I caught her eye across the room as I took my seat in the witness box; could tell she wasn't best pleased, but she managed an encouraging wink.

"Now, Rosie, can you please..."

"Before you begin, Mr O'Sullivan," growled Judge Victor Mumbles, QC, "what is your purpose in calling your client as a witness?"

Kieran looked flustered for a moment, and my heart sank into my boots.

"Well, Your Honour, I thought it might be useful for the court to hear Ms Carter's perspective on the evidence we've heard. I wish to demonstrate that she committed her crimes whilst under severe emotional and psychological stress, a factor which impaired her judgement."

"And what new evidence will her testimony bring to the court's attention?"

"Er… Well, none, really, Your…"

"In that case, I think I've heard enough. The offender will return to the dock."

Kieran stared at him in disbelief. I was totally confused as I walked back to the dock and sat down.

Judge Victor Mumbles, QC, looked down at the clerk of the court and gave a barely-perceptible nod.

"The offender will stand," called the clerk of the court.

I stood, my knees began to wobble as I prepared to hear the worst.

"Ms Carter," boomed Judge Victor Mumbles, QC, "you have been found guilty of a most heinous offence. Theft from Her Majesties Dockyard is a crime against the State and accordingly, must attract an appropriately severe punishment. I have little choice therefore, other than to award the maximum sentence of three years detention in Her Majesty's Prison."

Georgie's sharp intake of breath pierced the silence of the room. She looked across at me, her face distorted with agony.

"However," growled Judge Victor Mumbles, QC, "I have listened carefully to the evidence in support of mitigation and find the Basis of Plea to have a degree of merit."

As Judge Victor Mumbles, QC, spoke his final words, my hand flew to my mouth and a familiar feeling rose up inside me. The Judge's face began to elongate, becoming increasingly canine and drooping like melting wax. His gavel struck with reverberating thunder, echoing in my head, and Judge Victor Mumbles, QC, became a leering bloodhound lurching towards me, silvery strings of saliva streaming from under his floppy jowls. Then he went out of my vision, obscured by the rising wall of the dock. My cheek slid down the polished wood as darkness closed around me.

I came-to with the usual paralysis, but it lasted only a few minutes, Georgie flapping over me, crooning words of comfort and patting my hand, while next to her the uniformed court usher kneeled in to put a cushion under my head. Then Doctor Hardy appeared, beaming reassurance into my face then gently taking charge and calming everyone down.

When it was all over I walked arm in arm with Georgie down the stairs to the big hall, a static grin on my face that was beginning to make my jaws ache. John Hardy got us teas at the kiosk, and we found a table to wait for Kieran.

"Jesus!" said Georgie, "when the judge said he was giving you three years I nearly had kittens. Was it my imagination, or did he leave it hanging in the air just a little longer than necessary?"

"What, before he said…" I dropped my voice to a growl, "'The sentence shall be suspended for five years. You may go, young lady, and offend no more.'"

Georgie guffawed and said, "Sounds more like Winston Churchill, don't give up your day job, Sweetie."

Hardy arrived with two cups of tea then excused himself. "Got to fly, I'm afraid, needed back at the coalface. Glad it went well for you Rosie."

Kieran joined us, grabbing a chair from an empty table.

"Right," he said, getting down to business, "I've got three pieces of good news. First up, the Prosecution have agreed to waive costs. Second, the MoD aren't interested in claiming damages. So, there's nothing to pay."

"Except your fee." I said.

"Except my fee," he agreed with a wry grin. "Not much I can do about that, I'm afraid. My Firm would crucify me for an unauthorised pro bono."

Georgie patted his hand, "Don't worry, Kieran, we've got it covered."

"And the third thing?" I asked.

He slid a brown envelope across the table, "The Order of Release for your boat, you can go over and collect her anytime you   like."

30

My first sight of Pasha made me sick to my stomach. The MoD might have dropped their damages claim, but they'd certainly made sure I wouldn't benefit from my scams.

Gloomily, I surveyed the disorder of equipment piled on the greasy concrete: the genoa, folded but un-bagged; the mainsail still attached to the dismantled boom and spilling untidily out of its lazy-bag; the deflated dinghy and its bottom-boards, its outboard cast carelessly on top. In another heap, on top of a tangle of sheets, mooring lines and general-purpose ropes, lay my CQR anchor, now bereft of its chain, and my Danforth secondary anchor.

Alongside all this sorry clutter lay the mast, halliards wrapped round and round like a maypole, denuded of all its standing rigging.

"At least they didn't scrape off the antifoul," Georgie observed wryly.

"I wouldn't've put it past them," I said, "vindictive bastards!"

Georgie touched her shoe against the mast, "and at least you've got the chance to change the bulb in the anchor-light."

We locked eyes for a second, then both spluttered into hysterical giggling.

"Samink fanny?"

We turned and straightened our faces, or at least Georgie did, my attempt was still in progress.

It was the Yard Superintendent who'd let us in; a short, square man, blue work-coat and wellies.

"Private joke," said Georgie.

"When yer moving 'er art? Need this space."

"You haven't exactly made it easy for us," said Georgie, nodding at the chaotic jumble.

When he didn't respond I added, "Ever heard of *Duty of Care*?"

"Naffink to do with me, Lav, blame the filf. Ya got to Wednesday, arter that, it's an 'andred paand a day."

With that, he turned and stumped off.

They lifted her in for us on Monday morning, the mast and boom lashed down along the coach-roof, all the other gear stuffed haphazardly into the two lazarettes. We motored down the creek to the nearby commercial marina and boatyard.

"Now what?" I said, after we'd tied up at a finger-pontoon.

"What a silly question! Now, we talk to the boatyard and see what deal we can do to get the old girl back on her feet."

She studied my face a moment, then smiled and patted my cheek. "Don't worry, 'bout a thing, cos every little thing's going   to   be   alright."

Part Two

31

I awoke to the change in sound and motion, the rattle of sheet-blocks, the rumple of lazy sails; instead of heeling firmly to leeward *Pasha's* motion had become slack and lollopy. I slid out of my sleeping bag and checked the chart-table clock: 0220. The barometer read 1026, a rise of three millibars since midnight.

With a tired groan I shrugged into my heavy foul-weather jacket, climbed the ladder to the cockpit and peered through gummy eyes at a monochrome seascape under a frozen universe. The wind had dropped to little more than an icy breath that turned my exhalations into clouds of vapour.

Pasha drifted at the mercy of a smooth but precipitous easterly swell that by now had begun to rock her violently from beam to beam, the mast waving erratically at a cradle moon set against a cloudless, richly-jewelled sky.

Shivering in the still night air, I sheeted in the boom to stop it's mad swinging, fired up the engine, and quickly got to work on the genoa sheets and inhaul.

Five minutes later, with the headsail furled away and twenty-seven horses grumbling us southward at four knots, I sat in a kind of frozen stupor, too numb with tiredness to drag myself below to my warm bag.

The past forty-eight hours since leaving the Solent - weaving through the dense shipping of the Channel, brief catnaps in the cockpit when my eyes refused to stay open, watching my nav-track to stay clear of the separation zones, and forcing my tired brain to stay alert - had left me mentally exhausted.

It was early March, and I was some 200 miles southwest of Land's End, having altered course to the south at 1am, on the edge of the Bay of Biscay and reasonably clear of shipping, and had hoped for a few hours of uninterrupted sleep.

Some hope.

In that moment of leaden quietude, I saw my Aunt, wrapped in a winter overcoat of Mum's, thick scarf and woolly hat, waving from the pontoon at Gosport as I'd motored *Pasha* out of the marina.

It would be a warm balmy evening now in Florida, and I imagined Georgie sitting out by her pool with her partner Anna, sharing the sorry tale of my stupidity and misfortunes, and what it had taken to get me and *Pasha* back on track for our Great Adventure – a Med Cruise, as far as she was concerned.

In addition to replacing all the confiscated gear, I had invested some of Mum's money in the purchase of an AIS system, a kind of electronic beacon for ships that displayed vessels on my chart plotter and gave an audio warning of potential collisions. It also allowed them to see me. All very modern and high-tech – just call me Gadget-Girl.

With a resigned sigh I scanned the cobalt horizon once more then took myself back to bed, hoping for the returning wind that would get me to Cape St Vincent in a week or so. If this high-pressure, unusual for March in the Bay, stayed with us we could be motoring for days, would need to refuel at Vigo or Porto, and this first leg of my trans-Atlantic voyage would turn seriously long and dreary.

Not that I was in any hurry. It was far too late in the year to attempt a crossing now, so I planned to sail to Gibraltar, stay a few weeks there, then head on down to the Canaries where I would wait for the trade winds in November. Christmas in Florida seemed an attractive idea, and in the meantime, I was going to enjoy myself and wash out the misery of the past few months.

The calm continued into the morning. After breakfast, Weetabix with the last of my fresh blueberries, I sat in the cockpit reading, already sick of the monotonous rumble of the engine, the *gigglegurgle* from the exhaust, and the stink of diesel wafted into the cockpit by the slipstream of our windless passage; the sea, an undulating sheet of rippled glass, a westerly swell that rocked us relentlessly from side to side as we sliced our way southwards.

The sky remained obstinately clear throughout the morning, no sign on the horizon of clouds that would signal the returning wind.

The change began in mid-afternoon, mare-tails of wispy cirrus high in the western sky, a slight darkening on the horizon. A front was approaching.

By 4-o'clock a battalion of grey cumulous clouds had risen above the razor-sharp margin of sea and sky. Despite having wished for it, an approaching front always gave me a touch of the collywobbles, and as that familiar anxiety washed over me concentration on reading became impossible.

"Time for a cuppa," I said aloud, getting up from where I'd been lounging lazily since lunch.

"No, Rosemary, time to shorten sail."

Startled, I froze where I was, half out of my seat, gripping white-knuckled onto the console support. Hearing voices wasn't so unusual, especially when the engine was running. But this was no *gigglegurgle* delusion, no flight of fancy conjured up by tiredness and prolonged solitude. This was a real voice, almost a whisper, close to my ear, intimate.

And strangely familiar.

I'd heard it a couple of times before on *Pasha*, canned it as imaginary, perhaps a symptom of my depression. But now I wasn't so dismissive.

Was my boat talking to me?

I gripped onto that thought, willing it to be true because the alternative explanation was unthinkable.

I was reminded of what Dad used to say on reefing, one of his favourite aphorisms: 'If you watch and wait, it'll be too late."

"Okay…" I said, feeling faintly ridiculous, "you're right, whoever you are."

By the time I returned from below with my harness on a faint breeze had sprung up from the southwest, and the clouds in the west had burgeoned, towering dark and ominous.

I loosened off the mainsheet and dropped the mainsail down to the second reef, then hooked my harness onto the jackstay and made my way gingerly along the rolling deck to the mast.

Hooking the two reef toggles onto the ramshorn was straightforward, but back in the cockpit I struggled with the reefing lines to untangle them from the lazy-jacks and the end of the sail. It took longer than expected because I needed to put back the bimini frame to reach the end of the boom. By now the wind had strengthened to such a degree that the loosened boom swung about dangerously, swinging me with it as I fought to loosen the fouled lines.

Finally, I got both reefing lines hauled taught on the winch and the surplus sail stowed into the lazy-bag with a couple of lashings to keep them there.

Fuck it! I thought, as I sat down to catch my breath, I should've been ready for that, instead of sitting on my arse reading.

By the time I had the genoa out, unfurled to the third reef marker, about one third of its full size, the anemometer was reading fifteen knots from broad on the starboard bow, a close reach, and we were making seven knots. Still cursing my foolishness, I killed the engine, waited for the speed to fall off then trimmed the sails. I went below to put the kettle on.

An hour later the wind was gusting 25 and we were creaming along at eight knots, the wind vane now in charge of our steering.

I was learning the hard way that preparation is everything and delayed precautions can be fatal. Without Dad there to prompt me I had become lazy and complacent in my seamanship.

Get your act together, Rosie.

32

"*Hola, bueno tarde*, and welcome to Alcaidesa Marina."

The office felt refreshingly cool after the blazing afternoon heat outside. The receptionist was young, attractive, and business-like, and I was relieved she spoke excellent English so wouldn't need to assault her ears with my half-forgotten *Spanglish*.

"Hola," I said, "I need a berth for about a month?"

"No problem. Can I please have your passport, your boat registration and insurance?"

I smiled and handed over the documents.

I'd decided I wasn't going to stay in the Gib marina, and after fuelling up on duty-free diesel, motored around to the one in La Linea, on the Spanish side of the frontier, where it was quieter and had better berths on floating pontoons.

It was also much cheaper. I would have to watch my pennies if I was to spend almost a year away. I'd used up most of Mum's trust money on *Pasha* and had only my small navy disability pension to live on.

Of course, there were Dad's two pensions that were accumulating nicely while he was out of it, but I was working on the assumption he would eventually recover – and even an empty house generated bills that had to be paid. So I'd decided I wouldn't raid his bank account except in the direst of emergencies.

After the necessary form filling, the issue of my key card for the security gates and showers, I climbed back aboard

Pasha and motored into the marina where two guys from a boat next to my berth leapt ashore to take my lines. How kind, I thought.

Once moored up and connected to shore-power, I looked up at the mainsail lying in untidy folds where I'd dropped it, half-in half-out of the lazy-bag, wondering if I should climb up and stow it properly.

"Nah!"

I grabbed my towel, washbag and a change of clothes, and hurried along the quay to take my first shower in two weeks.

Afterwards I felt like just falling into bed and sleeping for a week. But no, I had things to do. Instead, I took my laptop up to the marina bar, chose one of several empty tables outside, and ordered a beer from a nice young waiter.

My first email was to Dad's hospital ward, asking for an update and adding a few newsy lines to be read to him on my progress so far.

Next, I composed one to Doc, whom I hadn't seen since the weekend before my ill-fated trip with Gary in February, though we'd kept in touch. Windy was in the Caribbean on a three-month stint as Guardship.

And finally, I squirted one off to Georgie to tell her of my safe arrival.

"Mind if we join you?"

I looked up, closing the lid of my laptop. He was a bearded grey-hair, a fit-looking fiftyish; she, a little younger, blonde frizz, open face and toothy smile.

I'd barely noticed the noise level increase as the place had filled up around me. All the tables were now occupied, and three chairs stood empty at my table.

"Please do," I said, smiling back.

"Just arrived?" she said, pulling up a chair as he went off to get drinks.

"About two hours ago." I said, "sailed from UK."

"I'm guessing you're a single-hander," she stuck out her hand, "name's Kate, by the way."

"Rosie," I said, shaking her hand, "is it that obvious?"

"Nah, not really," she gave a giggle, "saw you come in, that's all. No one else on deck, 'she must be alone', I said to Bill – that's my old man." Her accent was straight Essex, vowels as broad as her smile.

"When did you arrive?" I asked.

She laughed again, "about seven years ago. Liked it here, so we stayed. We're on that Westerly over there," she pointed out a smart-looking boat three pontoons up from *Pasha*, "blue hull, white sail cover."

"Early retirement?" I hazarded.

"Nah., I wish. We both got jobs in Gib. I work for a Property Agent, Bill's in the Marina, boat refurbisher. Self-employed, you know?"

"Pin money for me," Bill said, putting down three beers and passing one to me, "Kate's the earner, I just potter about."

His accent, I now discerned, was broad Geordie.

I'd intended an early night, but found myself rejuvenated by this gregarious, earthy couple, still bantering and laughing with them as the sun sank behind the Andalusian hills and night descended. It was only after I'd helped them devour a communal plate of chorizos, salad and fries that I felt myself drooping amid stifled yawns and excused myself.

Crawling onto my bunk I realised I hadn't paid for anything and made a sleepy note to settle with them tomorrow when I'd got myself some Euros.

Surprisingly, I was up at first light, feeling refreshed and alive with no ill-effects from what had been a rather boozy night.

After two weeks at sea, exercise was the first order of the day. I slipped on panties and shorts, a light cotton bra, t-shirt, socks and trainers, chopped up a grapefruit which I mixed with muesli and a yoghurt, and ate in the cockpit while the sun was still hidden behind the Rock.

Conscious of the coming heat and my un-acclimatised body, I drank down a cup of water, then donned my small backpack containing passport and purse, stepped ashore, and began my run, all the way to the frontier, through passport control, across the runway, and into Gibraltar's already busy Main Street. Here, soaking with sweat and huffing like a steam train, I bought a half-litre bottle of water from a kiosk and sank down on a bench to drink it.

Job done. Time to buy a phone.

Coming back towards the frontier, the demon addict in my head told me to call in at the airport duty-free shop and buy tobacco. I resisted, with some difficulty, and broke into a trot once more, this time to break the evil hex of temptation. I hadn't smoked since my trial and didn't intend ever to do so again.

Before going back onboard I called at an ATM and drew out two-hundred Euros, then a phone shop where I bought a SIM card with 50 Euros of credit. My new dual SIM phone was now UK and Spain enabled. My life was coming back together.

Back on *Pasha*, I connected my new phone to my laptop and loaded up the backup of my contacts, not a lengthy list, some people I hadn't phoned in years, but among them, some I might want to call again someday.

In my hand was a card I'd been fidgeting with for the past twenty minutes. It had been stuck in the back of my purse, half-forgotten until now.

Mateo Galindez

I thumbed the number into the phone and selected the Spanish SIM, then sat, undecided. Would he even remember?

The encounter had been so short-lived, and the circumstances far from convivial.

My finger must have brushed the screen; it was calling. I put the phone to my ear. Ringing out, then:

"Sí, Mateo aquí, quién es este?"

I couldn't speak, didn't know what to say.

"Hablame!"

I ended the call and sat fuming at myself. But what could I say, really?

My phone rang. It was the same number. Damn, I should have put my number on withhold. I swiped to answer.

"Dime, quién es?"

"Hi, Mateo, you probably don't remember me, but my name is Rosie. We met briefly last October. I was…"

"Ah! Rosey! Rosey! Rosey!" he chanted, mimicking the antics of my old shipmates.

"Yes, *that* Rosie," I said, laughing.

"Of *course* I remember you – I was hope for call, but no call. *Estaba decepcionado* – I… disappointed."

"I'm sorry. I would have called but something happened. I had to go home."

"Where are you now? You have Spanish number, yes?"

"I'm here in La Linea, I just wondered if…"

"Estupendo! You want we meet, Rosie?"

"Si, Mateo, I want we meet."

33

Anxiety began to gnaw at me almost as soon as I ended my call with Mateo. Since those sessions with Doctor Hardy, the shrink in Birmingham, I'd been scared even to masturbate; terrified the emotional high of an orgasm, or even the anticipation of it, would bring on another of my psychotic episodes. How would that play with a guy I was keen to impress?

But hell, I had to start somewhere, sometime. I wasn't going to live life like some celibate prude.

Take it slowly tonight, I told myself, and hope he isn't just up for a quick shag.

In the meantime, I busied myself with my laundry, stowing the mainsail, hosing down the decks and rigging, and cleaning up below.

We'd agreed to meet at seven at a small café on *Calle Caboneros* in the centre of town. I'd got a little lost and found him sitting alone at an outside table under a large parasol, spooning sugar into an espresso coffee. Coral-pink chinos, white canvas shoes, white shirt and cream linen jacket. He looked good enough to eat. And that mop of curly jet-black hair.

"Hi Mateo," I said breathlessly, "sorry I'm late."

He looked up, a momentary hesitation, then a wide smile and a flash in his deep-brown eyes that took me back to our all-too-brief encounter almost six months ago.

"Rosie," he said, standing up, taller than I remembered, "it is *so* good to see you."

I got a scent of sharp musky shower gel as he bent to give me an Andalusian greeting; thrice kissed on the cheeks, to which I responded awkwardly and then worried he might think I'd been going for an early lip-lock.

He stood back, grinning, and gave me the briefest of up-and-down inspections. Last time he'd seen me was in shorts and flip-flops. Tonight, it was a light blue cotton frock, high-heeled sandals with ankle-straps, and a little more makeup than just the usual smear of lippy. I'd even put on my dangly earrings and matching necklace which I hadn't worn in years.

"You look… nice," he said, flustered, and, as if realising his English might not adequately express his admiration, added, "*Muy hermosa!*"

Which was just as well. Dressing girly isn't easy on a boat, and this was my only outfit.

He pealed his eyes off me and pulled out a chair, "Please, Rosie, you sit? You grow your hair."

"Yes," I said, taking the seat and hooking my bag over the chair back, "I left the navy – now I can wear it how I like."

"It suits you longer. What can I get you for drink?"

"Er… *gracias, vino tinto, por favor.*"

We spent the next hour chatting, with me doing most of it, and him asking the questions: how come I left the navy, which I managed to hedge around; what I was doing now, which gave me the opportunity to steer the topic to *Pasha* and my plans to cross the Atlantic. He seemed genuinely interested in everything, but at the same time showed great sensitivity, quickly backing off and changing topics if I hesitated over something.

As I began to relax and that nagging anxiety I'd had dissipated, whether under his charm or the wine, or both, I found myself opening up about Dad and describing his locked-in state; and the story of my mysterious aunt, which he found both hilarious and amazing.

Afterwards, with darkness settling over the town, we moved up the *calle* to a charming little taverna where Mateo seemed to know all the waiters. We ordered more wine and talked. A waiter brought a basket of bread, and before long small plates of tapas began to arrive at our table, unordered but very welcome, and each time a plate was emptied it was replaced with a different delicacy.

"So, Mateo," I said in a pause in the conversation, "you know all about me," not quite true, I know, but some aspects of my life couldn't be told, not here, not now, "and I know nothing about you. Tell me, are you a secret agent?"

His smouldering features grew puzzled, "What is 'Secret Agent'?"

Devastated. My attempt at an amusing opening gambit lay in ruins at the gates of translation. I shook my head and laughed, then, seeing his annoyed reaction, reached across and put my hand on his.

"Forgive me, Mateo, your English is so good I forgot myself for a moment. What I meant to say, what do you do for work?"

To my relief, his frown gave way to a grin, "Ah, Si. *agente secreto* like James Bond." He turned my hand over and held it lightly in his long, sensitive fingers, smiling into my soul with those gorgeous eyes. "You are funny girl, Rosie. I like you."

"And I like you, Mateo. *Mucho*, in fact."

He chuckled, then sat up straight as I gently extricated my hand; the moment gone, for now.

"So," he said, "I am *cirujano veterinaria,* in English I think you say, veterinary surgeon."

I stared at him, then rolled my eyes, laughing.

"Is funny?"

"I thought that's where you lived. It's written on your card, *cirujano veterinaria.* I assumed it was a place."

"You think it...?" He spluttered, and we fell into helpless giggles.

More wine came, and yet more tapas. It seemed like we'd been eating and drinking forever. The place was thinning out – it was already after midnight.

"Is your clinic here in the town?" I asked him a little later.

"No, I have no clinic," he said, but didn't elaborate.

"So... you make house calls?"

He smiled, reached over and took my hand. I didn't resist when his fingers stroked my palm. A queasy warmth spread into my deepest regions, a sensation I hadn't felt in a long time.

"In the morning I show you where I work," he said, cryptically, "you will like it very much, I am sure."

I froze. Was he suggesting spending the night together?

"Mateo, there's something I..."

He hushed me with a finger to my lips, and then he cupped the side of my face, his hand so warm and gentle I might even have leaned into it a little.

"I will walk with you to marina, then I will go home. I will come for you at 9-o-clock in morning with my car, and we will go to my work."

34

I woke up bright and early again next morning, and stretched luxuriously on my newly-washed bedsheet, and thought about Mateo.

We hadn't spoken much on the walk back to the marina, just strolled along the empty, tree-lined streets in companiable silence, apart from the occasional inane comment from me about how quiet it was and how clean the streets were compared to any British city centre at one in the morning.

I had wondered what was in store for me tomorrow, but didn't press him further on the matter, content to let him surprise me. I was quite excited.

At the security gate he'd predictably done that three-cheek kiss again, but then unpredictably planted a fourth one smack on the lips. I'm sure it was supposed to have been a chaste peck, but the wine took charge and I turned it into a full-blown snog.

Embarrassing, what was I *thinking?* I walked back to the boat feeling like a silly teenager. Still, he hadn't seemed to mind.

As instructed, I pulled on a pair of jeans, socks and trainers. I supposed the day involved time out in the country. Maybe he was a farm vet. With no specifics as to the top, I donned a bra and t-shirt, and packed shorts and flip-flops, spare panties (always) and a lightweight fleece pullover into my mini backpack. He'd told me I might need that too.

I'd been expecting something sporty and was surprised when he pitched up at the marina in a big Nissan 4x4, a truck, really.

"*Bueno Dias,*" I chirped, climbing in and throwing my bag into the back.

"*Bueno Dias*, Rosie," he replied with his usual bright grin, "and how are you today?"

"Looking forward to my mysterious day out."

"Ah, you will not be disappointed," he looked out at the clear blue sky, "the day for it is perfect."

We drove northwest along the city's coastal road, making fast progress as this was Sunday and the streets were relatively clear of traffic. Reaching the end of the conurbation, we crossed a motorway intersection, then climbed north up to the small hilltop town of San Roque.

From here Mateo took a narrow winding road that led up into the higher hills beyond, and the scenery became rugged and rocky; occasional cows and herds of goats grazed among the scrubby bushes and stunted trees, and small rivers wound their haphazard way through gullies and troughs in the hillsides.

"You work up *here*?"

He turned and grinned but said nothing.

We continued our winding climb for another half hour or so, Mateo shifting expertly up and down the gears, slowing for hairpin bends that opened spectacular views onto the glistening blue waters of Algeciras Bay, the Rock of Gibraltar, and the hazy Moroccan mountains across the Strait, then powering along the straight and level sections to gain momentum for the next steep climb.

The road levelled out and we cruised down into a wooded valley where the vegetation turned lush and the sky above was obscured by overhanging boughs. After another mile or so he slowed, then turned left onto a sandy track that led arrow-straight up to a white-painted wooden archway with a closed wicket gate across the track. I looked up at the name of the place, emblazoned in big letters around the archway.

PREMAGNIFICO
granja de caballos andaluces

I turned to Mateo and laughed. "Horses? You're a horse-doctor?"

"Not just horses," he said, opening his door, "the World's greatest horses, *Pura Raza Espanola* - Andalusian Pure Breads."

He stepped down, walked to the side of the gate, and pressed a button on an intercom box. A voice squawked, and Mateo bent to speak into it. As he walked back to the truck the gate swung slowly open behind him.

Beyond the gate the track continued straight, lined by small plane trees behind which ran a white-painted wooden fence. As we drove along I began to glimpse horses beyond the fence, and more fenced off paddocks and more horses. And then horses were everywhere, as far as the eye could see; wall to wall horses.

And what colours! Dark chestnut horses, piebald horses, pure white and pure black, and splendid greys with bright silver whorls. Some stood alone with heads held high and proud, others galloped playfully, their movements lithe and graceful, one or two pranced about in that showy high-step they do in dressage, some stood in pairs with heads close, seemingly in deep meaningful conversation.

I'd never been what you'd call a horsey girl, but even I could tell these were special creatures, tall and rangy, rippling with muscle, and beautifully groomed.

"Wow!" I said, "I'm impressed. And you're the vet for all these animals?"

He laughed. "We have more than three-thousand horses here – for one person would be impossible. There are six in my team. Is full time work. Even today, Sunday, there are two *veterinarios* on duty."

"Not you though?"

"No, not me." He turned to me and smiled, "Today I am yours."

The track suddenly opened out into a wide cobblestoned courtyard, fronted on one side by a big old house; broad steps tapering up to a marble-columned portico. Two other sides of the square led off to row upon row of stables, some with horses looking out over the half-doors. A dozen or so stable-hands milled about at their work; several looked up and waved as we entered the courtyard. Mateo drove up to the house and parked.

"What happens now?" I asked. I didn't have a clue why I was here, but willing to go along with whatever he had in mind; reigning in my curiosity, so to speak.

He grinned again. "Now, we get out and walk, bring your bag." was all he said.

He took his own backpack from the back of the truck and led the way past one of the stable blocks; the stink of horse shit, faintly with us all the way up the drive, now became pungently overpowering.

Reading my thoughts, Mateo said, "In half an hour you will not notice it."

At the end of the block stood a huge barn with a small paddock alongside it. I followed Mateo inside, then stopped and stared, suddenly realising what he had in mind for my surprise.

There, in the centre of the sawdust-floored barn, stood two beautiful horses.

Two *huge* beautiful horses.

One, a brown and white piebald, was already saddled up, the other, a dappled grey, was in progress of being so.

Mateo, seeing my unease, came back and took me by the hand. "Come, come. These are gentle animals, come."

"You expect me to ride one of these? They're *giants!*"

He laughed again, led me up to the piebald, and patted her neck. "This is Abril, she is Pasa Fino, and she will take good care of you, don't worry."

The person who'd been preparing the other horse now sidled over, a short, stocky woman in blue coveralls and riding boots, grey hair tied back in a loose ponytail. She looked around fifty, with a weatherworn but friendly face.

"You ever ride Pasa Fino, honey?"

American accent, her voice deep and gravelly; a fifty-a-day voice.

"I've never ridden a *horse*." I said, gingerly stroking the horse's muzzle, "and I'm not sure I can, not without... you know, training? Have you got something smaller, a pony, maybe?"

She gave snort, "Phooey, any child can ride a Pasa."

She took the reins and led Abril over to a mounting block. I stayed put.

"Come over here, honey."

Reluctantly I obeyed, Mateo holding my hand and smiling encouragement.

"Now, just step up on the block and put your left foot into this here stirrup, Mateo'll help ya."

Well, I got myself mounted, impressed that Abril stood like a rock while I did so. It was a long way to the ground.

"See, that worn't so bad, was it?" she offered up her hand, "Name's Bonny bah the way."

I bent down and shook her hand, it was hard and calloused.

"Rosie," I said.

"Now, there's two ways to make her go forward, yer kin snick yer tongue in yer cheek to start her off slow or kick her gently with yer heels to make her go faster. Every time yer kick her, she'll go a little faster. Not hard, mind. Pasa's don't need no hard kickin'.

"When ya'll want her to stop or slow down, just ease back on the reins. When you wanna go left, ease back on the left rein, and same on t'other side.

"Now, I'm gonna walk ya around the paddock out there till you feel comfortable, then we'll see how ya do on yer own. Ready?"

I'd fully expected to be holding on for dear life while the horse bucked and bounced beneath me. But this was amazing. Abril's legs moved in an odd kind of fast trot, and she snorted a lot, but the ride was no worse than a pushbike on a cobbled street. And once I'd got used to using the command signals I began to really enjoy myself.

By the time Mateo's mount was ready I felt confident enough to go further afield. And that's exactly what we did, riding far out into the forested valley and up into the wild hills, lunch on a charming riverbank, and back at the stables by late afternoon. A truly wonderful day.

35

Before we drove off I leaned over to Mateo, hooked my arm round his neck, and gave him a big wet kiss on the cheek.

"Thank you," I said, "that was a lovely surprise, and a fabulous day."

"It is not over yet," he said, grinning, "now we go to my house and I cook dinner."

"Oh, really?" I said, piqued but also faintly amused by his presumption. "And what if I had other plans for tonight?"

His grin faded, "I am sorry. Okay, I take you back to La Linea."

Well that backfired.

"No, no, I don't have plans, I was just saying… you know?"

He turned to me, a solemn expression, "Rosie, do you want to come to my house for dinner?"

"Yes, Mateo," I replied meekly, "that would be lovely."

"*Bueno*, we go." He pushed into reverse and backed out of the courtyard.

Teach me to be a smartarse.

Was this to be it then - the moment of truth?

As the craggy scenery whizzed past I felt my anxiety rising once more. There had been no attempt at intimacy between us during the day, Mateo had acted the perfect gentleman. There'd been ample opportunity beside that gurgling river in a secluded glade for things to have got steamily romantic. But he'd barely moved from his grassy mound, back against a solitary rock, while I sat on the bank dangling my feet in the cold rush of water. And while the horses grazed contentedly nearby, we ate our sandwiches and talked.

I told him about my childhood, growing up in England, and stories from my time in the navy. He told me about his past and his work at the ranchero. At one point he became quite animated on the history of the Andalusian pure-breds but that's as passionate as it got.

Even if I'd had the nerve to move things on a bit I suspect it wouldn't have gone down well. It was becoming clear to me Mateo was a guy who compartmentalised his life; everything in its time and place.

Okay, that's cool.

Still, I was nervous about the next part.

His house.

I'd discovered during our riverside chat that Mateo was thirty-six, was originally from Cadiz, had studied at Madrid University then returned home to work in a small veterinary practice, and had moved here five years ago when he was offered the job at the *granja*.

"You live alone, then?" I now ventured.

"Si, my house has two bedrooms, but I use one for office. I prefer live alone."

He paused, and turning, grinned brightly, "Maybe one day I will feel different, eh?"

At San Roque we turned into the town's main thoroughfare - not much there, a small supermarket, a couple of shops, a taverna, all closed – and came out into a residential sprawl; houses festooned all around with colourful flowering trees and shrubs, and a couple of nondescript low-rise apartments. Leaving these behind the road narrowed and began to descend, and there once more spread below, the grand sweep of Algeciras Bay.

Presently we pulled up at a pair of iron gates, which Mateo opened with the click of a fob from the glovebox.

The house was too square and modern to be called beautiful. But it was spaciously luxurious and had a view from its wide patio to die for; a stunning panorama with the Rock of Gibraltar at centre-stage.

After my wander round, I found Mateo busy in the large kitchen, at a sink with a knife and some kind of dead creature.

"What's for dinner?" I said, peering over his shoulder.

He spoke without looking up from what I now saw was a cuttlefish. "*Zarangollo, paella negra, y Escabeche de conejo,*"

I let out a guffaw. "I haven't a clue what you just said, except I did catch the word paella in their somewhere."

"Si, black paella."

"What makes it black?"

"Ink." He looked up, saw my wrinkled-up nose, and gave me a cheeky grin, "from calamar, squid."

"Oh, how… nice."

He ran his hands under the tap and picked up a towel.

"You like my house?"

"Yes, roomy and all the mod cons… er modern conveniences – great views too. Mateo, I need a shower, do you mind?"

"Yes, please use the shower, everything you need is there."

I picked at my damp top. "Er, you haven't got a t-shirt I could borrow by any chance?"

"Can I help with anything?"

"No, everything is under control." Mateo said, then turned from what he was doing, "it is almost…" he positively gaped.

"What?"

"You look… can I say, sexy?"

I laughed. I'd put on shorts and the Barcelona t-shirt he'd given me, which was far too big and hung on me like a marquee. I was bare-foot and my hair was still wet from the shower.

"Yes, you can say it, but I think we need to talk about your... huh? *Mateo* mmm."

I was stunned by how suddenly it happened. One moment he was feet away, the next, his lips were locked on mine in open-mouthed urgency, one hand cupping my wet head while the other caressed the naked small of my back under the t-shirt.

Thrilled by his spontaneity I melted into his delicious embrace and gave it my all. Our tongues met and explored; my fingers laced into that luxurious hair as his hand crept down inside the back of my shorts and into my panties, pressing me firmly into his lean hardness, leaving me in no doubt about his aroused condition; a thrilling warmth spread into my lower regions, making me shudder with desire, generating involuntary squeaks and moans in my throat as I pressed harder into him.

But amid my wild abandon another urgency nagged for attention. If I gave myself to him I should at least warn him of possible consequences. I pulled my face back from his and looked him in the eye. A slight frown grew on his brow. I kissed him again for reassurance.

"Mateo," I said, my voice thick and husky, "whatever happens to me, you're not to worry, okay?"

He gave me a puzzled look. I kissed him again and lowered my hand to his inner thigh, ran my fingers up his jeans and found the bulge, drawing a loud groan from deep within him.

"Whatever happens to me, it's only temporary, remember that."

I found his lips again, kissing him deeply, passionately. His hands went around my waist and lifted me, so I wrapped my thighs and arms around him, our kissing unabated as he walked us through the house and into his bedroom.

He sat me on the bed and stood back. The light of lust still shone in those gorgeous eyes, but concern was there also.

"I no understand, Rosie, what does this mean, if something happens to you?"

I gazed up at him. Such a lovely man. Only fair to prepare him.

"I might... I might, just might, you know, go all floppy during sex, maybe fall asleep. I might not be able to move for a while – if my eyes are open you can talk to me and I'll hear. I'll answer your questions by blinking, once for yes, two for no."

Now he looked worried. With a reassuring smile I reached over and grabbed the belt of his jeans, pulled him towards me. He was still massively erect, and I gasped when it throbbed under my open palm.

"I want you, Mateo," I breathed, "I want you now."

In answer, his hands came down to my damp hair and I rotated my head in ecstasy as his long fingers curled around my ears and caressed my neck.

Slowly I unbuckled his belt, slid the zipper down over the bulge, letting his jeans drop, then eased the elastic of his silky grey underpants over his pulsating cock and slid them down his hairy, muscular legs to his ankles.

He groaned when I curled my fingers around his large penis; feeling it's metronomic throb in my hand drove my hunger, and I knew he couldn't hold back much longer. I kissed its purple dome and looked up into his eyes.

He smiled down through a glaze of lust, reached down and pulled my t-shirt over my head, so I had to let go of his ready manhood. While he stepped out of his jeans and removed his shirt, I half stood and whipped down my shorts and panties then hitched myself back onto the bed, watching his dark, muscular torso revealed. He had a great body.

Moments later we were in the throes of a passionate kiss, tongues searching, his hairy chest grazing my nipples erect, his hands stroking my neck, teasing my ears with his fingers, while my own fingers played over his broad chest, his well-developed shoulders, down the muscles of his back, down his firm stomach, and curling around his pounding member.

His control was impressive, but I could wait no longer. I curled a leg around his thigh and pulled him over onto me. Resting on his elbows he smiled down into my eyes, filling me with love and desire; nothing else mattered than to have this man inside me, to be soundly fucked, all thoughts of what might happen blown away on a wind of overwhelming lust.

We reached our orgasms together, a surging flood that drew cries from us both and rippled through our conjoined bodies again and again.

Then.

A bright purple flash, a blinding roar. Pure pleasure shudders through me as never before; Mateo's face morphs into waxy, abstract shapes as it draws up over me, and I float away on a sea of sublime contentment.

"You are awake?"

Mateo's face came into focus above me, a lustful expression. I felt his gentle hand caressing one of my breasts.

I blinked.

"Are you okay, Rosie?"

His hand glided across to my other breast, his palm light over the hard nipple.

I blinked.

"Is okay to touch you?"

His hand now cupping my cheek, his fingers touching my ears, softly stroking.

I blinked.

"And..." his hand moved onto my belly, then slid slowly downwards, "down here?"

I blinked. I wouldn't have moved now, even if I could. This was *so* erotic.

"You like I touch you, Rosie," almost a whisper, his eyes half closed.

I blinked.

His face descended, kissed my slack lips. I felt my right thigh lifted, bending at the knee, lowered gently outwards, slowly with great care for my comfort, the sole of my foot resting on my left calf. His hand stroked upwards from my foot to my thigh, then came to rest on my pubic mound, soft fingertips brushing my exposed lily.

"And here?"

I blinked.

His fingers entered me, first two, moving slowly up then out, then three long fingers, in, in, deeper, curling in to touch that incredible spot behind my pelvis, the spot other fingers never reach. My eyes closed, my mind trembled in delight, though my body couldn't. My abdomen convulsed as heat flooded my vaginal cavity, a liquid gush around those wonderful fingers.

Lights flash behind my closed eyelids, then I'm falling, falling...

Conscious. I opened my eyes. Mateo, smiling down at me. "Good?"

I blinked.

When I recovered we showered together, soaping one another down, playful, laughing, careful not to arouse one another again. Afterwards Mateo resumed cooking while I fixed us gin and tonics, then took mine out on the patio to watch the sunset.

And think about what just happened. Weird. Passive sex, who knew? I was getting aroused again just thinking about it.

Over dinner Mateo asked me about the sleep paralysis thing.

"It's called Hypnagogic Hallucinatory Narcolepsy," I told him, "HHN for short."

He looked surprised.

"You Hallucinate?"

"Oh yeah, like you wouldn't believe," I twirled a finger by my temple, "all sorts of weird stuff going on up here. The black rice is lovely, by the way."

"Thank you. Doesn't it frighten you, when it happens?"

"A bit, sometimes. I'm getting used to it I suppose. And sometimes it's quite nice, you know, like an amazing dream you don't want to wake up from."

"And this happens only with sex?"

I laughed and shook my head. "I wasn't sure it would until today. It only started happening to me a few months ago. No, it's whenever I get overemotional about something that happens. I try to keep cool about stuff, and that sometimes works, sometimes not."

I reached over and stroked his face, grinning, "You can make me lose my head anytime you like."

"You like it, when you cannot move?"

"Mateo, it's the best orgasm ever. Well, you know, not…"

"I like it too, with you helpless. It is very, how you say?"

"Erotic?"

"Si, erotica, is same in Spanish."

I nodded down at his empty plate. "You finished."

"Yes, I finished. You want…"

"Good. Let's go to bed."

36

The next morning Mateo asked me if I wanted to stay at the house for a few days. He would be at work during the day but there was selection of DVD movies, some in English, and would you believe it, a swimming pool at the back of the house, shared with a neighbour who also worked during the day.

I said yes, but not today. Would he drop me at the marina to get some things, then he could pick me up after work.

As much as I loved *Pasha*, the opportunity to live in comfort for a few days was not one to be missed. And there was Mateo; my god, I was getting addicted to submissive sex – I could see now what the turn-on was with bondage. But first I wanted my deodorant and makeup bag, my battery toothbrush, swimsuit and a few changes of clothes. Oh, and my Kindle; laddish DVD's weren't my thing.

When I got back onboard I changed into running gear and went for a long jog up the eastern seafront to clear my head and punish my body. It was another hot day and I came back with my shirt and shorts clinging wet, tingling and revitalised.

After my shower I took my laptop up to the bar and wrote a long email to Doc, telling her about meeting up with Mateo again, what he was like, the horse riding, and described his house. I knew she'd be impressed, and maybe just a smidgen envious, but in a good way. Of course, I didn't go into detail about the intimate stuff, that would just freak her out, but I left her in no doubt that I'd shared his bed and would be spending the next few nights with him.

There was also a reply from Julie at the hospital, sent yesterday afternoon.

> Hi Rosie,
> Thanks for your email.
> I'm delighted to say I've got some positive news about your Dad. While I was reading your message to him this morning his blood pressure rose slightly, as did his heart rate. This has never happened before, and is a good indication he is fully aware, and his brain is undamaged, which is also born out by his latest scan.
> Mr Murchison says we're still a long way from any kind of moto-neural recovery, but the signs are good for an eventual positive outcome.
> On a lighter note, he also seems to like quiz shows on the television, or maybe he hates them. No way of knowing for certain but he certainly responds to them more than other programmes.
> Anyway, the staff here all send their greetings and best wishes for your voyage.
> Stay safe
> Best regards
> Julie Myers
> Senior Staff Nurse

Mateo came by at six and we stopped at a nearby beach bar for a drink before driving up to his house on the hill. I shared my good news about Dad, and he said he couldn't wait to get me into bed. We gulped down our drinks and made haste to the car. He drove home like a man possessed.

"Mateo," I said, feeling deliciously reckless as I unbuttoned his shirt, "I want you to know, when I'm paralysed you can do anything you want with me, anything. I won't mind. Whatever takes your fancy."

I spent the next three days sitting quietly by the pool reading, and the next three night in a haze of sex, mad hallucinations, and being sexually manhandled and shagged to a quivering orgasm while incapacitated.

I finally came to my senses when Mateo took things a little too far and scared me.

He began by straddling me and stroking my breasts then slid his hands up to my face, putting his fingers in my mouth and playing with my ears, which I loved. Then his hands were around my throat, gently at first, as he done a few times before and I'd enjoyed the vulnerability of it, the potential danger, but then a strange look came into his eyes and he began to squeeze, increasing the pressure little by little as if experimenting with how far he could go. My choke reflex couldn't work in paralysis, and I felt my breathing starting to labour. Fear gripped me, and I blinked rapidly to let him know of my distress. Even then, it was a terrifying moment more before he released his grip.

"I am sorry, Rosie," he whispered, then climbed off me and out of my vision. I heard him leave the room, closing the door behind him. A few minutes later I recovered and began to gather my things together. With my bag packed I went in search of Mateo and found him out on the patio, just sitting, staring out across the bay.

"Take me back to the marina, please," I said coldly.

We drove back in tortured silence.

Mateo phoned me the following morning, apologising for his behaviour, but offering no explanation.

"When I said you can do anything, it obviously didn't include killing me. What were you thinking?"

"I just… I don't know what happened, but I promise it will not happen again."

"Damn right it w…"

"I love you, Rosie, come back to my house, we talk about it, not make love, okay?"

I hesitated, almost caved, but then remembered the fear I'd felt, how close I'd come to being strangled.

"I can't, Mateo, not now. I've got some important jobs to do here on the boat. But listen, I'll call you at the weekend, we can talk then, give us both time to cool off a bit, eh?"

A long pause.

"Okay, Rosie, you call on Saturday, I wait."

I ended the call.

There was no way I was seeing that latent necrophile again. Fun while it lasted, but now it was over. I planned to sail early on Saturday morning, the day after tomorrow. Destination: Lanzarote.

37

Feeling better at last. Inexplicably I lost my sea legs during that week in La Linea (probably because of that boozy night out on Friday with Kate and Bill) and had spent most of the last two days huddled up wishing I were under a tree. Huh, seasickness, the worst feeling in the world. Didn't throw up though.

Saturday was the worst, not weather-wise, that had stayed fairly consistent till this morning, but the amount of shipping in the Gib Strait and Separation Zone meant I had to keep lookout when all I wanted to do was curl up down below and die. And on Sunday when I was over a hundred miles from land and hadn't seen a ship for hours, I did exactly that, coming up just once an hour for a quick recce.

Now I was up and about feeling fresh and revived. To celebrate my recovery and build up my lost calories I cooked myself a fried breakfast: egg, sausage, bacon, fried bread, and good old baked beans. Dad-style; all in the same pan to save washing up.

After breakfast I stripped naked and settled down in the cockpit to read. A gorgeous morning; azure sky with a scattering of fluffy cumulous scudding towards Africa on the warm north-westerly breeze, the sun rising over the lee quarter, giving the cockpit maximum shade from the bimini, and a slight sea that *Pasha* shouldered with barely a shudder.

Around noon I got a visitation by a big pod of dolphins. Just one or two at first, leaping up beside the cockpit to get a good look at me, then streaking along underfoot and playing in the bow wave. And suddenly there were dozens of them, their clicks and squeaks clearly audible above the sea and boat sounds, surfing down the short waves in formations of three or more, leaping joyously alongside and generally having a load of fun. I hitched up onto the counter and called to them, mad nonsense, really.

"Hey, how's the water?"

"Want me to join you down there? Sorry, no can do…"

…

But why not?

The sea was calm enough. Something on everyone's bucket list. Would they hang around if I stopped the boat? Only one way to find out. When you're alone on the ocean spontaneous insanity is common. The anticipation of doing something so outrageously beautiful and dangerous thrilled and almost overwhelmed me.

I took the wheel in hand, and turned upwind, sheeting in the main as I went, and watching to make sure the dolphins stayed with us. They did, so I continued through and when the headsail backed, reversed the rudder. *Pasha* hove to gracefully, as always.

Without another thought I climbed onto the counter and dived over the stern rail.

I gasped as I broke surface, the water colder than I'd expected, but my body quickly adjusted. I looked around for my new friends.

Then, a nudge in my back. I turned around, and there, not an arms-length away, a grinning head upright in the water. I reached out to touch it, and it was gone. Something brushed my legs, and another one, or perhaps the same one, surfaced next to me, moved its shiny flank close in to my shoulder.

I reached up, stroked my hand along its sleek back, its head rose and gave a squeak, rows of tiny teeth lined its grinning mouth. Another brushed by, going quite fast so I spun round in its wake.

Another nudged up to me, its narrow snout digging softly into my naked breast. I moved around to the side of the beast and laid a hand just behind the blowhole, then ran it slowly back towards to the dorsal fin. The animal hung as calm and still in the water as Abril had done when I'd mounted her. I took hold of the dorsal fin, and suddenly we were off, not too quickly, but I had to hold on with both hands. In the thrill of that moment I got only a fleeting idea of the danger I was now in; dragged through the water by a wild animal far out in the open ocean, alone and out of physical contact with my boat. I felt just in the moment, oh the joyful abandon of it.

A ripple of muscles down the dolphin's flank, its head rose, then began to dip, I managed a deep breath, and then we were under, going down still. All around us dolphins streaked to and fro, some at tremendous speeds, leaving a matrix of turbulence trails hanging in the clear water.

And the *noise*. Down here it was awesome, a cacophony of clicks and pips, squeaks and squeals, an all-consuming crescendo that penetrated beyond mere hearing.

But we were still descending; my lungs were starting to deflate under the pressure – I would soon lose buoyancy. I prepared to let go and claw my way back to the surface, but just then, as if aware of my limitations, the animal's back arched and we headed upwards once more. We burst from the water with such force that I lost my grip, falling backwards with an ungainly splash. When I surfaced again, I found myself within a few yards of Pasha's stern. My water taxi had dropped me off at the perfect spot.

My ride rose up in front of me, an open-mouthed grin, eyes sapient and friendly, making that odd squeaking noise, almost like laughter. Perhaps it was.

"Thank you," I called, "thank you, my friend."

Then suddenly, as if by signal, they all turned away, and were gone, leaving me feeling strangely empty.

Come back soon, guys, we'll do it again.

I came-to lying sideways on the banquette, my left knee aching where it swung at an awkward angle to the movement of the boat as she cut through the shallow waves. As I waited for movement to return, I reflected that I wasn't disappointed my incredible dolphin swim was mere hallucination, it had seemed real enough for a fond and lasting memory.

38

Wednesday 27th March
1243: 32 01N 11 34W Co 180 Sp 9
Trip Log: 401 miles
Wind WSW 28kts+ Sea 4m with heavy westerly swell.
Main fully reefed, 1/3 genoa

I laughed, mainly to stop myself from crying, though I suppose there was a funny side to my beef stew dinner slopping around the galley sole boards. The saucepan had been held 'securely' on the gas hob by roll-clamps.

Not secure enough, evidently. Not when a freak wave smashes into your weather side like a demolition ball, not when the gimbles on the cooker reach their limits and the boat keeps on going over.

So I laughed, laughed hysterically, for goodness knows how long, and then pulled myself together. Then I staggered aft through the saloon, holding grimly on each time a wave hit us, and made it to the head. Here I dragged out a bucket, a dustpan, and a large deck cloth. I half filled the bucket with seawater and staggered back to the galley clutching all three... and promptly skidded in the stew. I fell on my bum with a painful squelch, feeling the hot stew soaking into my shorts. Miraculously the bucket remained upright, but then slid down the deck to leeward, lubricated on its merry way by the stew, and collided heavily with the base of the cooker, and lost most of its contents in a cascade of seawater to dilute the avalanche of gravy, meat and vegetables.

"Oh dear."

"Oh, Fuck off."

I hung my head between my knees and despaired. But not for long. The stink of the congealed stew and the motion of the vessel was beginning to nauseate me. I grabbed the dustpan and started to scrape up the mess and shovel it into the bucket.

It was too rough to risk trying to empty the sloppy gunge over the side, so I flushed it all away down the sea toilet. Of course, I could just as easily have stepped up the companionway ladder and emptied it into the cockpit where it would be flushed away in seconds by the almost continuous wash-over.

When it was all cleaned up I staggered aft and fell back onto the lee banquette, utterly spent. In weather like this the simplest task became exhausting and fraught with difficulty.

I had a decision to make, and after a while heaved myself up from the banquette. First, I checked the wind. A little south of east at 28 kts, gusting 33. I checked the chart plotter. We were well to the east of track, nearer to Morocco than Lanzarote. I had two options, and our current course wasn't one of them; I could heave to and wait for the gale to abate, or, the more prudent, run downwind and take refuge in Agadir, where I could wait at leisure for better wind.

A no brainer.

I donned lifejacket and harness and went up to adjust the sails and windvane for a downwind run.

"We're going to Agadir. No arguments, okay?"

"You're the boss."

Eighteen hours later we entered the port and were directed to a finger-pontoon in the spacious and sparsely populated marina. Despite the blustering wind at my back it was already baking hot under the fierce, southern Moroccan sun and I'd stripped down to shorts and t-shirt during our approach.

Once tied up I grabbed the wallet containing my passport and boat documents, donned my floppy sun hat and shades, and made my way quickly along the pontoon and up the gangway to the quay, towards the lighthouse at the end where the Pilot Guide book said the marina reception, customs and immigration were co-located.

A few people were already out and about, browsing the high-fashion shops and taking morning coffee. I began to get hostile stares from head-scarfed women, some pointing and whispering to one another. I hurried along, wondering if I'd grown a second head or something, when a young woman who was plainly not Moroccan crossed from a cafe and intercepted me.

"Excuse me," she said politely, her accent Germanic, "are you checking in?"

She was about my age, slim and pretty, and wore a white cotton shirt with sleeves and blue calf-length pedal-pushers with flip-flops, blonde hair tucked into a white baseball cap.

"Yes, why?"

"I do not mean to be rude, but if you go in there dressed as you are, they may refuse to process you. You must cover your arms and legs. Do you have something more suitable?"

I shook my head, "Only some winter clothes. What's wrong with this, it's not indecent or anything."

She laughed. "This is a Muslim country, and here in Agadir they are quite conservative. Come with me, I have something onboard I can lend you."

I followed her back down onto the pontoons, bemused and mildly shocked by this novel development. Of course, I knew about niqabs, bourkas and headscarves worn by some Muslim women. You saw them everywhere. And though I was aware their culture had a thing about showing naked flesh, in all my travels in the navy I'd never had to conform to another country's dress code. But then, when I thought about it, I'd never visited a Muslim country. We live and learn.

Helga was another single-hander. Her boat, a 40-foot aluminium sloop, I thought rather ugly-looking compared to *Pasha's* more traditional lines, but she was roomy and comfortable below.

I sat in the saloon while she went to find me some clothes.

"Where did you sail from?" she called from the quarter-berth.

"La Linea, in Spain. You?"

"Funchal, Madeira was my last port, and before that, Horta, in Azores."

She came back into the saloon carrying a pair of lightweight boat-trousers in one hand, and a shirt like the one she was wearing in the other.

"These will suit you, I think, try them on."

When I was dressed she gave me the critical once over and declared me fit to be seen in public.

"Be sure to keep your hat on when you are out," she added, eyeing my shoulder-length hair, "and tuck your hair up inside."

"Thanks," I said, "I'll bring your clothes back when I've bought some stuff."

She waved a dismissive hand. "Ach, there is no rush, I am here for another week," she hesitated a moment, studying my face, then smiled brightly. "If you like, I will show you where to shop. Come to me this afternoon and we can go in the town."

I resumed my mission to check in, thinking about my new friend. How nice, to help a stranger like that. I was finding a new world in the boating community, where mutual support and easy friendship seemed a given, and made a vow to myself to watch out for opportunities to reciprocate.

39

Running along the wet pontoon barefoot, flipflops in hand, as the rain belted down in great billowing swathes on the wind, slicking wet clothes onto our skins, and ripping at my floppy hat so I had to stuff it into my bag of newly-bought clothes. We reached Helga's boat laughing like drains and helped each other aboard, clambered below and dashed around closing hatches.

Helga spread a big towel on the banquette and we both slumped down, still giggling, and then she turned to me, a sudden look of concern.

"Are your hatches closed?"

I thought a moment, then relaxed. "I didn't open them," I said, "and my washboards are up."

She sighed heavily. "Ah, that is good."

I watched her take off her baseball cap and shake out her long blonde hair, which was still mostly dry, unlike mine which was plastered to my scalp and neck.

The furious squall had hit just as we'd reached the marina gates, sending hundreds of shoppers and holidaymakers scurrying every which way for cover while Helga and I dodged and weaved between them to reach the gangway down to the boats.

"Don't you find long hair a nuisance on a boat?" I said.

"It is difficult," she said, fisting hers into a ponytail and flipping it into a scrunchy from her wrist, "but it does not suit me short, so I suffer."

She looked at me and touched my wet locks, "But your hair is quite long, and now it is slicked down so, I see it would suit you better short."

"Mm," I nodded, "You're probably right, but can you find a hairdresser when you want one?"

She got up and went to the head, came back with another towel which she handed me.

"I am hairdresser," she suddenly announced, a gleam in her eye.

I towelled my head in silence as the rain thundered down unabated on the coach-roof. Was she offering to cut my hair? Did I want her to? Finally, I folded up the towel and put it in my soggy lap.

"At least your sole boards got a good wash," I said, running my toes through a puddle by my feet, one of many pooling the deck, "where do you keep your cleaning gear? I'll help you mop up."

"This is very unusual," Helga said, standing up, taking the folded towel and shuffling past me, "it absolutely never rains here. All their water is desalinated from the sea."

"My fault," I said, "it must have followed me."

She laughed, "Oh, so it is English rain, that explains it."

With the awkward moment behind us we set to mopping the deck. Afterwards I took my new clothes into the head to change out of Helga's damp ones. I stared goggle-eyed at her spacious bathroom; walk-in shower, full-length mirror and double sink unit, and still room enough to move around easily. *Pasha's* was a shoebox in comparison. And a shower? In my dreams.

I'd bought a long-sleeved cotton smock, white with a colourful arabesque design embroidered on the front, and pink cotton trousers, loose hanging and comfortable. I dropped my damp panties and bra into the bag and hung her stuff on a rail over the sink unit to dry.

Checking myself in the mirror, I paused, picking at my hair, now all frazzled from the rubbing I'd given it. Maybe Helga had a point. I'd always worn it short in the navy, and now realised I'd only let it grow because I could.

Returning to the saloon I found Helga had also changed. It had stopped raining and she'd re-opened the hatches, letting a breeze waft through the boat.

Helga, wearing a short black kaftan, sat cross-legged on the banquette rolling a cigarette from a cellophane bag stuffed with olive-coloured fibres.

"I made coffee," she said, nodding to a steaming cafetiere and two mugs on the table, "help yourself."

"Thanks, just what I need." I pressed down the plunger and began filling the mugs, surprised at this unexpected revelation.

"I hope you don't mind," she said, looking up from her makings and smiling, "it is time for my daily fix."

"It's your boat," I said, "not my place to judge you."

"That is good, but I ask if you don't mind me smoking marijuana in your company – I don't want you to leave because it offends you."

I snorted a laugh. "I've smoked weed before, it doesn't offend me. Fill your boots. I might even have a toke or two if there's no tobacco in it."

She nodded wisely, licked the paper, and rolled it up with a practiced flourish. "I would never touch tobacco, such an addictive substance."

I blew down my nose and gave her a wry grin. "Tell me about it."

She reached over for her lighter.

"Er, Helga, before you light up, I want you to cut my hair short."

She dropped the spliff and lighter on the table and gave me an impish grin.

"Take off your clothes," she said, untucking her legs and jumping up, "I will get my clippers and comb."

She set up her improvised salon in the bathroom; a folding chair facing the mirror, a plastic sheet covering the deck, and me sitting with a proper hairdressing cape velcroed around my neck. All very professional. Except I was naked under the cape, which felt kind of odd.

"It is too damp for the clippers," she said, raking my hair with her fingers, "I will need to dry it first."

She switched on a blow dryer and began training it back and forth while teasing out tresses with her fingers. The heat in the bathroom quickly became uncomfortable, and as sweat trickled under the cape I was thankful my new clothes wouldn't be so soon in need of washing.

When the drying was finished Helga plugged in a portable fan to cool things down, then picked up the electric clippers.

"Number three, I think, okay?"

"Perfect," I said.

"Now, Rosie," she said, poised with the machine like an executioner, "last chance to change your mind."

I laughed. "Go for it, girl."

She worked with expert efficiency, great clumps of hair falling in my lap and around me, her fingers gently roving along the furry furrows where the clippers had been. Every so often she would stop and stroke the new stubble against the grain with her palm, which was incredibly cathartic, erotic, almost.

When our eyes met in the mirror her smile suggested she sensed my pleasure, and when she began working around my ears I could have sworn she knew how sensitive they were to touch for she continually brushed them with her fingers.

Pull yourself together, Rosie!

I couldn't believe I was fantasising over the ministrations of another woman, one my own age who was probably straight as a die and behaving quite innocently.

When she was satisfied by the evenness of the cut, she removed the attachment and shaved off the hanging hairs at the back of my neck, then swept around my face and neck with a soft brush.

"There, all finished."

Her fingers swept gently across my newly mown scalp, then her hands landed either side of my head, open fingers straddling my ears. I watched her in the mirror. She removed her hands.

"What do you think?"

"Amazing, Helga. Thank you."

And I didn't just mean for the haircut - it was only a crewcut after all - it was the sensuality of the process that was amazing. But I wasn't going to tell her that. God, how embarrassing that would be?

Smiling broadly, she unfastened the cape from my throat and gently shook it loose, spilling the remaining tresses onto the deck covering.

"Now, into the shower with you," she said, "I will clean up here."

I came into a saloon pungent with the haze of marijuana. Helga sat in the same place as before, again cross-legged, smoking dreamily on her spliff. Two glasses and a wine bottle on the table in front of her. She was unclothed and clearly unselfconscious about it.

I sank down on the opposite banquette, not knowing where to look, feeling a little out of my depth. I had a towel wrapped around me, and wanted the security of my clothes, but they were on the banquette beside her.

"The nightlife in this town is a little difficult for unattached women," she said, "I thought you might like to join me in a glass of wine."

She handed the spliff across the table, "Here, take some of this."

I eased it from her fingers and took a shallow drag while she filled our glasses with wine. Red, I was pleased to note. Okay, she's a hippie throwback from the sixties, that's cool, just go with it.

I took a drag deep into my lungs, gasped at the searing cut of the smoke, and suppressed an almost overwhelming urge to cough. With watering eyes, I handed it back to her and took a slurp of wine.

She chuckled, "I think you have not smoked in a long time, Rosie."

"No," I said hoarsely, "not since Uni..." I inhaled noisily, "seven years ago."

"Well catch your breath and then try again, but not so deep this time." She patted the seat beside her, "Here, come sit by me."

She saw my hesitation.

"My nakedness makes you uncomfortable?"

"No, well, yes, I suppose it does."

"But I have seen you naked. Why are you embarrassed to see me so?"

"Well, because you're just sitting there... I mean..." I giggled, "Oh hell, I don't know what I mean."

I stood and walked around the table, threw my clothes over to where I'd been sitting, and sat next to her.

"Sorry." I said.

I took the spliff from her and toked, not so deep this time, kept it down, then breathed out slowly, letting the heady smoke drift around my nose and mouth.

"You would feel less self-conscious," she said softly, reaching across me and untucking the towel from my chest, "if you were naked as well."

Heat rushed into my face. Hardly aware of what I was doing I eased up my bottom to let her pull the towel away.

"There, that is better," she murmured, "you have a beautiful body, such a shame to hide it."

Was she trying to seduce me? How I would I react if she tried it on? I took another suck on the weed and told myself to relax. She's not gay, just liberated. I passed her the joint and looked at her properly for the first time.

Like me she had small, tight breasts with well-formed nipples. Her straight-backed posture showed off her stomach muscle-tone to perfection. Shapely hips without a hint of cellulite curved down to fine thighs, attractive legs lying comfortably across one another, and feet so cute and perfect they could never have seen a high heel. With her flowing blonde hair and even, all-over tan, she could have been a goddess.

I suddenly realised she'd been watching me measuring her up, an open-mouthed smile and an expectant gleam in her dark emerald eyes.

I gave her a wide lazy smile. "You've got a better one," I slurred. I was feeling most peculiar, and slightly dizzy. I reached over and picked up my glass, brought it up to my lips and put it down again. I turned to find Helga looking at me strangely. I realised her hand was stroking the nape of my neck.

"Are you okay, Rosie?" concern in her voice.

"Have you got some water?" I croaked.

"Of course."

In a moment she was back with a glass of water. I gulped it down, then took a deep breath. I felt sick.

"I think I need to lie down for a while," I murmured, "if that's okay."

Without waiting for a reply, I swivelled my bum on the seat and threw my legs up along the length of the banquette. As I slumped back she eased my head down into her lap.

Into her lap!

But I was too stoned to care.

Her fingers caressing my brow, cooing softly.

"It is fine, Rosie, it is okay. Rest now, you will feel better soon."

Her breasts, inches from my face, shimmered golden, above them her beautiful face gazed down, smiling kindly. I reached up to touch it, grazed a perfect nipple, dropped my hand again.

Too stoned to care.

She picked up my hand, placed it back over her breast. "You want to touch me," she murmured, "it's okay."

"I cupped her small breast, felt her nipple come erect, tickling my palm."

I giggled.

"Feels nice," I said, "I think I love you."

I giggled again, stroking her breasts, first one, then the other.

Too stoned to care.

Her fingers slid down over my ears.

"You like your ears caressed," she whispered, "I knew it, earlier when I cut your hair."

Her fingers slipped over my ear, tracing its curves, slipping into the cavity and out again, around and around, so gentle, so sensual. I wanted it never to stop. I was in heaven.

Her other hand settled onto my right breast, gently tweaked the nipple as she gazed down into my eyes.

"I know you are not gay, Rosie," she whispered, "but sometimes it can be nice with a woman as well."

"So I'm finding out," I said, smiling back up at her. I was coming out of my stupor, but my libido was running wild and undiminished.

For a girl.

That was an enigma I wasn't yet ready to analyse.

"Are you gay, Helga?"

She nodded, smiling.

"Do you think we could, you know… I'd like to, kind of try it, with you, now?"

Her smile widened, and smoky love came into her eyes. Her hand travelled down my belly, bringing with it a flood of hot anticipation that spread deliciously into my loins.

"Helga, there something you need to know."

"What?" she whispered huskily, as her hand crept between my thighs,

"Oh, nothing…"

40

I spent that whole night with Helga. We smoked more weed, drank more wine, and made love often.

By morning the wind had eased and shifted into the southeast, bringing with it a haze of Saharan sand that covered the boats in the marina in a fine layer of ochre dust.

Helga made us breakfast, and then we said our goodbyes; she had to stay and suffer the dust while waiting for delivery of a part for her engine. Then she would be heading for the Med.

I wasn't prepared to let *Pasha* get any filthier that she had to, and the online forecast was perfect for a fast crossing to Lanzarote.

By ten-o-clock I was motoring past Helga's boat. We waved madly at each other.

"Bon Voyage, and fair winds," she called.

"And to you," I replied, "hope your part comes soon."

She grinned and waved again.

So, was I now bi? It was good with Helga, but I was not inclined to do it again with a woman. But who knew?

What was more interesting was that I had not once succumbed to my HHN. I could only guess it was the weed, and that was a compelling theory I would need to work on.

At 0930 on Sunday 31st March, *Pasha* and I entered the marina at Arrecife, a fast passage of two days. No trauma, no incidents, just enjoyable, exhilarating sailing. And to cap our success I got a cheap deal on a six-month pre-paid booking with water and electricity included.

When my phone connected to the local network, I had fourteen missed calls from Mateo. And one text message, saying simply.

"You bitch!"

I deleted it and put a block on his number. That guy was out of my life. I had other fish to fry.

The marina served WIFI to the pontoons, so I wasted no time in logging in and catching up on my emails. The first was from Doc.

Hi Sweetie,

Great news about your meeting up with your Spanish beau, and glad to hear he lived up to expectations. Looks like you've fallen on your feet after all that crap you went through, though as far as the stores thing is concerned... well you know how I feel about that.

Had any more of those funny turns? I do hope you get over that, it must be so traumatising. The way you described it, it sounds like a recurring LSD trip, you know, like that guy in Pink Floyd? Drove him nuts in the end. Don't want to worry you or anything.

So, right now we're in Kingstown, St Vincent for a whole week, and tomorrow I'm booked on a trip to see an active volcano, how cool is that? Well, no, not cool exactly, but hey, you know what I mean.

I take it you're still determined to cross the big pond to visit this mysterious aunt? (Still don't get why you don't just fly over.) Shame I never got chance to meet her, she sounds a lovely woman.

More news soon, stay safe on that boat and give that hunk of yours a big wet shnozzer on the mouth from me.

Much love
Doc. Xx

I took a deep breath, then rattled off a reply.

Hi Doc,

My Beau, as you call him, is history. I won't go into detail but there's a dark side to him that scared me.

Think I might be getting over the sleep disorder thing, haven't had an episode for quite some time now. And what was that comparison with Syd Barrett about? You know I don't do drugs. Silly bint!

Yeah, the transat's still on for end of the year. I know you don't get it. But then you can't unless you've got the bug for sailing. Bit crazy I know, but if you met some of the people I met, even you might see what this cruising life is about.

Now parked up in Lanzarote and going to stay here for six months. So if you want to come out and join me during your summer leave, you are of course welcome – the accommodation's a little cramped, but free. And if you want I'll take you out for a day sail, though I can guess your response to that suggestion lol.

Anyway, I'm on line for the duration now, so email anytime. We can even Skype if you fancy a tete a tete.

Love Rosie x

PS. Ever experimented with girly sex? ☐

I wasn't sure about the mischievous PS, how she'd interpret it, I mean. Anyway, I hit send and damn the consequences.

Next, I emailed Aunt Georgie and made up a story about being in Cartagena; only because I went there once and remembered enough to make it plausible.

And finally, Julie at the hospital, with a few more lines for Dad.

The remainder of my day was dedicated to *Pasha*; first hosing down the mast, rigging and sails, and then scrubbing and washing down the weatherdeck to remove the Saharan muck I'd accumulated in Agadir and on passage across. While the wind was in the east that corrosive and cloying red dust would continue to plague our boats, even this far out, so I was thankful not to be on metered water.

While I worked I planned in my head what exactly I was going to do during six months on a small volcanic island. The next day it soon became apparent I would need to spend some of that time improving my Spanish. Arrecife was not a holiday town, and apart from the waiters and staff in the marina and waterfront bars and restaurants, few of the locals spoke English, as I found out when I went to buy a bicycle. I got there in the end, but only with the help of a friendly expat Irishman who happened to be browsing in the shop.

By the end of that first week I'd downloaded a Spanish Course and joined a language club that met every Tuesday in one of the town's bars, where you paired up with a Spaniard who wanted to improve their English. I was pleased to learn that most of the English-speakers were fellow yachties; an opportunity to gather up some friends.

And I got myself moulded into the saddle of my new bike, a hybrid roadster with 18 gears and quick-release wheels. So now I could tour the island at leisure and stow the bike in the forepeak when I sailed to explore other islands. Rosie was getting her act together.

And then, suddenly, she wasn't.

It happened, right out of the blue, one bright, sunny afternoon when I was walking back from the supermarket with my weekly provisions. A motorbike came roaring out of a side alley and into the road that ran parallel to the cobbled quay where I was walking. There was nothing unusual about that, motorbikes were popular with the young men of the town and they just *loved* to show off.

I watched the rider accelerate past me, and gasped as he skidded sideways and lost control.

It is night time, overhead streetlights casting orange light onto a dual carriageway, a bike screeching along the road, a slim female body impaled upon its frame as it barrels over and over in a shower of sparks and cigarette cartons, a severed foot, still wearing a beaded sandal, landing amongst the debris. My knees give way as flashing blue lights and helmeted policemen arrive on the scene.

...

Lots of voices, urgent, shrill. Spanish gabble.

I opened my eyes. My cheek lay pressed against a wall of hot grey cobblestones. A face appeared, inches away, a young man, dark stubble, eyes wide and sharp with alarm. It was only then I remembered I'd fallen.

"Señora, can you hear me?"

I blinked at him.

I was on my left side, right hand down flat on the hot stones, legs bent at the knees, one in front of the other. Coma position. Someone knew first aid. Except those cobbles were *really* hot, burning the side of my left leg and face.

The man moved out of view.

More Spanish chatter, too fast, indecipherable.

Please someone, get me off these fucking stones.

As if answering my silent plea, unseen hands rolled me carefully onto my back. The same man's face came into view, still wearing a worried frown, but smiling down at me.

"We are going to lift you now."

He moved back, and three men and a woman, all in green outfits, bent down over me, then...

"Listo? ...uno... dos... tres."

And I was airborne, moved sideways, and lowered onto what felt like a canvass stretcher. My face and leg felt numb and tingly from the heat of the cobbles.

My leg twitched even before they'd closed the ambulance doors, and seconds later my motor function returned.

"I'm okay," I said sitting up and swinging my legs over the side of the stretcher, "I'm fine now."

I looked at my watch, twenty minutes, tops. I forced a grin at the four paramedics looking at me with stunned expressions. "Thank you, really I'm fine now," I scissored my legs. "See? Good to go."

My bag of groceries was on the floor of the ambulance. I stood and picked it up.

"Señora," said the woman, "we should take you for check in hospital,"

"No, honestly, I'm okay now." I jumped down and turned back to them; they still looked shell-shocked. "*Gracias, mucho gracias*. Sorry to cause you so much trouble."

I looked over to where I'd seen the accident. The road was quiet, people going about their business, no sign of any recent kerfuffle. I'd hallucinated the whole thing.

Ignoring the bystanders looking on open-mouthed I turned and legged it quickly back towards the marina.

41

"Good evening, Rosie, how are you?"

"Buenas tardes, Enrico, er... esta muy bien, gracias. Y cómo estás?"

Enrico was my partner in the language club. He was around twenty, bright and not bad looking. This was my second session with the group and I was already becoming quite adept in the language, speaking it at least. The audio lessons were helpful, but you couldn't beat the real thing.

He said, "Your Spanish is coming along very well. Have you practiced him... it?"

His English was much better than my Spanish, but then he'd learned it as part of his school curriculum. He'd told me he was brushing up to get a job as a waiter in the resorts down south.

I thought a moment, and replied, *"Si, he practicada en el supermercado."*

"Very good," he smiled, "you remembered the gender conjunctive this time. You can also say '*sí, lo he practicada...*' this means I have practiced *it...* for better precision."

Our conversing continued thus for the next hour or so. Enrico was very patient and spoke his Spanish slowly enough for me to understand; it was obvious I was getting more out of the exchange than he was.

A delicate question had been forming in my mind, and finally building up courage and glancing around to make sure no-one from the nearby pairs were listening in, I said with lowered voice, *"Sabes dónde pueda comprar marihuana?"*

To my surprise, he didn't bat an eyelid. Just gave a chuckle and said, "Yes, of course. It is very easy to buy weed in most Spanish territories, including Lanzarote. But maybe not so easy for not Spanish people. Would you like me to get some for you?"

"Non-Spanish," I said.

"Que? Er... I'm sorry?"

"You said 'not Spanish'. It's non-Spanish."

He reddened. "Oh, yes, of course."

Incredible. He was far more embarrassed by his minor slip than by talking about supplying weed.

"And... " I lowered my voice again, *"Sí, por favor, podría conseguirme un poco?"*

He grinned and nodded. *"Luego. Ahora hablaremos nuestro propio idioma."*

I sighed and smiled my thanks. Job done. Though I wasn't sure what 'later' meant. This was Spain, after all.

We went on with the session in our own languages, learning to listen rather than speak, which for me was more challenging.

Enrico came through for me later that evening after a brief errand to a nearby corner shop. I walked back to my boat nervous of another episode and what would happen if my hundred grams of illicit herb was discovered during my incapacity. After so many attacks I was becoming inured to the episodes themselves. It was just *so* fucking embarrassing.

That night I tumbled into bed and dreamt narcotic dreams of bizarre encounters with people from my past interspersed with meaningless snatches of Spanish conversation.

At the top of the steep rise I dismounted and leaned my bike against the rocky escarpment that bounded one side of the road. On the other side a steel barrier undergrown thickly with aloe and cactus guarded a near-vertical drop overlooking an unattractive huddle of white, boxlike buildings, a sad legacy of the Island's pre-tourist past.

The barren slopes beyond levelled out, giving way to later human intervention; the coastal motorway and intersections a dividing river of cars glinting in the harsh morning sunshine, the airport runway and control tower encircled by a vast complex of industrial and commercial enterprise, and the candy-coloured holiday homes of Playa Honda, its ivory beaches leading around the sweep of the bay to the storied hotels and resorts of Los Pocillos and Bocaina.

And beyond, the windblown open ocean; the flecks of breaking waves and tiny white triangles of sailboats, barely discernible from up here, upon a vast tableau of startling blue stretching away to deepening violet at the hazed horizon.

In the cloudless sky, a pinpoint light at eye-level marked the approach of another planeload of early holidaymakers, and beyond that, another fainter landing light in the queue for the busy airport.

Still huffing from the exertion of the climb, I opened my backpack and dragged out a towel to wipe the sweat from my face and out of my eyes, then took a long swig of water.

It felt great to be out on a bike again after all these years - navy life had provided little opportunity for riding. The soreness now from the new saddle and lack of practice was more than compensated for by the exhilarating effort and the exquisite pain of returning muscle-tone.

Revived, I mounted up and continued pedalling up the steep, narrow road, occasional cars and small trucks passing or coming down, giving me a wide berth. After half an hour the road levelled and passed a small village of tidy houses and the inevitable cute, stone church, and then began to descend, opening a panorama of desolate volcanic debris leading down to the western shore and the hazy expanse of ocean beyond. I stopped pedalling and let the bike gain its own momentum as the downhill slope steepened.

Faster and faster I went, thrilling to the freedom of speed with no effort, leaning into the occasional bend in the road and sitting up on the straight sections to let the cool windrush blast my face and dry my clothes.

There was a scary moment when an oncoming car appeared from round a bend and I'd taken the corner a little too wide; the bike gave an uncertain wobble as I adjusted trajectory, and for a nanosecond I thought I'd lost it, but then the moment was past, and I blew out my cheeks in relief. A belated drawn-out hoot sounded behind me and I laughed, more in response to adrenalin rush than at the driver I'd just annoyed.

Ahead of me lay my destination, something called a Geopark with a mysterious cave, a feature I'd spotted on the map and been intrigued by. I began lightly breaking.

An hour later I was riding again, this time along the cycle path beside the wide straight highway leading south, through twenty drab kilometres of ejected magma, nothing to please the eye, nothing but twisted basalt and pumice ash, and down to the resort town of Playa Blanca.

I don't know exactly what I'd expected at the Geopark, but it certainly wasn't what I found. I guess I thought I'd be visiting a managed tourist attraction with colourfully lit caverns, stalactites and mites, and a tour guide to show people around.

What I found was a boulder-strewn, hollowed-out tube running beneath a deserted and desolate lava flow. The only concession to visitors, a faded sign that told me the cave was a over two kilometres long and had formed less than three-hundred years ago.

Not that I went very far inside; there was no lighting and I hadn't brought a torch. I found it all quite dreary and stayed only long enough to eat my sandwiches and a bar of chocky, sitting on the cave's roof and contemplating the ocean. And the prospect of six months on an island with little to offer but extinct volcanoes and countless acres of ash. There was not a soul in sight anywhere. Some attraction.

Ninety minutes after leaving that dreadful place I locked the bike onto a parking rack in Playa Blanca and walked along the crowded promenade, eying with dismay the noisy, wall-to-wall humanity that festooned the beach below me. Eventually, though, the crowds thinned, and then joy of joys, I found what I'd hardly dared hope for; a secluded and child-free beach, a handful of basking adults, some wearing nothing but shades and sunhats. I hurried down, dropped my bag on the sand, stripped down to my skin and ran into the sea.

Gasping at the first invigorating splashes on my overheated body, I plunged headlong into the water and struck out in an energetic crawl for a hundred metres or more, enjoying the primal thrill of swimming naked after the dust and heat of my ride through the lava fields.

I rolled over onto my back and just floated, heaving gently on the shallow swell and dreaming into the deep blue sky. I wondered lazily what would happen if I had one of my turns right now, probably drown. Oddly, the thought didn't scare me. Besides, I'd been taking my fix of weed every night, so it wouldn't happen. Would it?

I switched my thoughts to my aunt. She hadn't replied to any of my recent emails, and that worried me. I found I was missing her ribald company and dismayed at the thought of not seeing her for another eight months.

Pushing the maudlin mood aside, I turned and struck for the shore.

I took a different route back to Arrecife, joining the coastal highway, a flatter and more direct route of some thirty kilometres along a well-maintained cycle track. It took me a shade over two hours.

I'd been back onboard half an hour and was preparing tonight's dinner, cold chicken with salad, when a knock came on the hull.

42

Rosie was grating a carrot for her salad when she heard a knock on the hull, then a familiar voice called, "Hello, boat ahoy, *Pasha*, anyone aboard?"

She froze.

Surely not? she thought.

She stepped up the companionway ladder and poked her head out. And saw her Aunt Georgina standing there, wearing a stylish, summer dress and a broad-brimmed sun hat.

"Hello, Rosie, thought I'd surprise you."

Rosie's shocked expression faded, became a puzzled frown, then morphed into a delighted grin.

"Georgie!" she cried, stepping up into the cockpit, "What a wonderful surprise. Come aboard."

Georgina kicked off her sandals, stepped aboard, and they hugged in the cockpit. Rosie stood back and looked her aunt up and down. "You look fantastic," she said, "that dress really suits you."

"Thanks, Sweetie,

"I was just getting some dinner ready, you hungry?"

"Famished," said Georgina, following her niece down the companionway.

"Didn't have time to eat in Madrid," she said, sliding onto the banquette, "had to run and catch my connecting flight."

"But how did you know I was here?" Rosie asked, sitting down opposite.

Georgina grinned. "It was Anna who discovered your wicked subterfuge," she said, "Cartagena indeed, Phooey!"

Heat rose into Rosie's face. "But how…"

"Don't ask me how, something about server IP addresses an suchlike. She notices these things because she checks all our incoming mail. When she saw your message routed through a server in Lanzarote, she dug deeper and traced it right back to this marina. Clever huh?"

Rosie stared at her, dumbfounded. "Clever, yeah. Wow! I didn't know that was even possible."

"I told you she was a geek. Professional hacker back home in Finland, and now she looks after security for our US Corporates."

Rosie smiled, went over and gave her another hug, "It's good to see you, Georgina."

"Good to see you too, but why the silly lie, Honey?"

Rosie thought furiously, still determined to keep the plan secret. Her aunt would have kittens if she told her she was intending to cross the ocean.

"I… I didn't want to worry you, you know, about sailing out here in the Atlantic. If you thought I was cruising the Med…"

"…that I'd know my little niece was safely close to land. Okay, I get it. But…"

"Yeah, I know it was a stupid idea. Sorry."

Georgina gave her niece a long, searching look, then smiled. "Well, at least you got here in one piece. Say, any danger of a coffee round here?"

Rosie jumped up to boil the kettle. "So, when did you land?" she asked, "Did you fly direct? No, you said you changed at Madrid, sorry, I'm all in a tizz."

"Landed around eleven this morning. Been hanging around here most of the day waiting for you to show up."

A sudden thought struck Rosie. "I'll need to clear some stuff out of the v-berth for you, or better still, you can have my cabin and I'll bed down here in the saloon."

Georgina grinned, "Don't worry, dear, I'm too accustomed to my comforts these days to be sleeping on boats. I've already checked into that big hotel at the end of town."

Rosie spooned coffee into a mug and poured in boiling water from the kettle, secretly relieved. It would be pretty cramped with the two of them living onboard, and she didn't really want to give up her cabin, even if only for…"

"How long are you staying?"

"Oh, a few days. I got an open return."

Rosie added some milk from the fridge and put the coffee down in front of her aunt. There was a strange look in Georgina's eyes, staring up at her, silent, sorrowful, and something else…

"I'll just skip to the loo," Rosie said.

She closed the head door behind her and sat down on the toilet lid. Without warning her eyes filled and a great sob welled up within her and spluttered out in a stream of saliva. And the dam burst, her body convulsing uncontrollably as huge globs of snotty tears dripped off her chin in a tsunami of inexplicable grief.

Half an hour later Rosie came out of the bathroom and surveyed the saloon, looking mildly puzzled. After a moment she shrugged her shoulders and picked up her coffee from the saloon table, moved with it around to the galley area, placed it on the worktop. She paused. Funny, she didn't remember making herself a coffee. With a shake of her head and a rueful grin she picked up the grater and the carrot she'd been preparing for her salad. She hesitated a moment, crinkled her nose as a vague notion niggled at the edge of her consciousness, shrugged again, and continued grating the carrot while humming to herself.

After dinner she fired up the laptop and checked her emails. Still no reply from her aunt, strange. She rattled off another, just saying, "Please reply, I'm worried." and hit send, then went to check her dwindling bank account.

43

s/y Pasha Passage Log
Crew: Rosie Carter (solo)
Thursday 2ⁿᵈ May 2013
1025: Departed Arrecife Marina
Destination: Graciosa Island
Wind SSE 8kts Sea 0.2m.

Pasha and I were out on the green and crinkly once more. Our destination, the tiny island of Graciosa, less than a mile off Lanzarote's northwest shore and a half-day by sea from Arrecife.

Last week I'd taken advantage of a ridiculously cheap flight and gone home for a few days, gave the house and my jeep an airing, and went to see Dad.

Julie had seemed overjoyed to see me and gave me a big hug and everyone was thrilled with the bottle of wine and giant box of chocolates I'd bought them from the airport duty-free. It had been heart-warming to see Dad's vital signs reacting to my voice, especially lively when I held his big shovel hand in both of mine, though his unmoving eyes still gave me the heebie-jeebies and I avoided looking at them. Encouraged by his responses on the monitor I rambled on and on about everything that had happened in the past two months. Well, not everything, obviously, but you know, the swimming with dolphins, our unplanned diversion to Morocco, my *faux pas* with clothing which I liked to imagine caused an internal guffaw, success at Spanish, the biking adventures, and other trivial stuff I reckoned would interest him.

Returning to Arrecife and running out of useful things to do, I decided to go island hopping for a few days to broaden my horizons and find some new scenery. I'd told the marina to hold my berth, I'd be back in a week or so.

That evening I treated myself to the local fish in a rough-hewn wooden shack of a restaurant overlooking the little marina at Caleta del Sebo where *Pasha* rocked quietly with other boats on the harbour swell.

Finishing my meal, I looked up to meet the curious eyes of a middle-aged man on the next table, his younger female partner busy on her mobile phone.

"Hi," I said, "you here on a boat too?" A standard ice-breaker.

The woman looked up and gave me an indulgent smile.

"We sure are," she said, smoothly taking charge, "the clipper, a couple down from yours."

I scanned the line of boats near *Pasha*.

"Oh," I said, taking a punt at a small two-master, "the blue hulled ketch?"

"Yeah," drawled the man, still staring at me, "only she ain't a ketch, she's a yawl."

I grimaced and shook my head, appalled at my ignorance.

The woman laughed, "Excuse Jim," she said, "he's a boat-pedant. Give him chance and he'll bore the socks of you."

"I'll take the chance," I said, holding out a bare foot, "So, tell me, Jim, what's the difference between a yawl and a ketch?"

Jim's eyes lit up, suddenly transforming his demeanour from crabby to ebullient, "Why don't ya slide on over here an' I'll tell ya'll 'bout the Nantucket Clipper, best cruising sailboat ever built."

After introductions Joanie said, "We saw you come in. Pretty cool handling."

I preened at that. It had been a tight entry, but with nobody around to help me I'd manoeuvred skilfully into the berth, stopped her dead in the water as the fenders touched, and bounded onto the pontoon with both lines in hand. I didn't always judge it right, but I'd been proud of that one.

During the next hour over several wines I was fully apprised of the characteristics and benefits of the Nantucket Clipper. The difference between a yawl and a ketch, by all accounts, was the position of the mizzen mast in relation to the rudder post.

I excepted Jim and Joanie's invitation to look around their boat and stayed for a 'nightcap' that ended up wandering into the small hours. I found Jim to be not so much curmudgeonly as wryly indifferent, and once I got used to his dry humour, very funny.

I slept late.

Hurrying a cereal breakfast, I snapped the wheels onto my bike and set off for a leisurely tour of the island.

"Señora, señora! Please wait."

I stopped the bike at the side of the village street and let the young guy catch up.

"Qué pasa?" I said.

"Ah, tú hablas español," he gasped.

"Si" I said and waited for him to catch his breath. He was spotty-faced, not more than eighteen, I guessed, in tidy jeans and trainers with a red t-shirt splashed with the logo 'Trail Blazers'.

"Mi jefe," he said at last, *"él me dijo que corriera detrás de ti, para advertirte."*

"Warn me of what?" I said in Spanish

"Your bicycle, she is not suitable for the trails. She will be broken very soon, trust me. Your wheels, they will buckle in the gullies. Your tyres, they will puncture on the stones."

I looked again at his logo and began to suspect a scam. Oh, my suspicious mind.

"And your clothes," he said, eying my naked legs and floppy sunhat, "you must wear protection."

I blew out an exasperated sigh. Can't a girl go for a quiet bike ride around here? Several riders passed us on the street, all togged up for serious mountain biking. I looked down at my hybrid tyres, rugged enough for moderate trails, but…

Maybe the guy had a point.

He nodded at the departing riders who were now pedalling vigorously to race each other out of the village.

"For ten euro and a small deposit you can hire a mountain bike and knee and elbow pads," he said, "and a helmet. Please. Come back with me to my shop, señora, it is not far."

"Okay," I said, dismounting.

Ten euros, I reasoned, was really a no brainer.

Suitably attired with helmet and pads, equipped with a sturdy bike, thick knobbly tires and suspension fore and aft, I followed another small group of riders out of the village and onto a smooth but unmade road of fine grey sand. Apart from the occasional rough patch of stones the going was easy, and I began to think I'd been had. I shifted up to the highest gear and put on some speed, overtaking all but one of the bikes in front.

After a few kilometres the road surface began to deteriorate and narrow, until it became quite rough and I found myself having to swerve around protruding rocks and sudden deep gullies cutting into the trail.

The scenery here could only be described as treeless desolation, the only greenery, a few scattered shrubs growing low and dust-laden on the grey, volcanic ash and debris. The sea, clearly visible on both sides of the featureless terrain, heaved dark and sullen under an overcast sky, the only wind, that of my onward rush over the bumpy, winding path.

Ahead of us rose the only mountain on the island, a barren table-top, its yellow sides rising in steep, fluted ridges. The rider in front veered off the now almost indiscernible trail and on impulse I followed him, weaving among shrubbery and loose rubble for a hundred metres of more, until we came to a line of rocks that marked the shoreline, a sandy beach spread a few metres below. We'd come to the foot of the mountain escarpment.

I thought we would stop here, end of trail, but my unknown leader spun to his right and without hesitation rode up a steep gully, standing up on the pedals to gain power and traction.

Okay, pal, anything you can do…

I followed, shifting down to low gear and powering the bike upwards as scree and sand flew out from under the tyres. Up, up we went, the bike in front drawing gradually away as I puffed and panted and strained to keep mine moving up that incredible incline.

At last it began to level off, the trail a little smoother with hard-packed yellow sand, and I finally reached the plateau, heaving and panting for breath.

The rider in front had stopped, waiting for me, a white-toothed grin, breathing heavily but looking less exhausted than me. He nodded to me and pedalled off without a word.

I followed at a more leisurely pace until my breathing got back to sustainable, then powered forward to catch him up.

And this was exciting, a biker's playground, with unexpected twists and turns, flying rises and accelerating drops and sudden obstacles to challenge reactions. As I gained in confidence I got faster and more daring; my exhilaration level was off the scale, my energy, boundless. Soon I was behind the guy again, matching his lightening moves with increasing skill, feeling at one with the bike and terrain. Other riders crisscrossed our path, some making breathtakingly high leaps from the ridges.

We were reaching the end of the plateau, above the next ridge was the sea, stretching away grey and placid. My leader swerved sideways and halted just short of the ridge. Flushed with the excitement of the moment, I prepared to do the same. I squeezed both brakes.

Nothing happened.

I careered on helplessly, pumping the useless brakes, too fast to turn, too stupefied by terror to jump off.

I hit the ridge and took off, flying, with only the sea far, far below. I opened my mouth to scream, but no sound came, just the wind rushing past my ears. As my trajectory curved downwards I gripped hard onto the bike as if it might save me. The blue-grey waves rushed up, and cold darkness washed over me.

The man skids to a halt and turns to watch the girl who'd been following him. She's nearly up to him, and braking, when suddenly her body slumps over the handlebars.

"Oh Dios mío!" he exclaims as the oncoming bike topples sideways and spills the girl into a bush, where she bounces out like a ragdoll and flops face down on the hard-packed sand.

"Oh mierda!" he mutters, dismounting and letting his bike clatter to the ground.

Reaching the girl, he slips the backpack from her shoulders, eases her arms from it, and turns her over, carefully unfastens her helmet and removes it, then checks her pulse and breathing. Unconscious, but otherwise she seems okay. The bush must have broken her fall. He slips off his own backpack, places a rolled-up towel under the girl's head, and takes out his mobile phone. When he looks down again, her eyes are open.

44

My hands were shaking as I raised the water bottle to my lips and drank deeply. José was still staring at me, clearly freaked out by what had just happened; he'd freak out even more if he knew the horror I'd experienced. It had all seemed so real at the time, and I'd been totally nonplussed to find myself on dry land, with this helmeted face looking down at me.

I handed him back his water bottle and grinned, "You had better cancel that air ambulance."

"Are you sure you are okay?" he said, "maybe you should let them take you to the hospital."

"Please, José, call them. I will be fine to cycle back. There is really no need to panic."

He shook his head despairingly, clearly not happy, but began tapping the emergency number into his phone.

While he made the call I jumped up and dusted myself down, grateful now for the knee and elbow pads that had probably saved me a few nasty grazes. And the helmet of course, which I now picked up and donned.

"There, it is cancelled," José said, dropping his phone into his pack. He watched me fumbling to fasten my helmet.

"Here, let me," he said, stepping forward. I dropped my hands and lifted my chin to let him fasten me up. Close up he was no Leonardo di Caprio but had a friendly face, nice smile.

"Take it easy going back," he said, handing me my backpack, "I will stay close behind you."

I took it easy going back, mulling over this latest episode, still fazed by it and wondering at the randomness of the attacks. I'd evaded José's interrogation about what had happened; the paralysis on this occasion had lasted only seconds after coming to, and he probably hadn't even noticed.

Because of the late night with Jim and Joanie I'd missed my nightly weed fix. Today's frightful episode was further evidence that the remedy was effective.

The hard-braking, jolting ride down the slope was a bit hairy but with José gallantly taking the lead we made it to the bottom without incident. I parted company with him at the hire shop, thanked him with a hug and triple-cheeker, and wheeled my own bike back to the boat.

Jim and Joanie's boat had gone, along with most of the others; *Pasha* was only one of two visiting boats left in the marina. I guessed one day was long enough to experience the island's charms.

Before starting on dinner, I sat down and rolled one.

Saturday 4th May 2013
0730: Departed Graciosa
Dest: Santacruz, La Palma
Wind SE 12kts Sea 0.5m.

Early next morning, with the wind strengthening from southeast, I slipped from the marina and headed west on a two-day passage to La Palma, the most westerly of the major islands. The deadening clouds of yesterday had cleared away leaving just a few wisps of high cirrus which would soon burn off in the heat of the day.

Dolphins joined us just a few hours into the trip and hung around until mid-afternoon. After they'd left I sat in the cockpit and assembled Dad's boat rod, not used for several years but still in good nick. The multiplier reel span free and easy, but the line on it was a bit stiff and gungy, so I reeled on a new one. When it was all good to go I unwrapped the big yellow jelly-lure that I'd bought in Arrecife, armed with two vicious-looking hooks, and let out a long trawl over the stern.

It was approaching sunset, and I was below, making tea, when I heard the reel give a short zip. I froze, teabag poised above the mug. It zipped again, then stopped, then started again, and suddenly the line was singing off the reel.

Squealing like a schoolgirl I legged it up into the cockpit and heaved the rod out of its holder. The line was zipping out at tremendous speed, but I didn't want to strike dead for fear of losing my catch. Slowly I moved forward the drag lever until the line slowed. Then it stopped, so I locked the reel and struck tentatively. The response was immediate and violent, almost ripping the rod out of my grip.

"Fuckfuckfuckfuck!" I held on tight, bracing my thighs against the counter edge. I'd only ever caught dogfish in the Channel, this was a whole new ballgame.

I struck again, and began to pump the rod and wind in.

"Shit!" I said, through gritted teeth, *"Come... on."* It was too hard to turn the reel, my quarry too strong. I'd need to play it and try to weary it out. Suddenly the line went slack, and I reeled in frantically. When it tightened again the fish had shot out to starboard. Again, I went back to playing it, trying to force it back to astern.

And then I saw what I was up against, and my heart sank. Out of the water flew a monster, a magnificent animal and one I knew I'd never land. At least six feet long, its sleek blue-grey body convulsing furiously through the air as it struggled to break loose, proud dorsal sail rippling along its back, spiked bill waving like a conductor's baton.

And then it was gone. My blue marlin, the first I'd ever *seen* in the wild, let alone hooked. As I reeled in my slack line I reflected how privileged I'd been, and how fortunate to have lost the fight.

And I only wanted a little bonito for my supper.

Sunday 5th May 2013
1223: 28 48.3N 16 18.1W
Co: 260 Sp 6.5kts
Wind SSE 18kts Sea 1.5m. Swell: E. Heavy.

The dolphins returned this morning but didn't stay long. The wind had gradually increased, forcing me to shorten sail, but we were going as fast as I wanted; no point in reaching La Palma before first light tomorrow. The sea was now quite rough and uncomfortable; a long swell from ahead clashing with the wind fetch from the southeast.

I spent most of the day reading under the bimini, until a freak wave during late afternoon washed into the cockpit and nearly drowned my poor Kindle. I went below and dried it off, then myself, glad I wasn't wearing clothes. I set the collision alarm and lay down in the saloon to get a couple of hours in before dark; we were now within a hundred miles of land, and there were likely to be tuna boats around overnight. It was going to be a long, sleepless night. At least I had my evening joint to look forward to.

Dawn found me bleary-eyed in the cockpit, huddled in my foully and eying a pair of fishing boats manoeuvring a couple of miles off the starboard bow. Eight miles ahead the twinkling lights of Santacruz were beginning to fade as the sky lightened from astern, and I could now make out the jagged volcanic skyline high above the town. I shivered in the cool air and stirred myself. Time for a nice cuppa.

Two gigantic cruise ships lay alongside the quay, towering over me as I transited the length of the commercial harbour to reach the marina lock entrance. Depressing to think I'd be spending my first day in town with hundreds of rubber-necking cruise passengers crowding the streets and cafes. Still, at least they'd be gone this evening. Maybe I'd just grab a shower after breakfast and get my head down until then.

I found Santacruz a universe away from Arrecife's provincial modernity; pretty, Italianate facades, complete with green, slatted window-shutters and ornate wrought iron balconies above sympathetically discreet shopfronts and restaurants.

The dimly-lit cobbled streets opened onto delightful little plazas with whimsical public art, trickling water-features, and orange and plane trees under which white-shirted waiters flitted between chintz covered tables to serve amiable groups of diners.

Smells of freshly baked bread from late-night *panaderías,* and delicious spicy aromas from crowded restaurants wafted on the warm Atlantic breeze, rickety tables spilled out from tavernas onto the basalt cobblestones like estuaries of demand.

And this was only Monday, I thought, weaving among sauntering family groups with their frisking youngsters, what would it be like at the weekends? Not that I would find out; I planned to leave on Wednesday.

I dined *al aire libre* at a pasta house overlooking a square commanded by the statue of a rather squat, napoleon-like figure (though he struck me as more reminiscent of O'Brien's dissolute hero, Jack Aubrey) and beyond it, a life-size replica of a sixteenth-century caravel. After finishing my Chicken Alfredo I got chatting to a trio of Chinese girls who were flying to London tomorrow and wanted to brush up their English. They grinned preeningly when I told them their English was already better than most of that city's inhabitants.

I brought the bike to a halt, panting like an overheated dog, and took in my surreal surroundings; the clouds swirling on the vertiginous slopes far below on one side, and on the other, the dark, igneous rock of the caldera's outer rim, raw and spectacular, towering near-vertical to its jagged lip hundreds of feet above.

I checked my watch. Five hours! *So* pleased I'd left at first light. Five hours of gruelling slog up the winding road from Santacruz, around the northern slope of the volcano, a climb of some 1500 metres, I calculated; higher than Ben Nevis; the highest I'd ever been while in contact with the Earth. And I'd *cycled* it. Well, most of it, anyway. There'd been sections I'd had to walk due to sheer exhaustion.

I drank down the last of my water, the last of two litres, then popped a boiled sweet into my mouth to up my sugar-level and keep the saliva flowing.

I leaned heavily on the handlebars. *Phew!* It was hot work, this.

Ahead of me wisps of clouds crept up the mountainside and burgeoned at eye-level, and through them poked the pale green domes of two mountain observatories. There, I knew from my map, was one of the caldera's many visitor centres where I could buy more water, maybe even a coffee. Beyond that the road continued upwards, winding around the rim-wall where a steel crash-barrier defended an almost vertical drop into misty treetops far, far below. The visual incongruity was dizzying.

I moved aside as a car ground up the hill behind me, and when it had passed I pedalled off after it, presently taking a slip road left down towards the visitor centre. At the carpark I dismounted and locked the bike to a railing, then stretched and shook out my burning, tingling leg muscles. They would be stiff and aching tomorrow and for days to come.

Sitting on a wall outside the small kiosk, sipping my coffee, I found myself looking longingly at a guy lighting a cigarette. The craving could hit at the most inappropriate times.

He saw me looking and tapped his cigarette box, "You would like one?"

I am constantly perplexed as to how we Brits are so easily identified by Spaniards. How do they know?

"Mataría por uno," I said, smiling ruefully, *"pero no, gracias."*

"Ah, you have given up recently," he said, reverting to Spanish.

"Not recently," I said, "but the urge to smoke is always there, such an addiction, yes, *such* an addiction."

He smiled then. "Your Spanish is very good. It is unusual for the English to use colloquial speech like that."

"Thank you," I said, flushing slightly. I'd been giving him an 'up yours' for his presumption but now felt oddly moved to have Enrico's efforts recognised; he'd coached me relentlessly in colloquial *idioma*, including the Spanish way of emphasis by repetition.

"I have a good teacher," I added, getting up and dropping my empty cup into a waste basket.

I took a walk along a paved footpath leading through a gap in the rim and ate my lunch gazing down into the heart of the caldera; inside walls festooned with small trees and shrubs clinging precariously to the naked rock, and down below the hanging folds of cloud, bigger, denser forestation as arboreal nature reclaimed the tortured remains of ossified magma. And far below that, where the western side of the volcano had collapsed into the sea, and where the town of Tazacorte had, countless millennia later, been built in its ruins, on the margin of a glittering ocean that stretched away uninterrupted for two-thousand
miles.

Part Three

45

s/y Pasha Passage Log
Crew: Rosie Carter (solo)
Wednesday 2nd October 2013
1140: Departed Arrecife
Dest: Mindelo, Sao Vincente, C. Verdes
Wind ENE 12kts Sea 1m. Swell: Negligible.

We were 180 miles south of Grand Canaria when I noticed the barometer starting to fall quickly, too quickly, three millibars in the past hour.

Although the weather had been close to perfect for the past two days, four months alongside in Arrecife had once more robbed me of my sea-legs, and I'd been feeling quite queasy and a tad apprehensive about the 800-mile passage south. Yesterday was the worst, my birthday, and the most miserable ever. I toasted myself with a small voddy and coke, and promptly started bawling. Oh, the lonely tears. Pathetic really.

Okay, the trip down from UK had been longer, but these were not those benign European waters and I was acutely aware that the land a hundred miles to the east was just a vast empty desert; it might just as well have been another ocean for all the help I could expect if the worst happened.

I *know*. I was just being a wuz. But for maybe the first time since setting out from Pompey I was feeling horribly exposed and vulnerable. Which wasn't helped by the battalions of black clouds now towering up from astern. With the sun on the starboard beam an hour from setting,

"Snap out of it, Rosemary. There's work to do."

I still wasn't sure if the voice was real, or in my head. But it was true, I needed to secure the boat for a rough night.

When depression calls, action is the key, and as I worked feverishly at the mast to hook on the reef toggles, I felt my mojo returning. *Pasha* was a sturdy sea-boat, after all, and I rated myself a reasonably competent skipper.

"What can possibly go wrong?"

"Everything."

"Oh, shut up, it's cool."

It was with that complacent thought that I missed one necessary precaution, giving little thought to the probable wind shift the approaching gale would bring. Something a *truly* competent skipper would never have missed.

In short order I had all three mainsail reefs down and hauled taut, extra lashings on the boom to hold down the lazy folds of sail, the bimini folded back and lashed, and the genoa furled in to the size of a docker's hanky. It was almost dark, and we were bumping nicely along on a beam reach in a strengthening Force Six, the sea rising from the port quarter ahead of the oncoming blow.

I now disabled the windvane and engaged the autopilot to make taking the wheel in hand easier if it became necessary.

A last look around the deck and cockpit to see all was lashed or stowed, then swung below to secure everything that could move and put some clothes on. Feeling revitalised by the rush of activity I heated up a bowl of stew and wolfed it down straight from the saucepan.

Final tasks: nav lights on, instrument lighting to dim.

There, I was ready. Bring it on.

The wind came suddenly, half an hour later, a dull roar and a rush of power into the sails, heeling us over hard to leeward. I fastened my lifejacket over my fouly and climbed the ladder to the cockpit, where I was greeted by a stinging lash of spray in my face. Closing the hatch and slotting home the washboards to keep water out of the saloon, I plonked down with my back to the wind and pulled up my hood.

I watched the anemometer display; the wind had backed ten degrees and strengthened past 25 knots. I eased out the main sheet a few inches, then likewise on the genoa.

The stern was beginning to buck and slew on a rising, quartering sea that was worsening by the minute. The autopilot was working too hard, overreacting to swing then overcompensating. I heaved myself up to the control box and reduced the rudder gain.

"Better."

A few minutes later the anemometer read 32 knots, but *Pasha* was holding well. The wind backed another 15 degrees, and I let out more mainsail, left the genoa where it was; letting out more would put it in the lee of the main.

The wind backed further, just fifteen degrees off dead-astern now. It was then I realised what I'd forgotten. I hadn't put the preventer on the boom.

"How fucking amateurish!"

"Yup. Too late now."

To get a preventer on I would need to crawl along the lee side with the rope's end, with the sea breaking over me while I threaded it through a block on the forward deck cleat and dragged the end back. Even with a harness the thought was terrifying. And then I would need to haul in the boom to reach the end of it to tie on the rope. Single handed it was all a bit too hairy.

"Shit shit shit!"

I pressed the button on the Autopilot for ten degrees port, then another ten to be on the safe side, and hauled in the main as she turned.

We were on a broad reach, safe for now, I reckoned, from an accidental gybe, but heading way off course. Oh well, not the end of the world. Just have to ride it out and hope it doesn't last days.

By now despite my foully I was soaked to the skin from waves breaking over the counter (and me), the cockpit continually filling and draining. Time for a cuppa.

I was waiting for the kettle to boil when it happened. The deck heaved up dizzyingly beneath me, then a dreadful graunch above from the labouring autopilot and we began to come upright. In a cold dread I turned off the gas and hurried back up to the cockpit to prevent a gybe.

Too late. The boom flashed over my head at lightening speed, snapping taut the sheets with the sound of a cannon shot, sending sickening shockwaves through the boat.

I quickly disengaged the autopilot and took the wheel. As we turned upwind I applied full starboard rudder, and *Pasha* heeled over to port as the gale leaned hard against the backed genoa, pushing the lee rail deep underwater while furious waves battered the upturned weather-side of the hull.

There, we were safely hove to. Time to check the damage.

I hauled in the mainsheet and watched the gooseneck, the swivel attaching the boom to the mast, for signs of misalignment. It seemed okay. I looked along the boom to check for buckling or cracks. That seemed okay. I noticed one of the mainsheet block shackles had contorted; I'd need to change that.

I looked up at the sail. I couldn't see much in the darkness, but it was definitely *not* okay; it should have been bellied out tight to the wind, not rippling and flogging like that. I pulled the torch out of its pocket and shone it upwards.

"Oops."

"Oh fuck!" I breathed.

A big rip from luff to leach grinned down at me like a malicious demon.

In that buffeting wind and precipitous heel to leeward it took an exhausting hour to get the ruined sail down and zipped up in its lazy-bag. Afterwards I just went below and flopped into my bunk, content to remain hove to till morning. I was in no hurry, after all.

Friday 4th October 2013
0635: 24 51N 17 43W
Hove to
Wind NE 12kts Sea 0.5m. Swell: Easterly mod.

After breakfast I went up to empty my organic waste box: a few stale breadcrusts, fruit and veg peelings, cooked chicken bones and skin.

The gale had subsided, and it was a bright sunny morning with a warm, moderate breeze from the northeast. The sea still heaved a little from the gale but looked set to quieten down in a few hours.

I threw the waste overboard and turned to go back below. An agitated splashing made me turn back, curious. The water seethed and churned where I'd thrown the stuff in. I stepped over to the rail and gawked. Beneath the surface of the crystal water a frensy of flashing dorados were gobbling up my slowly sinking throwaways. I looked up as another leapt from the water, proudly-raised dorsal sail, translucent flank glinting multi-hued in the sunlight. Then I saw more of them, leaping and cavorting all around the stationary boat.

"Wow!" I murmured, "mahi-mahi for dinner tonight, maybe?"

My stomach tightened with excitement as I lifted the rod out of its holder and swung the line out over the transom. I flicked the rod and dropped the lure a few metres out, and immediately three fish arrowed in towards it.

I squealed with delight as the smallest of the trio took the shiny hook, while the two bigger ones snapped in frustration at the lure hanging from of its closed jaws. I pulled back on the rod with both hands and my fish came on with little resistance, on too short a line to put up much of a fight. I reeled in rapidly then swung it easily up and over into the cockpit sole, where it flipped and flapped around in frantic indignation.

"Yes!" I hissed, punching the air.

Gingerly I took hold of the shredded lure and inched my fingers to the shank of the hook protruding from the gaping mouth, then, avoiding the rows of small but sharp-looking teeth, managed to twist it free.

Aside from the ugly, bulbous head, it was a beautiful animal; a youngster, clearly, only two feet long, but a true pelagic predator, a sleek torpedo of shimmering blue-green. It seemed a shame to kill it. Should I throw it back?

"Nah, sorry. You're dinner, my little friend."

I reached for the winch handle to despatch the creature, hefted it, then paused - a sudden vision of Gary with blood pouring down his face, glowering dangerously at me across the cockpit.

I shivered and dropped the handle back into its pocket.

"Try alcohol, Rosemary."

Something Dad had told me years ago flashed into my mind. I dived below and retrieved the vodka bottle from the drinks locker and poured a little of the spirit into the fish's panting gill. The effect was instant; the animal stiffened, convulsed a few times, then lay still. Within seconds its bright lustre had faded to dull green.

"Yup, that worked. Thanks Dad."

Tuesday 8th October 2013
0947: 16 59N 24 58W
Co 250 Sp5
Sailing (headsail only)
Wind E 16kts Sea 0.2m. Swell: NE Slight

I sipped my breakfast tea and gazed at the unrelieved starkness of the rust-red volcanic ranges rising to port, and the more verdant heights of the island to starboard.

We'd been fortunate to make such good time. Without our mainsail any wind from ahead of the beam would have given us problems, but the gods had smiled upon us and kept it blowing conveniently between northeast and southeast, and with enough strength to average a comfortable six knots.

Now, seven days after leaving Lanzarote, our destination was at last in sight. Two miles ahead stood the conical rock called *Ilhéu dos Pássaros,* beyond which lay the harbour and town of Mindelo, its low-storied frontages tinged pale pink in the morning sunlight.

46

"Here, let me give you a hand."

I stood up from the untidy heap that was my unrigged mainsail and looked at my saviour.

"Thanks," I said, palming sweat from my brow, "I could do with one."

He was American, forty-something, clean-shaven and handsome, with light brown hair tied in a ponytail. His most striking feature though was the shiny metalwork extending from his left knee to a canvas boat-shoe.

Cautioning myself not to stare, I stooped and gathered up two arms-full of the stiff laminate sailcloth and manoeuvred it over the guardrail to his waiting hands, and together we managed to feed it all over onto the wooden decking of the pontoon.

"Ooh! Nasty," my new friend exclaimed as we spread out the sail and the two-metre-long tear showed itself, "what happened?"

I looked glumly down at the two halves of my sail, held together only by the line bonded into the luff and the reinforced hem at the leach.

"Don't ask," I said.

"Shit happens, eh?" he grinned with a knowing twinkle.

We folded and bagged the sail then heaved it onto the flatbed trolley I'd wheeled down earlier. I'd noticed while we worked how unhampered the guy was by his prosthetic, and how unselfconscious, too. I recalled watching the London

Paralympics last summer, and in the darkness of my unshared grief, had drawn comfort and inspiration from that same stoic, go-get-em attitude. I reflected also on the dismembered Afghan veterans I'd met at RCDM still coming to terms with their mechanical appendages. I wanted to think that they too had by now found purpose and inspiring challenge in their lives.

My friend glanced at his watch. "Hey, sorry, I gotta run, damn chandlery closes for lunch soon, and I need to buy stuff."

"S'okay," I said, "thanks for your help."

I watched him walk briskly and very ably along the swaying pontoon, then stooped to pick up the handle of the trolley.

I gaped disbelievingly at the guy in the sailmaker's shop.

"Three *weeks?*" I said.

He sucked his teeth, grimaced apologetically and waved a hand at the rows of stacked sails behind him.

"Got all dees before de ARC sail. When dey gone, we can do it, no before."

He handed me a canvas tag and a marker-pen. "Write down name of boat and berth number. I bring sail down to you when it ready, okay?"

"Can you give me a rough estimate of cost?" I asked as I wrote.

"Where de tear, and how long?"

"Above the second baton, about six feet straight across."

"Is on de seam?"

I shook my head. "No."

He frowned and began tapping figures into his calculator. Finally, he looked up with a careless shrug.

"Maybe, two hundred."

"Okay," I said cheerfully, handing him the completed tag and his marker, "ciao for now," and breezed out of the shop, leaving my sail on the trolley for him to take inside.

200 Euros was about £170, not as bad as I'd feared but still a good chunk out of my dwindling resources.

I sat at the crowded, floating bar with a cold beer and watched the bustle of activity along the pontoons. It was the annual gathering of the ARC Rally; the marina was already aflutter with their ostentatious blue and white flags, and more boats were arriving by the hour.

"Hey, it's the pretty girl with the busted sail," drawled a familiar voice.

I looked round to see my erstwhile helper at a table with a mixed crowd of other yachties. I threw him a smile, raised my glass to him, and turned back to the bar.

"Say, why don't you shimmy on over here and join us, lonely girl? We won't bite, ya know."

I flushed, and turned on my stool, bristling. But before I could find a witty retort he kicked out a spare chair from under the table, nodded sideways to it, and disarmed me with a cheery grin.

"Yeah, c'mon over, honey," enjoined a feisty, frazzle-haired woman with a deep neckline showing off her adequate cleavage.

With the grin of defeat, I picked up my drink and sauntered over.

"Alone, isn't lonely," I told my apparent admirer, "there's a difference." which sparked off a general discussion around the table about other single-handers they knew, and which quickly strayed into lamp-swinging anecdotes and ribald badinage.

"Name's Dirk," my friend said, holding out a hand.

"Rosie," I said, shaking briefly.

When the babble died down Dirk stood up.

"Everyone, this here *English Rose*, is, believe it or not," he paused for dramatic effect, "Rosie!"

When the polite titters died down he went around the table; I quickly forgot most of the names, but they included a big Swedish guy with flowing blonde locks and pale blue eyes whom Dirk introduced as Erik the Viking, and a Welsh couple called Terry and Karen.

Thing was, Erik the Viking held onto my hand a little longer than necessary, and I know this is a cliché, but really, a spark seemed to jump between us. Which I knew Dirk noticed because of the quizzical glance he gave me.

It was Terry though, the gregarious Welshman, who quickly commandeered my attention, with tales of starting up from nothing to build a chain of outdoor shops across Wales, which now, he at 72, Karen at 68, supported their world-circumnavigation adventure on their 32-foot cutter, which they'd eponymously named *Terkar*. I was impressed to learn they were heading, not across the Big Pond, but south to St Helena, and thence around the Cape and into the Indian Ocean.

Dirk, I discovered, was the full-time Captain of a 60-foot ketch whose owners would not join the vessel until they reached Antigua.

"Cap'n Ahab, that's me," he'd declared, knocking on his prosthetic leg.

The other Americans around the table, including the Bet Midler lookalike, were some of his crew and groaned at the oft-heard trope.

Making my spliff that night I noticed my stash was running worryingly low and wondered how I might go about getting some more. I'd had a few suspicious wafts this morning while walking across town to the laundrette but hadn't noticed any likely dealers hanging about. And if I had, would I have had the nerve to approach them? This was not Lanzarote, and I had no idea of the rules here. Except I knew the police had a reputation for intolerance and brutality with local people caught dealing.

Next morning, I dug out my wheelie shopping-bag and set out for the markets, first the fish market where I picked up a couple of fine tuna steaks for the pan, and the tail end of a wahu for a fish stew I was planning. Next, I found a huge indoor fruit & veg market, where I bought sweet potatoes, plantains, onions, carrots, an aubergine, and a weird-looking root vegetable I couldn't pronounce the name of but thought it might make an exotic addition to my stew.

Gosh, Aunt Georgie would be proud of me if she only knew.

I also paid fifty cents for a huge bunch of green bananas that I planned to hang on *Pasha's* stern-gantry to ripen. The rest of my staples, eggs, bread, milk, beer etc, I picked up at a little supermarket near the marina.

I was wheeling my overloaded trolley along the quayside when an emaciated Rastafarian, all hung about with colourful craft jewellery, crossed the street and intercepted me.

"You wan' buy, Missy?" he said, holding up a rather attractive beaded leather wrist-thong, "it suit you good."

"No thank you," I said politely and walked on.

"Aaw, c'mon, Missy," he wheedled, hurrying alongside, "you pretty lady, dis look fine on you, look." He flipped the thong over my wrist and tried to fasten it, but I pulled away and walked faster, making for the marina gate where the security guard would shoo him away. "Only two hundred escudo, Missy, I know you like."

I slowed my pace. That was what, less than two Euros? But I'd had another thought. I stopped and turned to him.

He grinned a brown-toothed grin, "You like, Missy, here, try on."

As I took the bracelet I got a whiff of him and tried not to recoil. I swear I saw things moving in his dreads.

I made a show of studying the thong, it really was very nicely crafted and probably wouldn't fall apart in a few days.

"I'll give you one Euro," I said.

"Aaw, no Missy, you pay me two Euro, I got wife, little childra, you pay me two for beautiful bracelet."

"What's your name?" I said.

"My name? My name *Motorman*. You pay me now?"

I moved close and tried not to breathe in. "I'll pay two Euro" I said, lowering my voice, "if you can get me some marihuana." I moved back and watched his face grow shifty. He peered at me through bloodshot eyes.

"Pay me now, fifty Euro," he said quietly, "I get for you tonight."

I blew out, "Fifty Euros for how much?"

"Ten gram, best weed in all Cabo Verde, Missy."

I grinned mirthlessly and shook my head. "No deal, my friend. I need one hundred grams, and for that I'll pay you fifty."

He snorted, then paused, saw I was serious.

"Okay, you pay me now, I bring tonight."

"No way, Motorman," I said, feeling quite the streetwise buyer, "you meet me tonight with the weed and then I'll pay you."

Motorman went away disgruntled but promised to be back there at 7-o-clock to do the deal. I grinned at my new wrist-ornament, pleased with my performance at dealing with the local low-life. And more to the point, it looked like I'd scored my weed.

Silly bint that I was.

Back onboard, I stowed my provisions and got started straight away on my stew while the fish was good and fresh.

First, I hauled out my pressure-cooker and set some coarse-chopped onions simmering in olive oil in the open pan.

Meanwhile I peeled two sweet potatoes, four large carrots, and my unknown root (which raw, tasted like tangy turnip), and cut them into thick slices.

Next, I prepared the liquor; I poured a little boiling water into a jug containing a vegetable stock cube, ground cumin, and a little madras curry powder and stirred it into a brown goo, which I then diluted with more water, white wine, lemon juice, and a splash of balsamic vinegar.

By now the onions were golden, and I added the vegetables to the pan, a good shake of salt, a tablespoon of chopped garlic from a jar, and poured over the liquor. I secured the lid and set the valve to full pressure.

Now I skinned the wahu tail and stripped the thick white flesh away from the spine, cutting it into sizable chunks. These I placed in a big polythene bag with a little seasoned flour, blew into the bag to inflate it like a balloon, and gave it a good shake until all the fish chunks were dusted with flour.

Finally, I washed the aubergine and cut it into thin slices. By now a glorious spicy aroma had filled the saloon.

When the pressure-valve tripped I turned off the gas and let it continue cooking until the pressure equalised, then added the raw fish, a can of chick peas from my tinned supplies, and some dried pulses that I'd soaked overnight. The last touch was to layer the sliced aubergines over the stew. I then resealed the lid and lit the hob.

When the valve tripped a second time, I turned off the gas and went for a shower.

The stew filled six portion sized plastic pots, which I sealed hot and left to vacuum-cool. They would later go in the bottom of the fridge to be used over the coming weeks.

As I washed up and seven-o-clock approached, I began to get nervous about my illicit rendezvous. I pulled on jeans, socks and trainers, and my least alluring top. I took ashore with me fifty Euros, my marina key-card, and nothing else.

"Missy, missy, you come now." Motorman, beckoning from the corner of a building. He was late; I'd been waiting there twenty minutes and had been about to give up. Pedestrians passed on the sidewalk behind him, so I felt it safe to go over.

"Have you got it, Motorman?"

"Yeahman, but not here," he cast around theatrically, "Police, yanoo. You come."

He stepped away and began across the empty street, where the buildings and alleys opposite looked dark and deserted. He saw me hang back and returned to my side.

"Just up dere, Missy, not too far."

Where he pointed, on a street leading up the hill, I could see lights spilling from windows and a couple of bars, people milling about.

"Okay, lead on." I said, with returning confidence. If I wanted to score here I'd better stop being such a wuz.

A little way up the hill just a few yards short of the first bar, Motorman stopped by a dark, narrow side-alley, and I felt the small hairs spring up on the back of my neck.

"Dis man," he murmured, as a tall figure moved out of the shadows, "he got you stuff, you pay him." And then Motorman was gone, shimmying quickly back down the street, leaving me alone with a stranger. My mouth went dry as fight shuffled with flight.

"Fifty Euro, right?" murmured the stranger. I still couldn't see his face in the shadows, just the tall lean shape of him. I took out the rolled-up ten and two twenties from my pocket but kept it tightly folded in my hand.

"Er… yes, have you got…"

"Here," he said, "you come in here, Police, dey everywhere, you done know."

I took a tentative step into the alley, ready to flee at the slightest sign of trouble. He handed a polythene bag towards me. I reached for it, but he pulled it back and waved a finger "De money, first."

I held out the cash and reached with my other hand for the bag. Suddenly the notes were snatched out of my hand and the bag dropped to the ground, spilling ash or something across the pavement.

"Hey!" I shouted as he pushed past me out of the alley, and foolishly grabbed at his collar, swinging him back to face me. A black face flashed angrily, then a sickening thud to my temple turned off the lights.

Dazed, I flopped to my hands and knees, but then staggered back to my feet to see a double image of my attacker weaving between duplicated drinkers outside the bar. I wobbled after him for a few steps, but overcome with dizziness, sank down again, my back to the wall, feeling sick but vaguely aware of some commotion up the street.

As I sat there in a semi-swoon, cursing myself for an idiot. Heavy footfalls, then a big shadow appeared in front of me, legs, slightly apart, silhouetted against light from the street lamps. I drew up my knees and clamped my arms around them.

"*Tenga nada,*" I said, sullenly, then, as temper overcame fear, I screamed, "I've got nothing left, so just *piss off*!"

The man squatted down on his haunches, a giant of a man. I squinted up to make out his face against the backlight, saw only that his hair was long.

"That black devil tried to scam me last week."

"Oh, it's you," I said.

"He dropped this when I punched him. It is yours?"

"Thank you," I said, plucking my fifty Euros from his big fingers. I sniffed back a sob. "Thank you, thank you so much."

47

"Mm, one can see this is a lady's boat, it is too tidy for a guy."

I laughed. "It was a *guy* that taught me to keep the boat clean and uncluttered. But then he was ex-navy and it was in his DNA."

"I am guessing that was your father?"

I raised my beer bottle. "Yup, good old Dad. Taught me everything I know, excuse the cliché."

Erik the Viking's bulk seemed to fill half the saloon; I'd had to drop the leaf of the table on his side so he could squeeze his massive legs behind it. He'd scrunched his blonde hair into a pony tail, which somehow made him look even bigger.

We clinked bottles and drank to Dad.

"It looks like he taught you domestic economy too," he said, eyeing my pots of stew lined up on the fridge lid.

"No," I giggled, "Dad used to despair of on that score. It was my aunt that got me into cooking onboard. In fact, she's partly the reason for this trip."

"Oh?"

I went on to tell him all about Georgina, my shock when she'd turned up out of the blue and how she'd flown over from Florida to support me when I'd nobody else.

Erik told me he was a professional delivery skipper, here on a brand-new 44-foot cutter on its way to its proud owner in the Virgin Islands. Erik was waiting for a replacement rudder from the boat's builders in Sweden, and the arrival of his crew for the final leg, both expected in a week's time.

"What happened to the rudder." I said, "or shouldn't I ask?"

"Something hit it, maybe a whale. Nobody saw it happen, we only felt it. Anyway, the post is buckled, so now they must replace the whole unit. They are sending an engineer and a diver down with it."

I puffed out my cheeks, "Expensive, who's paying for that?"

"Ach, probably the builders, or their insurers. It's not my business to ask. So long as they pay me, I am happy."

I suddenly felt hungry, and Erik didn't look about to leave, so I asked him, "Do you fancy some fish stew? It's freshly made, my own recipe. I'd be pleased to hear your verdict."

And I *was* pleased with his verdict. He couldn't praise it enough. Afterwards, over coffee, he asked me what I'd been doing going out alone in town at night.

After a pause, I said, "Erik, I have a bit of an issue with blackouts, random, you know. They don't happen often, but when they do, it scares me. I found, by happy circumstance really, that a little smoke of cannabis at night stops it from happening."

"Ah, now I understand, you were trying to buy weed. And instead you bought a broken face."

I spluttered a laugh and gingerly touched the side of my head; it felt swollen and tender, but the throbbing pain of earlier had melted away, thanks to two paracetamol and an ibuprofen tablet.

"Yeah, stupid, huh? Thanks again for getting my money back, cash is pretty tight right now."

He beamed sympathy. "I know what it's like. I used to cruise too before I found a better way of sailing the world, when somebody else pays. When you own your boat there is never enough money."

"Unless you're rich," I said.

"Ya," he nodded wisely, "then it is a different story."

He looked thoughtful for a moment, then said, "Come to my boat, a nightcap. I have some good vodka. And maybe something else you would like."

I flushed. "Erik, I don't..."

"No, nothing like that. I am not trying to seduce you," he laughed, "you have the word of a Viking."

Mildly ashamed of my presumption and perversely unsure I wanted the word of *this* Viking, I looked at the clock. Nine-thirty, early yet.

"Okay," I said, jumping up, "I'll just wash the dishes, then I'm ready."

The boat under Erik's charge blew me away. From her clean, classic lines and beautiful teak deck to her ingeniously clever control arrangements, *Thorfinn* was a yachtie's dream. Stepping down to the saloon, I let out a long, low whistle at the spacious, luxurious interior. Reluctant envy vied with the guilt of disloyalty to *Pasha*.

Erik lumbered down after me and went straight to his freezer, lifting out a frosted bottle of Karlsson's Gold and two equally frosty shot glasses.

"Please, take a seat," he said, filling the glasses, "you want a beer as well?"

"Mm, why not," I said, sliding along the banquette on cushions still wearing their shiny plastic covers, "Pretty tidy boat for a guy."

He cracked open two beers from the fridge and joined me on the seat opposite, sliding my beer and shot across the table.

"Ach, they keep sending potential customers to view her, the company use her as a showboat." he said. He raised his glass. "*Skal.*"

"*Skal,*" I responded, and we sank our shots together in one.

I gasped, and he laughed.

"Tomorrow I go to Santo Antao," he suddenly announced, "because I heard it is very beautiful. Do you want to come?"

"What, you're sailing over there?"

"No, no, we take the ferry, then a minibus tour, there will be other people. It is only a few hours."

"Okay," I said, "sounds like fun."

We chatted for an hour, more shots, and nursed our beers. He told me until recently he'd been paired up on deliveries with his girlfriend, but they'd split up and she was now working out of Greece as chef on a superyacht.

"Do you miss her?" I asked.

"I miss her cooking," he replied with a rueful grin.

When I got up to leave he said, "Wait a moment," and disappeared into the after cabin. Returning, he handed me a bulging polythene bag and said, "Something to help your blackouts and save you from another punch on the head."

Gobsmacked, I gaped up at him. "Wow, Erik, are you sure?"

"Sure, I'm sure. Take it. I can get more."

I weighed the bag in my hand; about 200 grams, I reckoned.

"Can I at least pay you something for it?"

"Ach, I don't need the money. I will come to your boat tomorrow at 8-o-clock."

I tippy-toed and kissed his cheek. "You're a star, Erik the Viking."

I left him blushing.

"You think we'll make it?" Erik said, leaning over me and grinning.

"No, don't say that?" came a startled woman's voice from the seat behind us.

The minibus was labouring up a steep incline at a crawl, a vertical drop to our right looking down on neat, cultivated terraces far, far below, carved out of the volcanic rock and planted with produce; and beyond the valley, rising majestically and fading into forever, jagged mountain peaks, between which we caught tantalising glimpses of the glittering ocean.

"Don't scare the tourists, Erik!" came the jocular voice of Dirk, aka Cap'n Ahab, from the back of the bus. He'd come over on the ferry with us, along with his busty First Mate, Sarah. The remainder of the passengers were a hodgepodge of British and American holidaymakers staying at a beach resort on the south side of Sao Vincente.

I gave Erik a nudge, and he turned and smiled reassurance at the unnerved woman, "Don't worry, I am sure our driver has done this before."

I'd almost bottled it this morning, feeling horribly self-conscious about my bruise, but my mood had lightened after pulling off what I considered a diplomatic triumph.

"Jesus, what happened to you?" Dirk had said loudly as we waited to board the ferry.

Having thus had their attentions drawn to it, some of our fellow passengers now eyed my contused temple, which had turned a livid purple and yellow overnight, and began casting suspicious glances at my large companion. A story of falling down the companionway clearly wouldn't do.

"Oh, just some drunk local guy in a bar last night," I told Dirk, loud enough for all to hear, "luckily Erik here came to my rescue," I'd then gripped his big arm in mine, and gazed up theatrically, "My Hero."

The mountain road levelled out, and we pulled up on a narrow ridge crossing between two peaks where another minibus was reloading its passengers. Everyone piled out and began snapping away with cameras at the stunning vistas on either side and taking selfies against the extraordinary backdrop from that precipitous causeway in the sky.

After two hours or so traversing those glorious mountains, we descended the steep and winding road down to the sea, passing women carrying enormous bundles on their heads and men driving sad-looking burros laden with water-containers and baskets heaped with farm produce.

We stopped at a fishing village and were herded into a rustically furnished restaurant where spicy aromas from a bustling open-air cooking range whetted eager appetites; to help ourselves to lunch from trestle tables groaning under the weight of all manner of hot and cold foods, then join other diners, from other buses, on long benched tables while a guitarist entertained us with songs in Portuguese and waiters came around with endless supplies of beer and local wine.

"Are you happy you came?" asked Erik, as I prepared to tuck in to my grilled grouper and salad. Unsurprisingly, he'd chosen something huge and meaty, and smothered it in a rich, gooey pea gravy, with a mess of fried potatoes, okra, and sliced, spicy plantains on the side.

"Of course I am, I'm over the moon."

I picked up my beer and chinked it against his.

"Thanks for inviting me."

"Thank you for coming. It is much better with a friend than alone."

I glanced across at Dirk, currently in deep conversation with Sarah, their food yet untouched. I guessed from their body-language she was a Mate in both senses of the word. No, Erik wouldn't have had much company from that quarter.

I turned back to my Viking, "That was a bus ride to die for, wasn't it?"

He nodded agreement, and levered a large, juicy chunk of meat into his mouth. I watched him chew thoughtfully, a glob of gravy on his lower lip, his pale blue eyes widening in delight, nodding his head slowly as the flavours hit his taste buds, and I was struck by the untethered expressiveness of his face; such an open, honest face and soulful demeanour that reminded me of that first electric encounter at the marina bar. Was I really falling for this oversized Swede?

After lunch the bus took us to a rum distillery, where, following a guided tour of the molasses-reeking plant, we sampled the wares and gasped as the fiery, ninety-percent spirit evaporated our lungs. We were delayed leaving by one of the older male tourists who couldn't decide which species of the rocket-propellant he wanted to take home to Granny, and so our driver had to risk all our life and limbs to get us back before the ferry left.

That night, after dinner together at the marina bar, and vodkas after coffee, and a shared joint in *Thorfinn's* cockpit, I told my big, honest Viking he needn't keep his word, and to please be gentle.

He was.

48

s/y Pasha Passage Log
Crew: Rosie Carter (solo)
Wednesday 13ᵗʰ November 2013
0940: Depart Mindelo
Dest: Antigua
Wind SE 16kts

It was mid-afternoon, when I could no longer see the distant peaks of Santo Antao astern, when that familiar feeling of utter aloneness crept over me. This was it, the Big One, and everything from now on was down to me, and me alone. Soon I would be out of VHF range, maybe already was, my last link with the rest of humanity. "Alone," I murmured, staring out at the breaking rollers, "just me and the great big ocean."

"Not quite alone, Rosemary."

Oh, of course, there was my invisible mentor, my ethereal guide, my... guardian angel?

"Hardly that."

"Why do I only hear you at sea?"

No response.

Erik had left two weeks ago. With his new crew, the second of whom had finally arrived only a day before sailing. They were probably in sight of the Antilles by now.

We went back to Antao, Erik and I, walking this time, roads unsuited to motor vehicles, but well suited to us. We took sleeping bags and food, stayed overnight in the lush mountains, and made love and slept under the stars. Perhaps we'd meet up again someday, me and my Viking man-mountain. It was a small world in yachting circles. I blew a laugh.

Only the world didn't look so small right now.

Saturday 16th November 2013
0830: 14 51N 31 19W
Co: 260 Sp 7
Trip Log: 394 miles
Wind: ENE 14 kts
Sea: 1m Swell: mod. Westerly

Day four. After breakfast I brought my tea up to the cockpit and sat watching the huge rollers piling up behind us, heaving the stern upwards before washing beneath with a roar, the windvane powering up to compensate as she tried to slew to windward.

The wind was almost dead astern; the genoa poled out to port and the newly-repaired mains'l flying slightly by the lee to starboard; Goosewinged, or Wing-and-Wing as Americans preferred to call it. After I'd solved the chaffing problem where the genoa sheet runs through the end of the pole (using a roller-block instead), I hadn't once had to touch the sheets.

Over the first three days we'd averaged 130 miles a day, not a bad start. I was firmly in the 'groove' now, in a routine, one changeless day following another so that time became meaningless, just an abstract figure to write in the log every four hours, then forget about.

Mealtimes were dictated by the sunrise, solar meridian, and sunset. After breakfast I'd haul up a bucket of seawater, tip it over my head, and soap myself down, then rinse off with a sparing spray of precious fresh from the deck-shower. I'd then spend the day reading in the cockpit, and after sunset would push back the bimini and smoke a joint while watching the stars appear one by one, until the bright panoply became hard to look at for long. And when tiredness called, I'd slip below and sleep till morning.

Tuesday 19ᵗʰ November 2013
0800: 14 23N 36 38W
Co: 250 Sp 4.5
Trip Log: 704 miles
Wind: NE 12 kts
Sea: 1m Swell: mod. Westerly

Made 140 miles yesterday, with wind gusting 20 kts or more. Not so good this morning, barely twelve knots and we were crawling along at a dogged four to five. Worse still, there were dark clouds piling up to starboard, converging with our course, slanted columns of rain beneath them.

"Happy with your sailplan, Rosemary?"

"I wish you wouldn't call me that, it's Rosie."

I looked at the poled-out genoa. Maybe I should furl it away. Dad used to say, "If you think something might go wrong, it probably will."

I watched the approaching squall. Might it miss us?

Shit, I was getting lazy.

Shaking my head in self-disgust, I jumped up and adjusted the windvane to take us further to windward, and sheeted in the main as she came up, until the genoa began to flog and rattle the pole. I took all but one of the turns off the sheet winch and paid out the sheet while hauling in on the furling line. Thankfully there wasn't too much wind and it came in easily.

I looked at the bare pole, standing out to port like a left turn signal, and judged it safe enough without the wind force of the sail. Next, I came further up to windward, to a close reach, and took in two reefs on the mains'l. Finally, I hauled up the windvane paddle and engaged the autopilot, then sheeted in the main and turned downwind, gybed onto the port tack so the pole would be on the weather side and not in danger of dipping in the water.

"Good thinking, Rosemary."

First came the wind, sudden and furious. The anemometer shot up to thirty-five as it veered wildly southwards. I took the wheel in hand and fought to steer to the ever-shifting wind, regardless of our compass heading, that was now irrelevant. The sea all around us seethed chaotically as the wind ripped the wavetops into whips of stinging spindrift.

And then came the rain. And such rain. Great torrents hurled down to flatten the sea and render visibility zero. Not that I needed to see far, only as far as the anemometer reading. And billowing under the bimini, so cold on my naked skin that goose-pimples sprang up like little volcanoes. I wished I'd put some clothes on while I'd had chance; even a t-shirt would have helped.

Friday 22nd November 2013
0805: 13 58N 43 51W
Co: 265 Sp 7
Trip Log: 1126 miles
Wind: NNE 16 kts
Sea: 1.5m Swell: mod. Westerly

There had been a series of those squalls over the past three days, some only minutes apart, as if the wild ocean were taking a breath before raging again with increasing fury as I fought to control the boat.

Now we sailed under clear skies once more. With the wind more in the north I had been forced unrig the genoa-pole and sail a beam reach to hug the Great Circle that would sweep us up to Antigua.

Yesterday afternoon, as the last of the squalls disappeared into the southwest, I was astonished to see a trio of egrets flying low around the boat. Why were they so far from land? I wondered, Egrets are not known for oceanic foraging, they're not even seabirds.

As I watched them, I realised they were trying to land on the boat. But there was no safe landing spot for them. The spinning wind-turbine above the gantry precluded any attempt there, and the deck was sloping too sharply to afford any traction for their wader's feet. One even tried to land on the sea but aborted at the last moment. They looked tired and desperate, and I could only assume that they were migrators that had somehow lost their way. After a few more aborted attempts to land, they flapped off miserably to the north, where the nearest landfall would be many thousands of miles away in the arctic circle. I felt so sad for them I almost cried. Wild Nature can be so horribly cruel.

Today's visitors had been more uplifting; a pod of huge bottle-nose dolphins. They arrived just as I settled down with my morning cuppa, and swam close to the cockpit serene and stately, watching me watching them as their heads broke surface before diving gracefully down once more, keeping pace with my seven knots with hardly a flick of their large tails. After an hour or so they leapt joyously out of the water and shot off into the blue.

Monday 25th November 2013
0803: 14 42N 49 33W
Co: 275 Sp 2
Trip Log: 1228 miles
Wind: E 4 kts
Sea: 0.5m Swell: slight. Westerly

Calm. If the wind dropped any more I'd need the engine. I calculated with my spare fuel I could motor for 400 miles if necessary, but that was a last resort. And I still had over 600 miles to go. At least the current was with us, pushing us along at around two knots. Patience, girl, patience.

Thursday 28th November 2013
0800: 16 25N 55 12W
Co: 280 Sp 6
Trip Log: 1593 miles
Wind: ESE 15 kts
Sea: 1.5m Swell: mod. Westerly

We lolled around all day and overnight in that maddening calm, genoa furled away to stop its lazy walloping, the boom creaking to-and-fro as the main struggled to fill with what little breeze offered.

But on Tuesday morning the Trades returned; a southeaster sprang up that had steadily strengthened over the two following days. The genoa was once more poled out and we were goosewinging on the home stretch with around 350 miles to go.

I was about to go below to make my noon sandwich when something caught my attention on the port bow, a large object in the water. At first, I thought it must be a cargo container some ship had lost overboard, but then I saw the spout of water. A whale! And a big one at that. I'd seen whale plumes before in the distance, but never one this close. And I was going to pass it very close, too close, perhaps. I tweaked the windvane to take us a point to starboard. As I watched the whale draw closer cold fingers began to crawl up my spine. Many boats had been lost getting too close to large cetaceans. And this one, I now recognised from its angular head, was a sperm whale, the most notorious of them all; Cap'n Ahab's whale, I noted, and pictured Dirk in the bows brandishing a harpoon.

Suddenly, the creature's head dipped, and its massive flukes lifted out of the water, so close now the slosh from its rising tail almost reached our bow. And then it was gone, a patch of swirling froth marking its departure. I realised I'd been holding my breath, and now breathed out in a long sigh of relief at danger averted.

But I'd been so transfixed with the spectacle to port, I hadn't noticed what was going on to starboard. I did now and let out a yelp of panic as another enormous set of flukes rose before my eyes, feet away, just a brief glimpse before a ton of water poured over me, and then I was hanging on to the wheel and gasping for air as *Pasha* beam-ended.

When she righted herself, water streaming off the mainsail after its almost total immersion, I sat there stunned in a cockpit full of water, the two scupper-pipes slurping and gurgling under the surcharge, hardly able to believe what had just happened.

"Er... oops."

"Oh, fuck off!"

While the cockpit drained I checked for damage. The rig looked fine, *Pasha* had picked up the wind and sailed along quite unaffected by the near catastrophe. Two of the starboard guardrail stanchions had stove inwards, cracked at the bases so would need replacing. No big deal.

Down below was not so good. The washboards had been out when the whale struck; a deluge had poured into the saloon and the bilge pumped was whirring away. Instead of lunch I would spend the next hour baling out.

Sunday 1st December 2013
0801: 17 10N 61 25W
Co: 270 Sp 6
Trip Log: 1957 miles
Wind: ESE 15 kts

This morning I began to see birds. Oh, there'd been a few ocean wanderers around during the crossing, an albatross, a couple of petrels, and of course those poor egrets. But now I saw coastal dwellers; first a solitary tropicbird that seemed to take a fancy to my wind turbine, then flocks of boobies and terns diving for fish, and a pair of frigate birds hovering above for a chance to rob someone of their catch.

By noon, a faint black line painted the horizon ahead. Antigua was in sight.

The following morning, I took a marina berth in Jolly Harbour, on the western side of the island. I took on water and provisions, got a metalwork guy from the boatyard to do a temporary repair of *Pasha's* cracked guardrail stanchions, got drunk as a skunk at the marina bar with a bunch of other up-for-it yachties. I got online and completed my ESTA for entry into the US and sailed three days later for Bahamas and the Florida Keys.

Part Four

49

"Hey, lady, how long ya'll planning stayin' here"

The guy had motored over in a dingy from ashore as soon as my anchor rattled down.

"Oh, till after Christmas if that's okay."

"It's okay by me, but ah'll tell ya, holdin's not great here, you might wanna think about takin' a mooring ball, especially if'n ya'll not plannin' to stay aboard."

"How much?"

"Five bucks a day, you can pay when ya check out."

"Okay," I said, "can you give me a hand to pick up the buoy?"

"Sure, no problem."

After we'd moored I unlashed the dingy on the foredeck and hoisted it into the water on the spare halliard, dragged it aft and lowered the outboard onto it. Within the hour I was motoring ashore with my passport, ESTA printout, and boat documents.

The small customs and immigration office processed me surprisingly quickly, and the girl at the marina office was *helpful* with my queries, in particular, the cheapest way to get to Miami.

"Well, ma'am, the cheapest is by bus, but you'll need to change twice to get to Downtown, an it'll take you more than six hours."

"Oh, I'm not going as far as Downtown. Do you know where French Country Village is?"

"Sure, that's easy. You'll need a cab from here to Mile Marker 98, there you get the bus to West Palm Drive, from there you walk to Park and Ride and get the 38 Max to Dadeland South, but you get off at University, and from there it's a ten-minute walk to French Country."

She smiled proudly at her mastery of geography and the public transport system, but then saw my look of blank confusion and frowned.

"Ma'am, do you have Google Maps on your cell-phone?"

I motored back to Pasha and went to bed. I'd been at sea a week since leaving Antigua and the last few days transiting the Bahamas had been gruelling to say the least.

I woke up mid-afternoon, starving. I showered in the cockpit, then took the dingy back to shore and looked for a decent eatery.

I was accosted by a man in sawn-off jeans and bare feet, a filthy, smock-style shirt, straggly unkempt hair and matching beard.

"Ma'am, can you spare an outa-work sailor a few dollars? I promise not to spend any of it on food."

I guffawed at his audacity, but then told him I didn't have any US Dollars, I was running on plastic. He wished me a nice evening wandered off.

I found a busy waterfront restaurant from which floated mouth-watering aromas and chose an open-air table on decking over the water. I ordered a beer, a shrimp starter followed by gator-burger and fries and a side order of Waldorf salad.

"I guess you're hungry, huh?" came a voice from the next table as the waiter left with my order.

He was thirtyish, his friendly smile and attractive green eyes somewhat let down by the shaved head and ginger goatee.

"Famished," I said, then turned away to look out over the water, where *Pasha* sat, still and restful at her mooring on the placid lagoon.

"Nice boat," the man persisted, despite my 'not interested' signal, "saw you come in the dingy."

I turned back to him, gave him a disengaged smile, "Thanks. She's old and a bit cranky, but she takes care of me."

"You sail alone, then? Gee, that's risky for a purdy young thing like you. Doncha git scared?"

I paused, put my chin in my hand, and gave him a patient stare, then said carefully, "Are you always so rude?"

His face went beetroot, but he rallied quickly, "Are you always so stand-offish, or is that just normal British arrogance?"

"Everything okay here, ma'am?" the waiter asked, placing a tall flute of beer in front of me then glancing at the man.

"Yeah," I told him, "we're all good, thanks."

The waiter hesitated a microsecond, then left.

I took a long drink and wiped the froth from my mouth, then said, "Look, I've had a long, exhausting trip here, and I'm hungry, as you said, and not the best company right now, so can we just leave it, okay?"

"Okay, okay, no problem, ma'am," he said, "I apologise for any offence," an obsequious nod of his bald pate, then turned to gaze out over the water, fingers drumming silently on the table.

I grinned to myself, then took out my Kindle and began reading.

Halfway through eating another beer arrived, unordered, to replace my empty one. I lifted an eyebrow at the waiter.

"Courtesy of the gentleman at the next table, ma'am."

I looked across at my ginger stalker, who was staring up into space with pursed lips, looking vaguely apprehensive. Despite myself, I snorted a laugh.

- 309 -

"Thanks," I said, "that's very kind."

He looked at me, and I gave him an apologetic smile. "Sorry I was a bit grumpy earlier."

He grinned sheepishly, "Gee, you were running low on glucose and I behaved like a dick. So why don't we just wind back to before I opened my big mouth?"

I raised my glass to him, "Done, and cheers."

He raised his and we drank a silent toast to our new-found cordiality. He left me to eat my meal in peace, then asked if he could join me. I pulled out a chair for him.

"I'm Chuck," he said, sitting down, "Chuck Masefield."

"Rosie Carter," I said, shaking hands, "but I'm afraid I can't stay long, I've got an early start in the morning."

"Me too," he said, "got to be on the road by seven. So, Rosie, where ya sailing to next?"

"Oh, I'm not sailing anywhere just yet. I've got an early bus ride up to Miami."

"Wow, that's some journey, ya gonna be all day on buses. Where ya headed, exactly?"

"French Country Village, it's where my aunt lives."

"And can't yer aunt come an' get yer, or don't she drive?"

"Oh, I'm sure she has a car, but she doesn't know I'm here. I want to surprise her, you know? Just show up on her doorstep unannounced and shout, 'Merry Christmas!'"

"Well that'll do it, but how d'ya know she's not away on vacation for the holiday? A lot of Miami folks head out when the snowbirds hit town, the white folks, anyways, the Hispanics stay around for the money."

That was something I hadn't considered, that Georgie and Anna wouldn't be home for Christmas. I'd made some pretty broad assumptions about their lifestyle here.

"Hadn't though o that, huh?"

"Er… no, I hadn't. But I'm in no rush to leave. If they're not home, I'll just hang on here till they get back."

"Hey, listen up. I'm driving up to Miami tomorrow, what say I give ya a ride up there, French Country's not far outa my way. Take ya two hours instead of five."

"Really? That would be fantastic."

"My pleasure," he drained his glass, "now, let's have one more at the bar, then I'm outa here. I'll pick ya up at 7am at the dingy dock."

50

"So, this aunt of yours, you must be quite fond of her to want to sail all the way from England just to give her a Christmas surprise, tell me about her."

I stared out at our speeding progress along the smooth Federal Highway. Beyond the flashing barrier posts of the causeway a brilliant turquoise sea shone yellow where shallow sandbanks rose, alternating with bright sandy inlets and golden beaches Small fishing boats left crisscrossed trails of wake on the pristine inshore waters, while further out, sailboats and motor-cruisers scudded the open ocean.

"Rosie?"

"Oh, sorry, miles away. Yes, Aunt Georgina, she prefers just Georgie. She's my mother's twin. I didn't even know she existed until Mum died last year."

"Oh, I'm so sorry for your loss." Chuck said, sounding genuinely sincere.

The car smelled of newness; a Toyota-something in metallic green. And the aircon worked rather too well; goose bumps raised on my arms in the cold air from the vent.

"Do you mind if I open my window?" I asked.

"Oh, sure," he said, switching off the aircon, "go ahead. Thought you might be unused to the Florida heat."

"Very thoughtful, Chuck," I laughed, sliding down my window to let the warmer air from outside caress my face, "but I've been in the tropics for months, I think I'm acclimatised by now."

"Yeah, I guess. So, you've got me intrigued. How come you didn't know your mother had a twin?"

"I'm not sure. Georgie won't talk to me about it, and I can't ask my Dad, because…"

I sucked back a great sob. No idea why it hit me just then. I couldn't trust myself to go on.

"Oh, I'm sorry, I hit on something, huh? You wanna talk about something else?"

I took a breath and gave a forceful sigh. "No, no, not your fault, just me being a wuz. My Dad's been in hospital for the past 18 months with Locked-in Syndrome. You know what that is?"

"Huh-huh, it's when they're fully aware, but can't move or respond, right?"

I nodded. "A fully functioning brain inside a body that doesn't work, cut off in every way from interaction with others, can you imagine?"

"No, I can't, it sounds terrifying, and extremely upsetting for you, clearly. And understandably so."

"Well, in Dad's case at least, there's a hopeful prognosis, there's a definite sign that he can see and hear, I witnessed it myself last time I spoke to him. And Julie, that's the nurse in charge of his ward, tells me his cognitive functions are improving week on week. His consultant says it's just a matter of months now before he's back with us."

"Well that's good news. And, Rosie, I hope when you get back to England your Daddy's going to be there, smiling and waiting give his daughter a humongous hug. That'll be some homecoming."

I looked out again and let the wind brush away the standing tears. "Thanks," I said, when I'd got it together, "I hope so too."

We sped on in silence, the engineered paradise of the keys gradually giving way to wilder, less managed places;

swampland greenery sweeping out to our left and burgeoning into dense mangrove and bigger, more established forestry.

"The Everglades," Chuck supplied, "gator country."

I nodded.

After another few silent miles zipped past, Chuck said, "So, back to your Aunt, does she work, retired?"

"She's probably due for retirement, she's 66, but no, she still works. Runs a software business with her partner, Anna."

"That's 'partner' as in... she's gay, right?"

"Yup, I suppose there's no denying it, partner in both senses."

He glanced across at me. "Hey, you're blushing, Rosie. Don't you know this is the Gay Capital of the World? Hell, I'm a part of it."

I stared at him, he flashed me a sideways grin.

"You're *gay?*"

He nodded, "Sure am. You thought I was hittin' on ya last night, right? Well forget it, my preference is strictly male."

I burst into laughter. "I'm sorry," I said, "I'm not laughing at you, just the comic situation."

"I know," he said, grinning hugely, "I had a good laugh about it last night in my room."

"Like a TV sitcom." I burst out again in helpless giggles.

"Yeah, Big Bang Theory, like when that girl thinks Sheldon's coming on to him and slaps his face."

"I saw that one, it was so funny, Sheldon just cracks me up."

I sighed, and a few moments later, so did Chuck.

"So, what business are they in, Georgie and Anna?"

"They run a software company, outsourcing for big banks, I think. Something to do with online security."

"Well here's a coincidence, that's my line of work too. Commercial, City Bank, that kind of thing?"

"Yes, I think so."

He suddenly snapped his fingers. "Wait a minute. Anna. She'll be around what... sixty now? Originates from Scandinavia somewhere?"

I stared at him. "Finland. You know her?"

"Anna Koskinen? Is that your aunt's partner?"

I shook my head. "Georgie never mentioned her surname. How do you know her?"

"Anna Koskinen? Everyone in my industry knows Anna. She used to be *the* big cheese in banking security systems."

I went cold. "Used to be?"

"She was called up to Washington two years back, works for the CIA at Langley, last I heard."

I relaxed. "Ah, that can't be her then. Georgina's Anna still works in Miami."

"Yeah, you're probably right," he said, "Anna's a pretty common name, and Finnish software people are all over America; Silicon Valley's crawling with 'em."

51

"Here you go, 1284 Seville Avenue," Chuck said, pulling over to the kerb. "Whoa! Nice place."

I stared in astonishment. On a slight rise and surrounded by lush sub-tropical trees and shrubs in glorious bloom, the house was a modern wonder; sprawled out over a huge area, a triple garage with a vast paved parking area in front. The well-tended lawns had several sprinklers on the go and two spreading banyan trees gave shade to the open porticoed porch. The top floor was half timbered, with numerous tall, Georgian-style windows. A decorative chimney rose from one side of the house. The tall hedgerow leading out from the rear suggested an extensive private back garden, and through the white gate bars of the separate entrance I could make out what looked like a swimming pool diving board.

"Looks like somebody might be home," Chuck said, nodding towards a silver Ford Pickup in front of one of the garage doors.

I'd been getting increasingly anxious as we'd driven through the Village looking for the address. Now my nerves were stretched to breaking point.

"Want me to wait?" Chuck said.

"If it's not going to make you late, I wouldn't mind," I said, "then if there's nobody in you can drop me at the nearest bus stop to get me back to my boat."

"Can do better than that," he said, "I'm only in Downtown for a two-hour meeting, then I'm driving home for the weekend. Did I mention I live in Key West?"

"Oh, that's great. And you don't mind, I mean if all this goes pear-shaped?"

He snorted a laugh. "I will mind if ya stall much longer."

Okay, Rosie, let's do it. I took a deep breath and swung open my door.

"Wait a moment," chuck said, "I don't mean to worry you, Rosie, but did you notice the name on the mailbox?"

I turned and looked at the mailbox on a post at the end of the drive

Koskinen

I looked back at Chuck, startled and confused, trying to reconcile the implications.

He reached into the glove box, "Here's my card, just in case, you know…"

"Thanks, Chuck" I said, "thanks for everything."

I stepped shakily up the drive and rang the bell. A ding-dong sounded faintly, then a dog began barking. A yellow shape approached through the frosted glass of the door, a wagging tail at near floor-level. The door opened, and a little terrier ran out and began licking and sniffing excitedly around my ankles.

"Hello, how can I…" Anna broke off and simply stared at me. "Georgie?"

"Yes," I replied, smiling broadly, "I'm her niece," I put out my hand, "and you're Anna, I recognise you from your photo. Is Georgie home?"

Ignoring my outstretched hand, Anna's mouth fell open, her face paled, she staggered back a pace and put a hand to her chest.

"I'm sorry," I said, unnerved by her reaction, "is Georgie alright, has something happened?"

She began shaking her head, then said, "This can't be happening. I'm having a nightmare. Who *are* you?"

"I'm Georgic's niece, Rosie. Look, Anna, I don't understand, whatever's the matter?"

She appeared to get herself together, took a breath, then said. "I don't know who you are, and if this is some kind of…"

Then her face grew hard. "Okay lady, show me some ID or I'm calling the police right now."

The little dog at my feet backed away and began growling.

Bewildered and growing tearful, I opened my bag and took out my passport. Without a word I handed it to her. She flicked through to the back page, looked at me, and then the photo, and a look of slow realisation came into her face.

"Rosemary Carter!" she almost whispered it, "Rosemary Carter. My god! You're Georgie's daughter. Oh, I'm so sorry, Rosemary, so rude of me, come in, come in."

The dog was wagging its tail again.

I turned and gave Chuck the thumbs up as Anna ushered me inside. Inside the door, I stopped, realising what Anna had just said. Bemused, I shook my head and followed inside. Maybe Anna wasn't well. Dementia can strike early these days.

"Go on inside, take a seat." said Anna, now the bubbly hostess, "I just made some lemonade, you want some?"

I walked into a big open plan lounge, nothing fancy, just stylish practical furniture, lots of pale woodwork, and a large potted plant in the high-arched fireplace, and a dining table on one side.

I took a seat on an ivory coloured leather settee corner-unit, and the little dog jumped up and began fussing me. I gave it a little scratch behind the ears, which seemed to satisfy it, and it jumped down and curled up by my feet.

Anna came into the room with two glasses of cloudy lemonade. "And how is your mother? God it's been how long? Almost thirty years now." She set the lemonade down on the small coffee table and sat down next to me.

"But I thought you knew," I said, "Mum died last year, didn't my aunt tell you?"

She stared at me, and tears sprang to her eyes. "Oh my, oh my... excuse me a moment."

She almost ran from the room, gushing tears, the little dog following with its tail down.

I sat in utter bewilderment. What on earth was going on here? And where was Georgie? Had they split? If so I'd need to ask where she was living now.

A couple of minutes later Anna returned, blowing her nose on a tissue, her eyes red-rimmed. As she sat down I looked at her, hoping for answers but not wanting to upset her further. She sniffed, then turned to me.

"I don't know your aunt," she said, "I never met her. I guess she must be on your father's side of the family, because Georgie was an only child. So you see, Rosemary, I had no idea Georgie, sorry, I mean your mother, Margaret, had died."

"Er... Anna..." I stuttered, dumbfounded.

"I assume you know we were once lovers, so naturally I was devasted to hear she died. I did wonder why I didn't get a card last Christmas, she never missed one before."

"You and Mum? I don't understand. It was you and Georgina, surely..."

"You're confused, honey, and I can see why. Georgie was my pet name for Margie. There never was a Georgina."

I sat back, staring at nothing, trying to come to terms with what I was hearing. No Aunt Georgina? But... this can't be right, Anna, or am I going mad?" I couldn't stay sitting, frustration forced me to stand up, pace the room, tears welled up, so I could barely see.

"Are you telling me," I bawled, "that the woman who came to find me, the woman who told me she was Mum's twin sister and lived with you in Florida, that she... that she *never existed?*"

Anna stood and hugged me while I blubbered on her shoulder. She spoke to me soothingly, "Give yourself a break, honey, now just calm down. I don't know what's happened to you or what's going on here, and it's confusing the hell outa me too. So come and sit down, and I'll tell you what happened all those years ago, and maybe we can make some sense outa this."

I returned with her to the settee. I picked up my bag from the floor. "I want to show you something," I said, pulling out my laptop.

"When I saw you at the door just now," she said, while I was waiting for the machine to start up, "I thought I was seeing my Georgie, aka Margaret, your mother. Because you look just like she did when I last saw her, a little younger sure, but as like as makes no difference. Of course, I knew that couldn't be right because she would have aged, but honestly, my brain did a somersault when I clapped eyes on you."

She watched me as I opened my email, knowing perhaps I'd only been half listening. I went to my Inbox, then stared at the screen. The last email from Doc was there, but... I scrolled down. Nothing, nothing from Georgie, nothing in Sent from me to her either. "I don't understand," I muttered, "she must be here."

I went to my Contacts but couldn't find her there either.

Bewildered and panicky. I looked at Anna, who was watching me with a concerned frown.

"She's not here. I *know* we've exchanged emails, but she's not..." my head was buzzing. I was suddenly very hot, despite the cool of the room. Feverishly, I pulled out my phone and went to Contacts. Again, nothing.

I stared at Anna again, "But how…"

"shh shh," she patted my hand, "let me tell you the whole thing, then questions, okay?"

I sniffed and nodded.

"So, Margaret and I met in 1980, at a weekend regatta at Chichester. She was sailing her father's boat *Spectre* and was one short in her crew. I was there just to help on the marina, and I stepped in. After that she asked me a few more times, and we found the two of us got along pretty well. Eventually we fell in love, but this was the eighties and it was England before the 'enlightenment', if you know what I…"

I put my hand up, "wait, just stop there a minute… I know all this, I thought from Georgie, but it wasn't was it? It couldn't have been."

"No, it…"

"Just give me a minute."

I leaned back and closed my eyes.

52

I'm five years old, Mum has been teaching me to read and I'm so pleased with myself I begin reading anything and everything I can get my hands on. Not just children's stuff, but mum's classics, newspapers, Dad's Navy News and Readers Digests. It's become a kind of obsession. One day I'm in Mum's study looking through her bureau, I find a book, hand written which I find hard but fascinating, but just another feed for my reading addiction. I sneak into her room every day and read a little more. Much of it makes little sense to a five-year-old, but that doesn't matter, reading's such fun.

"It must have stuck, what I read, you know, in my subconscious."

"I'm sorry?"

"Mum's diary, I read it when I was five."

"So you think maybe…"

"Could explain a lot about… never mind, please go on."

"Anyway, we decided to live onboard *Spectre,* so we could be together, you know, without raising suspicion. I mean it wasn't a problem for me, I was raised in Finland, and besides, petty prejudices didn't bother me. But Margaret's parents were, shall we say, more than a little conservative, and devout churchgoers. It was important to her to keep our relationship in the closet.

In '84 Margaret's father died and left her *Spectre* in his will, and a big chunk of cash in a covenant to keep her living with her mother in that big old house, 'My Golden Handcuff' she called it."

That tugged another memory, but I parked it for now, fascinated with all this stuff coming to light at last.

"Life for us was a little more difficult, but we managed. We still had every weekend and some weekday nights together. In '85, Margaret sold *Spectre* and bought *Pasha*, a brand-new boat and more comfortable as a live-aboard. Life was good, Rosie, believe me, we were so happy."

She was welling up again. I pressed my hand on hers, "I know." I murmured. Something was happening to me while I listened, I couldn't fathom it, but it felt good, as if my body was getting lighter.

"It was about then Peter, your Dad started crewing for us at races and regattas. He always had a soft spot for Margaret, probably was even in love with her, but knew about us and always kept his distance. A very honourable and liberal-minded man, your Dad.

"Then, two days before Christmas '85, we were both supposed to go to the Yacht Club Christmas Party in Mullhaven. I was working for a software company in Reading at the time and would have to work late to finish some urgent work before the holiday, so Margaret and I decided to meet at the Club and sleep on Pasha overnight. Georgie went, but I was kept quite late, missed the party entirely, and went straight down to the boat."

She paused to dab her eyes with a tissue.

"I knew something was wrong as soon as I stepped aboard. I found her sitting in a bathrobe with the electric fan heater on full blast. She was crying and there was a big bowl of hot soapy water, and water slopped all over the saloon, where she'd given herself a thorough washing, a birdbath."

She stared at me, "Rosie, your mother never wanted you to find this out, but…"

"She was raped. I worked that out, but I think I always knew anyway. Been locked away I suppose. I didn't want it to be true, so it wasn't."

"She didn't want anyone ever to know what happened to her. It was only when your grandmother deduced that she was pregnant, even before Margaret herself knew, that the shit hit the fan. They were Irish Catholics, your grandparents, and Margaret had been brought up in that strict tradition. Not only was she not allowed an abortion, but she had to be married before the baby was born."

"So, in stepped my Dad." I supplied, my voice quavering.

She nodded. "So, in stepped your Dad, only as you now realise, he wasn't your biological father. But he loved your mother, and he was more than ready to accept you as his own. And I believe from her occasional letters, they had a happy life together.

"For my part, well I knew Margaret and I were finished. I was devastated, and I believe she was as well, but with your mother, family values always came first. She was very strong-willed and always followed her own notions of what was right. We'd always planned to come to Florida together some day, both for its liberal attitudes and opportunities in technology. We were going to start a business together."

A long pause while we held each other's eyes. It was all still sinking in, but I felt a curious sense of peace settling over me. So many questions answered, questions I'd not dared to think about for most of my life. Questions that had been bubbling away inside begging for release.

After an age, I said, with heartfelt feeling, "Anna, that's so sad, you abandoned your happiness and came here alone, lost the love of your life because of bigotry and religious dogmatism."

With brimming eyes, she bore up heroically, "That's how I thought of it for a time, but now, looking at you dear, I think the sacrifice was worth it."

"Aww..." I spluttered and blubbed. We hugged again, Anna patting my back like Mum used to when I was upset.

"And you've made quite a name for yourself," I said, "so I heard today."

She pulled back and looked at me. "Oh?"

"The guy that brought me here this morning, he's heard of you."

She sniffed and nodded, dry eyed now.

"Small world, huh?"

We both laughed, the tension gone.

We chatted for another hour, Anna made sandwiches and coffee. I told her about the weird false memories I had of my imaginary aunt, walking the Malvern hills together, even going to see a play that I'd watched years before at Uni; Georgie in court, watching me – I'd wondered why nobody had said anything when she didn't clear the gallery with the others.

"When I think about it now," I told Anna, "nobody ever acknowledged her, even when she came out with her funny remarks and wise observations. At the time it all seemed, you know, normal behaviour, but I suppose that was just my mind reconciling the unreconcilable." I snorted a giggle.

Anna took it all philosophically; an understandable reaction to stress and loss, she said, and that it would all probably stop now I knew the truth. I thought so too; I felt different, as if I'd walked out into the light, like the Hebrew Slaves in Nabucco.

Then we laughed and reminisced about the good times in our lives. She'd never met anyone else she could live with after Mum but had had a rewarding career and now worked for the Federal Government.

I called Chuck and he agreed to pick me up on his way home.

"Are you sure you won't stay for the holiday?" Anna asked as I got ready to leave.

"Thanks, Anna, I'm tempted. The winds would be better later, but plenty of boats sail across from Bermuda after Christmas, and I want to get back to Dad. I want to be there when he wakes up."

When Chuck tooted his horn outside I asked the question I'd been holding back.

"So, who is my biological father, does anyone know?"

"I think I'm the only person Georgie told, but maybe I shouldn't tell you. What if you find him? What will you say to each other. He raped your mother, you might just wanna kill him. Patricide, huh, not a good ending."

"I'm just curious," I said, laughing, "I promise I won't go looking for him with a meat cleaver."

She measured me up for a moment, then said, "He was a nobody, honey, just a young apprentice rigger from the boatyard, he quit and went elsewhere after he crapped on his own doorstep. His name was Gary Palmer."

Epilogue

s/y Pasha Passage Log
Tuesday 4th February 2014
0955: 50 55N 01 28W Course 085 Sp 6
Wind SW 18kts
Sea: 1m Swell E slight.

I shivered, despite my two fleeces and full foul-weather gear. It would take a while to acclimatise to the British Winter again.

I was nearly home, St Catherine's Point lay on the port beam with the chalk cliffs of the Isle of Wight sloping away each side, Spit Bank Fort clearly visible ahead.

The crossing had been fast and furious, the winter storms giving me no end of grief, but determined to push on despite gales of 30 knots plus and monstrous seas, I'd made the Azores safely in just 15 days from Bermuda. I'd stayed only two days at Horta, having had the amazing news from Julie that Dad had kicked his legs, and was now blinking. That spurred me to press on for home, a night anchored off Falmouth for a much-needed rest, and then onwards once more. Yes, I was nearly home, and fighting to curb my excitement.

1425: Passed entrance to Mullhaven Marina
Trip Log: 4241 miles

As we approached the marina I saw a tall, familiar figure standing motionless on the pontoon, and as we got closer, let out a great splutter of unrestrained joy. As soon as the lines were secure I stepped ashore, and we stood for a moment, grinning achingly at one another.

"You look great," I said, meaning it.

"So do you, Rosemary, so do you. Quite the little navigator, I hear."

"Oh, Dad!" I gushed.

And ran into his open arms.

The End